Stamped Out

STAMPED OUT

TERRI THAYER

WHEELER
CHIVERS

This Large Print edition is published by Wheeler Publishing, Waterville, Maine, USA and by BBC Audiobooks Ltd, Bath, England.

Wheeler Publishing, a part of Gale, Cengage Learning.

A Stamping Sisters Mystery.

The text of this Large Print edition is unabridged.

Other aspects of the book may vary from the original edition.

Set in 16 pt. Plantin.

Printed on permanent paper.

LIBRARY OF CONGRESS CATALOGING-IN-PUBLICATION DATA

Thayer, Terri.
  Stamped out / by Terri Thayer.
    p. cm. — (A Stamping Sisters mystery) (Wheeler Publishing large print cozy mystery)
    ISBN-13: 978-1-59722-955-5 (pbk. : alk. paper)
    ISBN-10: 1-59722-955-5 (pbk. : alk. paper)
    1. Women artisans—Fiction. 2. Murder—Investigation—Fiction. 3. Fathers and daughters—Fiction. 4. Architecture—Conservation and restoration—Fiction. 5. Handicraft—Fiction. 6. Pennsylvania—Fiction. 7. Large type books. I. Title.
    PS3620.H393S73 2009
    813'.6—dc22
                            2008054921

BRITISH LIBRARY CATALOGUING-IN-PUBLICATION DATA AVAILABLE

Published in 2009 in the U.S. by arrangement with The Berkley Publishing Group, a member of Penguin Group (USA) Inc.
Published in 2009 in the U.K. by arrangement with The Berkley Publishing Group, a member of Penguin Group (USA) Inc.

U.K. Hardcover: 978 1 408 44130 5 (Chivers Large Print)
U.K. Softcover: 978 1 408 44131 2 (Camden Paragon Large Print)

Printed in the United States of America
1 2 3 4 5 6 7 13 12 11 10 09

ACKNOWLEDGMENTS

Thanks to my intrepid critique group, Becky Levine and Beth Proudfoot. Without their constant support and encouragement, I would still be writing stories in my head. And the ones I did put on paper wouldn't be very good. From their suggestions, and by critiquing their work, I learned how to write better. I'm blessed to have great friends who are wonderful writers and editors.

Thanks to Mary Hernan for trying to keep me on schedule. She made me laugh, which is far more important.

To Holly Mabutas of Eat Cake Graphics for making the wonderful skull stamp and project. She captured the essence of the book. Good job!

Thank you to my agent, Jessica Faust, for

liking my writing and encouraging me to stretch. Her belief in me, and her incredible knowledge of the market, got me to this point and I'm really grateful.

Thanks to my editor, Sandy Harding, and the copyeditors, cover artists and other professionals at Berkley Prime Crime who did their best work on my behalf. I benefited from their expertise, as did my book.

CHAPTER 1

"You're killing me with these shoes, April. How many pairs does one girl need?"

April glanced at her mother. Bonnie groaned as she pressed the small of her back and bent down to pick up a pair of sandals from the box and placed it in the closet beneath the loft. April had brought a lot of shoes. They were one of the only things left from her marriage that were all hers.

She said, "No one asked you to put away my stuff, Mom."

Deana, April's best friend, rolled her eyes and smiled. In fact, April had just asked her mother *not* to unpack her suitcases. April returned the grin. Deana and April had been friends since the first grade when April had traded the fancy chicken salad sandwich her mother had made her for Deana's pb and j. Now, with her best friend helping her to move in, April could almost tolerate her mother's overpowering nesting urges.

"Better Bonnie touch your shoes than your art supplies," Deana whispered. April nodded, glancing across the room, double-checking that the valises that held her sketchbooks, inks and stamps were safely under her father's desk. She would deal with them herself when she was alone.

"Lift," Deana said. She and April set upright the futon they'd assembled. Her futon, which had nearly filled the second bedroom in their place in California, looked like a tiny piece of beached driftwood in the barn.

She scanned the room. The vast expanse of hardwood floor gleamed, unbroken by furniture. She really hadn't brought much with her. Once the shoes were put away, the unpacking would be pretty much done. She'd already unloaded her clothes into the built-in drawers, and Deana had stashed her toiletries in the bathroom.

"Now, let's put up your drafting table," Deana said. "You'll feel more at home once that's up."

April smiled. These next couple of months in her hometown might not be so bad with Deana around. She hadn't spent more than a week at a time here since she was seventeen years old. Aldenville had not been good to her.

She'd come back only for a few months, to regain her equilibrium. A year tops. Then she'd move on to New York or Boston where no one had ever heard of April Buchert Interiors, San Francisco.

Her energy sagged as she thought about the mess she'd left in California. A trashed reputation, a soon-to-be ex-husband, and an impossible-to-keep promise to pay back everything he'd stolen.

Deana handed her a table leg and rummaged in the box for the caster. Even her best friend didn't know the worst of it. April's face burned in shame just thinking about Ken and the way he'd duped her.

If Deana suspected something about her problems, her mother was aware of nothing. All Bonnie knew was that Ed, April's father, had a job for her to do with his company, Retro Reproductions, and was lending her his restored barn to stay in.

"Plants," Bonnie said, backing out of the closet and shutting the door. "That's what this place needs. There's so much square footage, it looks unnatural without some green."

"I like it," April said. "Uncluttered."

"Nonsense," her mother said, shaking her head for emphasis. Her tight curls didn't move. Her hair was mostly gray now, with only a few vestiges of April's rich brown tones left.

"You need to get a bureau and a living room suite," Bonnie continued. Her pronunciation of *suite* hit a raw nerve with April. She thought she'd left this behind. Bonnie went on pointing out possible furniture placement. "Over there, a recliner for Ken. I'm off tomorrow. Why don't we go up to the mall and look around?"

"Thanks, Mom, but I'll be working."

"I could just go take a look for you."

April shot her a look that her mother would clearly recognize from April's teens. Get out of my room, Mom, it said.

Giving up, Bonnie hovered over Deana and April, who were nearly finished with the drafting table. Deana sat with her legs splayed out in front of her like a young deer. April preferred to squat. She grabbed the bag of screws just in time to prevent Bonnie from stepping on them.

Bonnie watched them closely. "Lefty, loosey, right, tighty. Here, let me."

April exchanged a knowing look with Deana. Bonnie's homemaking instincts were too strong. April had to find her something to do. Something that didn't involve April's stuff.

"How about making some coffee, Mom?

To go with those cookies you brought?"

Bonnie leaned on the long, heavy wooden table that separated the galley kitchen from the main space. Purple pendant lights hung over the surface and she had to duck to get a good look at the kitchen.

Every surface in the kitchen gleamed. Ed and his partner were house flippers, living in a space while they fixed it up. The kitchen was always the last room they finished, and the room they spent most of their budget on. Most of the high-end appliances looked as though they'd never been used. An espresso machine was the only thing sitting on the glittering black granite countertop.

Bonnie hesitated. April could swear she looked intimidated. "I don't know how to use that fancy machine," Bonnie said.

"No need," April said. "I brought my French press. It's in there." She pointed to a box on the table. "I packed the beans and the mugs, too." She'd made sure she'd have access to good coffee her first morning back home.

Bonnie agreed, setting out the things April had put in the box her last morning in San Francisco. Her special stash of organic fair trade Guatemalan coffee, the beautiful mugs from the ceramics show at the Cow Palace. April's heart ached from all she'd

11

left behind.

Deana noticed her sad expression and whispered, "You doing okay?"

April shrugged. "It's harder than I thought." She looked in Deana's blue eyes, so concerned. "I haven't been on the receiving end of Hurricane Bonnie in a long time."

"She loves you, and wants you to be happy."

Tears filled April's eyes at her friend's simple view of things. "If only it were that easy," she said.

"You're going to be okay," Deana said.

April nodded. She almost believed it when Deana said it. "I just need to get to work." Work made everything better.

They screwed on the last leg, hoisted the drafting table up and set it in place. April felt a rush of something akin to love when she touched the familiar white surface. This was the only possession April cared about. All she needed. The drafting table had been her first purchase out of art school, and even later, when she could have afforded a better one, she didn't replace it. She was convinced her muse resided somewhere in the faux Formica top.

"Here's your stool," Deana said, rolling the blue armless chair toward her. "You're all set. Now you can work."

"Coffee's ready," Bonnie said. Deana and April pushed the drafting table into position, next to an oak post that dominated the center of the room. Bonnie had put out the tin of oatmeal raisin cookies she'd made and folded paper towels into napkins. She'd found sugar and creamer packets and stirrers April had liberated from a Mickey D's in Kansas and put them into the fourth mug. The table looked almost cheery.

"One cup and then I've got to scoot," Deana said. "I've got six rubber stampers coming in an hour for a sit 'n' stamp."

"What's a sit 'n' stamp?" April asked. Deana hadn't told her about this part of her life.

Bonnie answered, pouring coffee. "Deana's the valley's newest Stamping Sister dealer."

At April's blank look, Bonnie continued. "You know, like scrapbooking. Rubber stamping, embossing. Stampers come work on their projects. Deana supplies everything they need. And she sells them more stuff. It's the perfect setup."

"Do people around here do that?" April asked.

Deana said, "Hey, you know there's not a big night life around here. We have fun. I

13

really look forward to Tuesdays."

April thought of a snag. "The stampers don't object to your place?" Deana lived over the funeral home. She and her husband, Mark, had taken over Deana's family business.

Deana grinned. "They say they like the quiet. You should come, April."

The three continued chatting quietly, and April found herself relaxing for the first time in months. The barn might be devoid of any hominess, but it was a safe haven for her.

Unfortunately, Bonnie shattered the mellow mood. "What was wrong with your life in California anyway? All that sunshine. And so much to do, there in the city. I thought Ken loved San Fran. I never thought I'd see the day when you called Aldenville home again," her mother said.

April struggled for an answer. Interior design was a small world. Once word spread about Ken's proclivity to steal objets d'art, jewelry, even rolls of coins, April's reputation, and then her livelihood, had been ruined. But she was convinced that the real source of vitriol directed against her from her clients had more to do with the emotional havoc Ken had left behind. Most of her clients could afford to lose possessions. It was the loss of Ken's charm that they really missed.

After that it didn't matter that she was the only stamper in Northern California capable of doing historically accurate walls. No one called. When her father's job beckoned, she'd jumped in the old Volvo and headed east, leaving the mess behind.

Her mother thought her father had bullied her into coming back. Her father thought she was running away from a miserable marriage. Both were a little bit right.

The real truth was that five years of living with Ken had left her broke, bitter and back home.

"I'm sick of painting tussie-mussies," April lied. "If I never see another overstuffed Victorian parlor, it'll be too soon."

Bonnie's brow furrowed. "Okay, don't tell me. You're just like your father. Always with the secrets."

Deana's cell phone rang. She said hello in her professional voice, low and confident, and walked outside for better reception.

Bonnie gathered up the dirty dishes. "You need to fill that gigantic refrigerator. Let's go get a food order."

A food order. April hadn't heard that phrase in years. Indigenous to the area, it had originated in the mining towns that dotted the area. Her mother's father had been a coal miner, paid in scrip. The company store would deliver what was called an order to the tiny row house. Her mother always used the antiquated phrase.

She didn't want to tell her mother she didn't have the money to go shopping.

"Not tonight, Mom. I'm tired and I've got work to do. I'm starting the Mirabella job in the morning."

Mirabella was famous in this part of Pennsylvania. It was a Tudor mansion that had been built in the late 1800s for a coal baron who had no qualms about spending money on marble floors, hand-carved ebony balustrades and a crude air-conditioning system while his miners lived most of their short lives below ground, dirty, poor and under his thumb.

Bonnie looked at her daughter closely, clearly not diverted by April's attempt at name-dropping. April averted her eyes. What was it about mothers? They always knew.

"You need money," Bonnie said flatly. Her eyes flashed with disappointment. Whether because April was broke or because she hadn't told her mother, April wasn't sure.

"I'll have a steady paycheck coming in soon." And no Ken to spend two dollars as soon as she made one. "Dad's promised me an advance."

Her mother snorted and reached for her purse. April stopped her.

"Really, Mom, I'm fine." Her mother's job as cook at the country club didn't pay much.

Bonnie relented. "Well, come for dinner at least."

The barn door slid open and Deana came in, her mouth drawn into a tight line.

"Sorry, but I've got to leave. I've got a body to tend to," she said.

April asked, "Who died?"

Deana's brow was furrowed. "George Weber."

Bonnie's hand flew up to her mouth. "George? But I just saw him."

Deana nodded. "Another death at Forever Friends, the nursing home."

"That place," Bonnie exclaimed in horror. "People are always dying over there."

"Well, Mom, it's a nursing home, full of old people," April said, looking at Deana for support.

Deana gave her a distracted smile, but April could see her friend's thoughts had shifted to the deceased. "There have been a couple of unexplained deaths there in the last few months. More than usual. The county coroner has talked about holding an investigation."

April realized Deana was going to be busy for hours and said, "What about your stamping meeting? Will you have to cancel?"

Deana said, "Yeah."

"I can have them here," April said.

"Oh no you can't," Bonnie said. "You don't have any furniture."

"The girls don't care," Deana said. She rubbed the wood of the table. "You've got this huge work space. This table is perfect. They just want a place to make a mess."

Warming to the idea, Deana went on. "You wouldn't have to do much. I've done all the precutting and kitting already. Everyone is working on the same Stamping Sister piece tonight, a photo book."

"Okay," April said.

"I charge twenty dollars a head," Deana said. "I know at least six are coming."

April felt her jaw drop. "You get 120 bucks for a couple hours of work?" That was two weeks worth of groceries. Bonnie frowned.

Deana said, "That's including the cost of the project."

"I'll pay you back for your costs," April said.

"You will not," Deana replied vehemently. "You're doing me a favor. They'll be lucky to have you as their teacher. I'll have Mark drop off the supplies."

"All right. I guess I'm a Stamping Sister for the night," April said. Deana walked away with renewed energy. April accompanied her to the door and waved to her until her Camry cleared the driveway. She was glad to help out, but she hoped Deana would be able to come back later.

April took in a deep breath of the clean, warm June night air. She could hear the busy stream that ran under the driveway. The wide-open feeling here was so different from California. She hadn't remembered what it was like to live without congestion, without the constant background noise of people, buses and cars. A birdcall punctuated the silence. It was a mockingbird, a distant cousin to the bird outside her California bungalow that mimicked the computer booting up. More than once, he'd faked her cell phone ring so well, she'd answered it.

Back inside, Bonnie was rummaging in the drawers and opening cupboard doors. Kitchens were her milieu and it hadn't taken her long to get over her initial shyness.

"What about hors d'oeuvres for tonight?" she said. "I'll go to the IGA. I can whip up a batch of cheese straws. You can't just have people over without feeding them."

"It's okay, Mom. They'll understand that this is all last minute."

She walked behind her mother, closing the cupboards and drawers. They were mostly empty. Bonnie stopped at the far end of the kitchen and watched her daughter.

"What can I do?" she finally asked.

"I need to drop off the trailer. It's nearly five, and I don't want to pay for an extra day."

Bonnie said, "I'll come with you."

April had been looking forward to the quiet, familiar space of her car, but she had no choice. Bonnie was getting her purse. Once they were both in her car, April glanced back at the trailer. She was struck at how small a space her prized possessions had taken up. She didn't have much to show for her thirty-one years on the planet. She looked at her mother, who was getting into the passenger seat. Was this the life she'd envisioned for her only child? Probably not.

As soon as April pulled the Subaru back into the barn's driveway, her mother said, "You're coming over for dinner tomorrow night, right?"

April didn't remember agreeing to that, but she knew when she was licked. "Okay," she said.

"Whatever goes on, you won't miss it? I

don't want any of your father's drama to get in the way of our first dinner together."

April looked askance at her mother. "What kind of drama?"

Bonnie looked straight ahead. "Well, you know. They might want you to go to their place for dinner. Promise me. I've got something special to show you."

"Did you redecorate finally?" April said, laughing to take away the sting as she reached for the car door handle.

Bonnie's eyes clouded. "Six o'clock. Tomorrow. No matter what."

"Okay. See you tomorrow night," April said.

Her mother's face lit up. "You know, I'm glad you're back in town."

Her mother was pretty when she smiled, the frown lines turning into happy creases. April's heart warmed at the sight. She'd never told her mother the worst of Ken's antics, partly because she didn't want to admit that marrying Ken had been a big mistake, but also to keep that smile on her mother's face.

The car door screeched loudly as she opened it, sending a flock of birds out of the oak tree.

April bussed her mother's cheek. "Lucky for me Dad landed a job that needed my

21

expertise."

"Luck had nothing to do with it," her mother said. "He's worked for that family before. Don't forget, he built that guesthouse back in the early nineties. Remember? The Castle."

Of course April remembered the Castle. She hadn't realized that it was connected to Mirabella. Her mother delivered her parting shot after April had slammed her car door shut.

She stuck her head out the window. "I just hope they don't cause him to go bankrupt this time."

CHAPTER 2

After a quick shower, April pulled on a knit top and snapped her khakis, smoothing the wrinkles with the palm of her hand. April filled up her mug with fresh coffee and dug out a pad and a pencil from her backpack. She had time for a few sketches before the stampers arrived. She sat at her drafting table and opened the book. The last page was one she'd done in her motel room in Ohio two nights earlier, filled with signs — octagonal stop signs, a triangle buggy caution sign she'd seen in Amish country, a cow crossing sign. How did the cows know where to cross anyhow?

The barn was quiet. Only the gentle whirring of the two ceiling fans broke the silence.

When she looked at the page again, she realized she'd drawn the turrets and crenellations of a castle. The Castle her mother had been talking about looked nothing like this, she thought. The townspeople had given the nickname to the guesthouse being built in the woods when the construction dragged into the third year — April's junior year in high school.

It was supposed to be a storybook cottage in a woodland setting: one story with low roofs and a huge fireplace that dominated the front façade. Her father had been the general contractor. But the job had been plagued by numerous setbacks as the owner changed his mind again and again. The Italian marble tile was replaced with Connemara marble. Then, a two-foot change in the bathroom led to a six-month delay as winter set in.

As a young teen, April had visited the site many times, bringing her father lunch in the summer, and after school started, stopping by to do her homework in the job trailer. Somewhere in her mother's house was a book full of drawings she'd done of the Castle. In her mind, she'd been the girl it was being designed for. But the building never seemed to get finished, and she had gotten busier. She lost interest in the Castle. By the time the job ended, she hadn't been on the site for nearly a year. Until that night.

The way she remembered it, the owner had gotten into legal trouble and stopped construction. Things at the Buchert household had gone haywire at about the same time, and her father's company filed for bankruptcy shortly thereafter. She'd never really thought about what job had led to the demise of Buchert Construction.

She shook off feelings of foreboding. Her father's current company, Retro Reproductions, was a successful company, unlike Buchert Construction. Surely, lightning wouldn't strike Ed Buchert twice.

April opened the plastic containers Deana had had her husband, Mark, drop off. Man, she loved the smell of rubber stamps. Making her way around the table, she laid out the kits Deana had made, each one packaged in a cute plaid paper bag, tied with a raffia bow.

April propped up Deana's finished sample. The photo board book was made of thick bound pages, about four inches high by eight inches long. Each page had been decorated with coordinating papers, ribbons, eyelets and inks. The theme was tulips. The designs and colors were sophisticated, using pale pinks and reds with a touch of turquoise. The coordinating papers were an interesting mix of polka dots, stripes and florals. April admired the artist who'd originated the design.

The stampers had only to follow the

example of the one Deana had done, and they could have a carbon copy — or they could add their own touches to create a unique design.

April heard a car outside and pulled on the main door. Her grip slipped. Her palms were damp, and she wiped them on her pants. Take a breath, she cautioned herself. There's no reason to be nervous. She pulled the door open.

The barn sat on a slight rise with stone steps leading to the gravel drive. The slope had been planted with blue rug juniper, pachysandra and sedum. Close to the barn, at the base of the stone foundation, were roses and peonies and lilacs, the smell of which was overwhelming. So sickly sweet, so redolent of spring, April nearly swooned.

The drive was lined with oaks, their large branches creating a green canopy. She'd gotten used to gritty brown summers of California. Now there had to be twenty different shades of green right in front of her. The artist in her sighed happily. She would only have to look out a window for inspiration.

A Chrysler sedan had pulled into the drive. April walked out to the car to greet her guest. A toothsome, athletic woman with a faded spring-break tan pumped

April's hand. She looked older than April, maybe midforties. She was wearing a pink cotton skirt with matching heels. Her V-neck top had crystals along the opening and showed a freckled cleavage. She smiled broadly. Her forehead didn't crease when she smiled, giving her a frozen look. Apparently Botox had made it to the hinterlands.

She talked quickly. "Mary Lou Rosen, Rosen Realty. Glad to meet you. When is your father going to put this place on the market? I've got just the buyer for it."

April felt her mouth drop open in shock. The woman clutched her forearm and squeezed.

"I'm just kidding, hon. I say that to everyone. You'd be surprised how many listings I get that way."

A pretty girl pulled herself out of the passenger side. She was hugely pregnant and tottering on wooden-soled clogs. Mary Lou reached in the back seat and pulled out a quilted bag, then took the girl's elbow.

The young woman said, "Don't mind her. She's like a shock jock, but without a radio show. She just says things for effect." The girl smiled to take away the sting of her remarks. April liked her already.

"This is my daughter, Kit," Mary Lou said. "And," she said, pointing to her daughter's belly, "those are my granddaughters, Chloe and Portia."

"Not even close, Mom," Kit said, still smiling. She shook April's hand. Her face was freckled, and she wore a blue and white sundress that complemented her twinkling blue eyes. She couldn't have been more than twenty. "See what I mean? My husband and I have decided not to know the sex of our babies, but my mother keeps hounding me."

April felt an immediate bond with Kit. "Mothers," April said. "Mine put the 'mother' in smother."

Kit laughed in agreement. "I hear that."

Mary Lou pointed to her daughter's big belly. "Seeing as you are on your way to becoming one yourself, I think I'll have the last laugh."

Kit shrugged. "I can't wait to see the inside of the barn," she said, her eyes turning upward to the hay window above the door.

Mary Lou followed her gaze and nodded. "We've tried every year to get your father to put this house on the charity house tour, but he never would."

Kit said, "Ed Buchert, the contractor, is your father? I never made the connection."

That stung. There was no reason someone Kit's age would know Ed had a grown daughter, but it still hurt. It reminded April of all the years she'd stayed away.

"Let's go in," April said, swallowing hard. Mary Lou took her daughter's arm, warning her about the unevenness of the steps.

April had left the main barn doors open. Her father had rigged a track so the original doors could be drawn back easily. The back door on the side wall near the kitchen was the one most often used, but it was very dramatic to have these big doors, big enough for a team of horses to pass through, open.

Their slow movement into the barn was halted as a muddy, sun-baked Suburban came up the drive. April felt an immediate kinship. Her old Volvo was as battered, well used and well loved as this old car.

"Here comes Suzi Dowling," Mary Lou said cheerfully. "Don't mind the dirt under her nails. It's permanent. You know, she runs the nursery out on Drums Road."

Another family business. April wondered how she got along with her parents.

Suzi gave a half wave but was distracted by the plantings. She poked a toe into the pachysandra and pulled a dandelion out by the root. She was wearing clean jean shorts and a button-down blue shirt with iron marks on it.

"I think the peonies came from my grandmother's place," April said, offering up the only gardening jargon she knew.

"Yeah, they're doing great. You're going to want to dust those roses soon and watch for aphids." Suzi tossed the weed aside and brushed off her hands.

"Thanks." April wasn't clear on how to "dust," but she'd find out. Suzi finally turned to her and held out a hand. Her hair was sun-streaked brown. Tousled with a slight curl, her short cut flattered her pointy nose and chin.

"Who else is here? Anybody inside?" Mary Lou chirped.

April shook her head.

"Tammy has Weight Watchers tonight. Lyle'll drop her off after weigh-in," Suzi said.

Mary Lou put in, "Unless she's lost weight, in which case she'll make him take her to Stewart's Drive-in for a frozen chocolate-chip banana-coconut mocha blend."

"That sounds good to me," April said.

That got a laugh and the group went in the door, with April bringing up the rear. Her face flamed as she saw them catch the empty interior. These women probably had suites of furniture, like Bonnie'd wanted. Most likely their towels matched their shower curtains and coordinated with their comforters. April felt inadequate in a way she never had in California.

"Whoa, you're going to need a decorator," Mary Lou said.

"I've got more stuff coming from California," April lied. Ken would have to sell everything they owned just to pay off his credit cards. The house was his, but there was no equity left. As much as he loved the house his grandmother had left him, he had gambled it away. That had been April's final straw. She knew then that their life together was beyond repair.

She shook off the sadness and directed them to the table. "I've laid out everything you need. I've got more papers and inks over there on the kitchen counter if you need to purchase additional items." God, that was lackluster, she thought. She was a rotten salesperson. Good thing Deana couldn't hear her.

Suzi pulled a book out of her floral bag. The cover was collaged with pressed flowers, ribbons and leaves. "Look, you guys. I finished my garden journal."

"May I?" April leafed through the day-by-day calendar, embellished with lifelike drawings of vines, flowers and birds. She recognized a Wordsworth quote, "Earth fills her lap with pleasures of her own." The colors used were sophisticated and the balance between illustrations and writing, perfect. The journal made April curious to see Suzi's real garden.

"Lovely." She handed it back to Suzi, who had seated herself. Kit studied the paper and inks offered by Deana's company. She pulled a selection, and April noted what she used for Deana's records.

Mary Lou opened a kit and set out papers and ink pads in front of her daughter. "This is going to be so pretty," she said.

A husky voice came from the doorway. "Hello, darlings."

A tall redhead in cream-colored shorts and a hand-painted silk blouse paused for dramatic effect on the threshold. Her Hollywood entrance was matched by long moviestar legs and a Veronica Lake hairdo. The sleeves of her shirt were carelessly pushed up to show off a handmade found-object bracelet, dangling with bits of metal and stone. She was relaxed in her elegant body.

Men must flock to her, April thought. But then, men were easy. The platinum toe rings would probably bring most men to their knees. The true test was to see if the women liked her.

"Rocky," Mary Lou, Kit and Suzi greeted

her in unison.

"I brought presents," she said, brandishing an expensive leather portfolio. "Wait until you see these handmade papers I bought in Philadelphia last week."

"Save them for show-and-tell," Mary Lou said.

She introduced herself to April. "Rocky Winchester." Her smile was broad.

"Of course, I remember you from high school," April said.

One grade ahead, Rocky had been impossible to approach but just as impossible to ignore. Deana and April had studied her at the club pool, unable to imagine themselves as poised and popular.

"That was a long time ago," Rocky said. She looked around the empty space. "You've got the simple life nailed," she said.

Not so much the simple life as the no life.

The plank floor of the refurbished barn was dappled with late afternoon sunlight coming in the high windows. The warm wooden post and beams that made up the framework soared overhead, offering a rebuke to her meager possessions. Shafts of light captured the dust motes that lingered in the air.

April said, "Have a seat at the table. Lucky for us, it didn't fit in my father's new place."

Mary Lou ran a hand over the smooth tabletop. "So nice. It's one of Mitch's, isn't it?"

April shrugged. "I know Dad had it made locally. I don't remember who."

Rocky sighted down the table with an imaginary level and said, "Oh yeah, it looks like his work. True and straight. Just like him."

The others laughed. April felt a little left out by the obvious in-joke.

She turned back to Deana's plastic container, finding the stick-on name tags. She hesitated. They knew each other, but she needed a way to remember their names.

She passed the stack with a fat red marker. Each one wrote her name down and stuck the tag on her shirt without a word of protest. Suzi embellished hers with the drawing of a daisy.

Building on her success, April sent around the envelope Deana used to collect the fee. To her relief, the stampers slipped money in it without her encouragement. They were well trained.

A cool breeze wafted in through the open door. April heard a car door slam and then the sound of the car noisily pulling away.

"Here comes Tam. I recognize that horsepower," Rocky said affectionately. "Her husband has a thing for muscle cars."

"Tammy doesn't drive?" April said. Even in San Francisco she'd needed to drive to get to her clients. Out here, with no public transportation, she couldn't imagine being without wheels.

"She has her husband to cart her around," Mary Lou said. "He's good about it."

An out-of-breath woman lumbered in. She didn't look like country-club material. She was wearing a bargain-store turquoise seersucker short set. Her sneakers were bright white with black polka-dot laces. But her face was red with exertion or something else. April couldn't tell what.

"Sorry I'm late." Her words came in short bursts, followed by large intakes of air.

"Oh, Tammy, what is it?" Rocky said, leaving her chair to put an arm around her friend. "You've been crying."

"We lost another one." She sat down heavily in the chair next to Rocky's. She dropped the canvas bag she was carrying. Her eyes brimmed with tears, and she half sobbed, half burped. Now that she was with friends, the tears flowed easily. Her words became incomprehensible.

"Take it easy," Suzi said. "You're going to make yourself sick."

Rocky rubbed her shoulder. Tammy took

another shuddering breath and managed to get out a full sentence. "George Weber died on my shift last night."

Suzi and Mary Lou shared a significant look. They looked to Rocky for guidance, but she was staring at Tammy, stroking her hair.

"Another one?" Suzi muttered. She quieted when Rocky shot her a look.

"They can't put me through this again. I just can't do it," Tammy said. "They're always blaming me."

April busied herself with Deana's stamping supplies, straightening the papers on the kitchen counter. She started to put two and two together. Tammy must work at the nursing home her mother had mentioned earlier. George Weber was the body Deana had gone to fetch.

Rocky said, "They couldn't run that place without you, sweetie."

"Damn straight," Tammy said unconvincingly.

"Come on, Tammy," Mary Lou said, shoving a kit her way. "You know there's nothing you can do for him now. Do some stamping. Take your mind off things."

April looked back at the table. The stampers were getting back to their projects. Rocky straightened and gave Tammy a squeeze on her shoulder and a fortifying smile.

Tammy wiped her eyes. She shuddered once. Her face was returning to a normal color. "I'm okay. Just mad, that's all. George was a nice guy."

She reached into her bag and brought out a pair of scissors. A long cord was attached to the handle. Tammy put the cord around her neck so the scissors rested on her ample bosom, accessible for quick work.

She finally saw April and stuck out her hand. "Sorry, that was rude. My name is Tammy Trocadero. It's nice to meet you. April, right? I think you were a couple of grades behind me."

April's notoriety in high school was not her fault. She wanted to change the subject. And away from nursing-home deaths.

"Shall we get started?" April said, then, noticing one unclaimed kit on the table, she asked, "Is this everyone?"

Mary Lou said, "We're missing Piper Lewis. She's always late."

That was another familiar name. When April had left town for college, the Lewis family owned the bowling alley and bar, a gas station with convenience store and a huge farm. A mini empire. Not rivaling the Winchesters, with their tentacles into all the old money in the valley, but impressive just the same.

Work on the project began. April found the group didn't need her help. Deana's kit was self-explanatory, and the stampers helped each other. She relaxed and picked up her sketchbook, letting the conversation eddy around her. She started to draw, the creative energy in the room feeding her own. This was not the way she'd expected to spend her first night back at home, but it was nice to have voices surrounding her instead of the empty air of the barn. And the even emptier space that Ken had once occupied.

"How long have you been stamping together?" April asked.

"We've known each other since school," Suzi said. "We started stamping back then. We'd send secret messages to each other. Rebus puzzles."

"What's a rebus?" April asked. She thought she remembered the term from *Highlights,* but she couldn't recall.

Tammy said, "You take simple images and string them together to make a message."

"Like this," Suzi said. She quickly drew a circle and a bird.

"I don't see the meaning," April said, after studying the proffered note.

Rocky looked over her shoulder. "Simple. Round Robin. We were far more sophisticated than that," she said. "Try to get this one."

She drew a prone stick figure, wearing a T-shirt that said, "Rocky." Above that she wrote the word "over."

She drew a line between the two, tapping her pencil for emphasis. April shook her head.

"Over my dead body," she said, laughing.

"Wow," April said. "I guess your teachers could never bust you for passing notes."

Tammy said, "They never caught on. It's fun. Rocky and I still do it, just to keep our skills tight."

"Her husband can *never* figure out what we're talking about." Rocky laughed. "It comes in handy when we're planning our stamping sessions."

"Did you hear Henry locked up Piper's son Jesse again?" Suzi asked.

So, Aldenville's part-time police officer Henry Yost was still harassing teenagers. He kept an eye on every kid over the age of thirteen. April remembered being chased by Yost one long-ago Halloween, dropping her dozen eggs in a neighbor's flower bed as she ducked between houses to get home before he caught her. Every kid was a potential criminal in his book.

Mary Lou said, "Lucky for Jesse, he's still a juvenile."

Suzi said, "It's not like Piper didn't try with him. Remember last summer when she sent him to that boot camp out west somewhere?"

"He came back ornerier than ever," Mary Lou said. "Only difference was that he knew how to forage in the woods and build a fire without a lighter."

Tammy said, "That's when the VFW building on Main Street burned."

"What can you expect?" Rocky said. "His mother is Piper and his father is missing in action."

Suzi explained, "Piper lost her husband when Jesse was very young."

"Even when he was around, he never paid much attention to that kid," Mary Lou said.

A wind knocked some of the papers off the table. All the stampers looked up and saw a tall brunette standing in the open doorway. From the expression on her face, she'd heard every word.

"It's not Jesse's fault that his father died," the newcomer, who April assumed to be Piper, said. "Hi, everyone."

"Plastic cups will be fine," she said, crossing the room and handing April a box of white wine. Wine in a box. April cringed as she remembered the Russian River Valley Zinfandels she'd left behind.

Piper's hair was swept off her face with a black headband. Her eyes were faded blue, the leached color of the sky on the hottest summer day, and narrowed.

Those eyes flitted about the barn. "This was my grandfather Leo's place." Piper's sense of ownership raised hackles on April's neck, reminding her of how she didn't belong. Piper continued. "My father's family built this barn in the 1800s. They hid provisions here during the Civil War. I think there's a secret room underneath."

April swallowed the need to say, *My daddy owns it now.* She didn't want to get into that game. Being measured by one's family was more dangerous for April than most.

Rocky sniffed as though she smelled sewage. "That's fab, Piper. But the *original* barn was built by my great-great-great-great-great-granddaddy while your relatives were still tossing cabers in the Scottish Highlands. The Lenape Indians burned down that barn — twice."

The two women stared at each other. Piper looked away first.

April had to keep the peace, for Deana's sake. She didn't want to be responsible for

41

ruining Deana's stamping business. "Come in and take a seat," she said.

Piper parked herself at the head of the table, where April had been sitting. April gritted her teeth and smiled, moving her sketch pad out of the way. She put the cups and the wine on the counter and poured a glass for Piper. No one else asked for wine.

April's cell rang. She walked away from the group, grateful for the interruption, cracking her neck and rolling her shoulders as she moved away. There was a tension in the air that she felt in her body.

"Hey, Dad."

"How'd you know it was me?" her father whined.

When April didn't answer right away, he answered his own question. "Oh, that blasted caller ID. I hate that people know it's me on the phone. What's wrong with a little surprise?"

April cut him off. "So, what's up?" Her father's rants about technology could last hours.

"Did you find the key okay? Get the notes I left you?" Ed's tone was worried, more than usual.

"It was under the mat right where you'd said it would be. And your notes were very helpful." His "notes" filled a loose-leaf binder with emergency numbers, warranties and an illustrated map to the gas shutoff.

Ed said, "Sorry I couldn't be there. I spent all day on the phone to Italy, tracking down these fixtures the client wants."

April knew the last place he'd wanted to be was stuck for hours in the barn with his ex-wife, Bonnie. "No worries. Mom and Deana helped me. We were done in no time."

"We're meeting the client, Mrs. Harcourt, at nine tomorrow. Don't be late."

Mrs. H. was the woman who was restoring Mirabella.

She bit back the statement that she was never late. "I won't be."

Ed wasn't finished. "Don't park in front of the house. Look for a drive that goes straight back. That'll take you to the —"

April interrupted. "Servants' entrance?"

"No, not for the past fifty years," Ed said. "Be cool. I don't need to hear any of your California everyone-is-equal BS tomorrow. This is a rich client, April, and we need to treat her right."

"Dad, I know how to conduct myself." April wondered if her father knew how many millionaires lived in San Francisco. Granted, most of the ones she'd worked with had decidedly middle-class backgrounds, but rich people, whether newly fortunate or the latest in a lineage, were the same.

"And bring your sample boards. Mrs. H. will want to see your ideas."

April felt her panic rise. "What sample boards? I thought this was just a walk-through. I've got to see what the place looks like. I don't even know what stage the renovation is in."

"I'll give you the tour tomorrow. The walls were stamped, but they've been painted over a zillion times. You need to have designs ready to show Mrs. H."

"You could have told me," April protested. A couple of heads cocked her way, so April lowered her voice and moved further into the great room.

"Just do it, okay," her father said. "I don't want to screw this up. Use my computer, go online. Get some ideas, make a few sketches. Just something we can show the client to-morrow."

April swallowed her anger. There would be no sleeping for her tonight. "All right, but I have a question for you. When do you think I'll get paid?"

"Don't worry, I'll take care of you."

"You promised me I wouldn't have to wait."

Ed's voice faded. "You're breaking up. I can't hear a thing. I'm hanging up. See you in the morning."

"Dad . . ." she protested.

His voice was suddenly clear. "Drive carefully. Officer Yost has been handing out speeding tickets left and right."

There was dead air. Hopefully, pretending to have bad cell coverage was her father's idea of a joke, and he'd come through with her advance. She needed that money.

She glanced at the huge schoolhouse clock that dominated the stone wall. It was only eight o'clock. Deana had said the stampers liked to stay until ten or later. April sighed. How would she ever get the sketches done for tomorrow's job?

She dialed Deana's cell. Maybe she was finished with her body and could come by and help out. There was no answer.

"April, I'm not doing this right. Can you help me?" Tammy called out.

She squared her shoulders. It was her and the stampers. The faster they finished, the quicker she'd get to her research. She leaned over Tammy's shoulder and picked up a brush. "Try this. If you drag that brush, you'll get a fine line and then a fat line. See that?"

"Cool. Thanks. So you've just moved

back?" Tammy asked April as she drew the brush across the page. She drew with such expertise that April knew this had been a ploy to talk.

"First day back in town," April said.

"And you're going to work on Mirabella?" Tammy asked. She shrugged as though apologizing for eavesdropping. This was a woman tuned in.

No harm in telling Tammy. "I am. I'll be restoring the walls to their original finishes. Are you a nurse?" she asked, hoping to deflect Tammy's interest in her.

She shook her head. "I'm just an aide." She drew another squiggle on the page. "Rocky's dad used to own that place," Tammy offered.

April glanced Rocky's way. Now she made the connection. Rocky was one of those Winchesters.

Rocky shrugged. "Used to," she said, her face impassive. April wondered why her father had given up the mansion. Was he dead? If so, why had Mrs. Harcourt inherited the house and not Rocky? This was awkward. She must have stepped right into some family drama.

Tammy gave Rocky an apologetic shrug.

Rocky said, "Aunt Barbara bought the place from Dad. Her dead husband, Harry

Harcourt, left her plenty of money."

Suzi changed the subject. "Isn't today Jesse's birthday, Piper?" she said.

"Tomorrow," she said. "June 14. I remember his birth like it was yesterday. I fell in love with him the first moment I set eyes on him."

Tammy said, "He's out on bail, right? Are you doing anything to celebrate?"

Piper didn't answer but shot Tammy a withering glance. Tammy returned to daubing the edge of her page.

Suzi said, "God, remember the night he was born? Your graduation party, Rocky? Jesse was born the day after we got out of high school. Well, the middle of the night, really."

April froze. It couldn't be the same night. "When did you graduate?" she asked warily.

Suzi said, "1993."

April had been just finishing her junior year. She'd heard about Rocky's party that day. Everyone had. Plenty of kids crashed it. She'd been one of them.

"I graduated high school in 1978," Mary Lou said dryly. The others laughed. Mary Lou pointed to her daughter. "2005," she said.

Suzi ran her tape gun over a page and glued down a pretty swirly pink paper. "We almost didn't get her to the hospital on time."

Mary Lou said, "Ahem. My daughter is listening. Your party stories are not meant for everyone's ears."

Rocky did a long scan of Kit's belly. "Your daughter looks like she's had a few good times of her own."

Mary Lou smirked at Rocky. Kit came to her own defense.

"Mom, really," Kit said. "I'm twenty-one. Do you really think I didn't party?"

Mary Lou pointed a hole punch at her daughter. "It's not you I'm worried about. It's me. *I'm* too young to know the truth about your high school years. You lived through it, I didn't know anything at the time, and I don't want to know now where you did your underage drinking."

"Nicole Munson's basement," Kit said quietly, her eyes twinkling. Her mother covered her ears. April laughed. Bonnie had had the same head-in-the-sand attitude.

Rocky put a hand on Mary Lou's arm. "Mary Lou, sweetie, I know this may come as a shock to you, but your daughter is no longer a virgin."

Everyone laughed, and Mary Lou stuck out her tongue at Rocky. That was enough to change the subject.

"That's enough talk about sex, drugs and partying. What did you all bring to share?" Mary Lou said.

"Okaaay," April said. She tried to remember the last time she did show-and-tell. It had to be Mrs. Whitebread's third-grade class. Still, the process had to be the same.

Mary Lou took out pictures and passed them around. "Kit and I have been painting furniture for the nursery. We cut stars and moons out of sponges and stamped the drawer fronts. It really came out cute."

The rest of the group murmured their approval, except for Piper. She kept her head down, only surfacing to blow embossing powder off her page. She gave Mary Lou's pictures a cursory glance and went back to her project. Her arm was positioned in front of her page to ensure privacy. April wondered what she was doing that was so secret.

Mary Lou looked to Tammy, who said she had nothing to show. Suzi passed around her garden journal again. It was clear her love of plants permeated her life.

Rocky pulled out her portfolio. She handed out the papers she'd purchased, but a collage underneath caught April's eye.

"May I?" she asked, picking it up when Rocky nodded yes.

The collection of stamped images on the

page was thick and layered. April thought she saw a baby doll, leaves and a bird. She thought she saw a hammer. A ghostly image of a building was rendered, covered in brambles.

"Is this yours? It's wonderful," April said, admiring the colors and the disturbing, three-dimensional quality Rocky had produced on a flat piece of paper.

"Rocky sells her collages at Peddler's Village," Tammy said proudly. "She gets a lot of money for them."

"I can see why." April moved the page closer. She recognized one image. "Is this the Castle?"

"Yes," Rocky said. "My aunt is getting rid of the Castle once and for all, so I've been doing a series on the building. That's an old photo that I transferred onto organza."

"Oh, that's why it looks so ethereal," April said.

"The Castle has always been an illusion," Rocky said.

The stampers were quiet. Rocky's words were somber, so different from the teasing just minutes before. April didn't know how to transition back to the stamping night that Deana had set up.

"The collage is beautiful," she said inadequately.

Piper lifted her arm and began tapping her foot on the floor. She was clearly ready to show her project. Rocky pulled her collage from April's grasp and gave Piper the go-ahead, with a frowning expression.

Piper didn't notice. She stood, holding her piece close to her chest. She turned it around slowly.

"How do you like my 'get-out-of-jail-free' card?" She smiled at April, ignoring everyone else in the room.

April wasn't prepared for what she saw and she had to swallow a gasp. The image was dark and sinister, nothing like its counterpart in Monopoly. Piper had taken the pretty tulip photo book and used a sponge to create a black-striped background on each page. She'd stamped delicate and wispy angels and dressed them in bright orange jumpsuits. Their wings were outstretched, but their hands looked oddly empty. In the spaces for the photos were pictures of a tow-headed boy, at various ages.

April searched for an appropriate response. Rocky beat her to the punch. "Drama queen, thy name is Piper," she muttered.

"Be supportive," Piper warned.

"Great balance, Piper," April said finally,

resorting to critiquing the card and not the contents. "I like the way you used dragging for the background. And your handwriting is amazing. Are you a trained calligrapher?"

Piper nodded. "I've studied."

"Classes by mail that she found on the back of a matchbook," Rocky said.

"You should know. That's where you got your art degree," Piper said.

April felt panic. Why hadn't Deana told her there was such animosity between these women? Maybe Piper wasn't usually this mean. It could be because her son had been arrested.

Rocky was leaning back in her chair. She yawned loudly, fingering her ear as though to pop it. April could see these two were not used to sharing the spotlight.

The last page in the book was a depiction of a cell. "Jesse, getting out of jail." Piper held up the card for all to see.

The image of the blond boy grinning into the camera was shocking against the dark jail cell.

Great big tears gathered in the corners of Piper's eyes, hanging there like dewdrops off a rain gutter. Despite feeling sorry for anyone whose kid was incarcerated, April suspected the tears were as authentic as Ken's medicinal marijuana card.

April felt that she had to say something. "Piper, great juxtaposition of images. Good use of irony."

"Irony, schmirony. This is my life," Piper shot back.

Rocky frowned at her. "Get over yourself, Piper. If you've come for sympathy, you've got the wrong group of girls. I believe it was my fence that your darling son drove his four-by-four through last winter."

Piper looked around for another victim. "Ask Tammy what happened to her first boyfriend, April. He left town in a hurry."

Tammy started to protest, but Rocky stepped in this time. "Tammy's had one boyfriend. Lyle. Stuff it, Piper. Pick on someone your own size."

Rocky picked up the project she'd been working on, dug out her car keys and stood. "Thanks, April, but I'm ready to call it a night. Come on, Tam, I'll drop you off home."

April stole a look at the clock. It was only nine, but this stamping event appeared to be over.

The rest of the group gathered up their cards and purses, studiously avoiding Piper's gaze. Piper stood, tapping a pensive finger on her lips. She looked off into space. "April Buchert, right? I know that name."

Something in her soft voice caught the stampers' attention and they stilled. Noises abated. Like a wolf pack, they waited for the strike.

April caught her breath, steeling herself. She knew this moment would come. She just didn't think it would happen so soon after she arrived.

"Buchert. Now I remember. Didn't your father leave his wife for a man?"

CHAPTER 3

April took her hands off the wheel to scrub at her eyes; she'd spent all night preparing for this morning's meeting and she now felt gritty and a bit euphoric. After the stampers had gone, she couldn't shake the bad feeling left behind. She'd wasted time fretting, waiting for a call from Deana that never came and generally not doing the work on the project until finally knuckling down after midnight.

She made the turn off Main Street that would lead her deeper into the valley. The sample boards lay on the passenger seat. She couldn't wait to show her work to the client. She'd had a creative brainstorm at about three in the morning, and now she was thrilled with the results.

Piper couldn't have known, but she'd said aloud what had been bugging April since her mother connected the Castle to the Mirabella mansion. She was returning to the scene of the crime. That job had led to her father leaving her mother.

In her teenage April-centric world, she'd thought her parents' marriage was fine. After all, they never fought. Instead, her father had been away a lot that spring, and Bonnie had saved all her venom for April.

And then, her father ended the marriage and followed his heart. To Vince.

Everything changed the day he left. April felt the sting of humiliation daily until she finally escaped to art school and California.

The right front tire hit the edge of the road, bringing her back to the present. April grabbed the wheel, heart pounding. The two-lane blacktop rose and fell over small rolling hills and snaked around wooded lots and farmland, following routes deer had laid out centuries ago.

She passed the house where Samantha Eggar had stayed during the making of the move *The Molly Maguires* in the late sixties. People still talked about how sweet and beautiful she was, just the opposite of that Sean Connery, who had not stayed locally, preferring instead to be secretly limoed in and out of Allentown each day.

The sun was out, dappling the verdant countryside. A hawk hovered just beyond the car, reluctant to give up its wobbly thermal.

She caught a glimpse of three chimney pots and a slate roof. Suddenly, around a curve, Mirabella came into view. Built on a ridge, the Tudor hunched over the country club and surrounding homes like a vulture, the wings threatening to sweep lesser homes into its maw.

The house disappeared as she turned onto the private road marked by a short metal sign with the Mirabella crest. As she drove, the road rose steadily. There were at least ten acres of grounds, mostly woods. The rich knew how to maintain their privacy — buy up all the surrounding land.

The driveway curved to the left when the house came back into sight. To her right, she saw the rolling bluegrass of the golf course.

She slowed and studied the façade. The siding was tan stucco studded with decorative half timbers. A brick walk led to a massive carved front door. Tudor wasn't her favorite style, but she could appreciate the beauty of this house.

A crow squawked. This was where she would be working the next few months. This was the place where she could lick her wounds and repair the damage done to her by Ken. Work was the balm for her soul.

She always felt more comfortable in a stranger's home than in her own.

Following her father's instructions, April went off the paved drive and followed a dirt-packed utility road past the stucco garage and matching garbage can enclosure. She pulled in next to her father's pickup. He was standing on the first step of a brick porch leading up to a utilitarian door, hugging a clipboard to his chest. He was tugging on his bottom lip. "Hurry. Come on, let's go," he called out.

April reached into the passenger seat for her sample boards. She knew it wasn't even nine o'clock yet. "Good morning to you, too."

"Hi, sweetie." Vince, her father's business and life partner, came from the truck and greeted her, a set of blueprints rolled under his arm. He had a broad, rubbery face that was friendly and open. He was nearly handsome, but his nose was a bit too big. The short sleeves of his blue oxford shirt showed off nicely tanned arms — a construction tan that probably stopped abruptly where his sleeves began. He was wearing the gold chain bracelet that April had helped her father pick out online for their last anniversary.

He smiled and hugged her with his free

arm. She leaned in and squeezed him back. It had taken years to get used to the idea that her father shared his life with another man, but she really liked Vince.

"Don't mind him," he said to April, pointing to Ed. "He's always like this on the first day of a new job."

April had thought they'd been on this job for months. What would she be doing if the rooms weren't ready for the walls to be finished? She felt a glimmer of unease. She'd jumped on her father's job offer so quickly. Now she couldn't remember if they'd talked about the details.

She stated her question. "New job? But I thought —"

Vince said, "New phase, I should have said."

Protesting Vince's earlier observation, her father commented, "I'm not *like* anything." But his manner belied his words. He walked down the steps and back up them again. Pieces of nervous energy came off him like embers off a Fourth of July sparkler. Harmful, but only for a second. Bright, but no real danger.

April gave her father a quick kiss. "It's good to see you," she said. The last time they'd all been together was when Vince and Ed came to San Francisco in February.

"You too, hon. I'm glad you're here," he replied.

Vince smiled at him, but Ed reverted to form. "Listen, about Mrs. H. Don't look her in the eye."

April reared back, unable to keep the surprise out of her voice. "What is she, royalty or a pit bull?"

"Little of both," Vince said. He and April shared a laugh, but her father wouldn't budge.

"She's a very important client," he said.

"Come on, Dad. I'm a grown woman. I ran a successful design firm in San Francisco for ten years. I know how to present myself."

"Yeah, in California," Ed grumbled. "This is the Commonwealth. We don't do things like you granola eaters."

"Don't worry, I traded in my Birkenstocks at the border," she said dryly.

Even frowning with worry, her dad was a good-looking guy. Age became him. Or maybe it was being with Vince instead of her mother. His crew-cut hair was silver. He was over six feet, with a barrel chest. Today he was wearing an argyle vest and pink shirt.

Maybe she could tease him out of his mood. "When did you start dressing like a duffer?" she said.

He looked down. "Like it? Vince bought it at the Presidio Golf Course when we were out there visiting you."

April punched his arm lightly. "So you *do* borrow Vince's clothes? You're practically the same size."

Vince winked at her, on board with her joking.

"It's my shirt," Ed protested.

"I always suspected," April said. She tapped her teeth innocently. "There's so much I don't know about the gay lifestyle."

Vince said, "You probably know more about being gay than we do. We're just living our life here."

April grinned. "Well, I did march in last year's Gay Pride parade. It was a hoot. I walked right next to a guy with this giant pineapple over his —"

Her father had heard enough. "Okay, April, not now. Mrs. H. could hear you."

Ed started for the door, but Vince put a restraining hand on his arm. "Before we go in, I've got something to tell you," he said. Ed stopped, his brow furrowing even deeper. Vince indicated they should move away from the door, so they went down the steps and onto the lawn. A stone elf smiled at them from the flower bed. April hoped he was a portent of good luck.

Vince said, "There was another drug raid on the Mirabella property, night before last, out near the Castle."

Ed swore. "Damn Henry Yost. He's always after the kids."

Vince shook his head. "This is not just Henry compensating for the fact that he's never passed the state trooper test. It's serious."

"How can the kids be having parties there?" Ed said. "The Castle has practically fallen in on itself. There's only three walls still left standing." He began to pace.

Vince shrugged. "Kids don't need walls. Yost says he found cocaine, crystal meth. He arrested a couple of kids."

"Piper Lewis's kid," April put in.

Her father frowned. "How do you know?"

April said, "I met a few of Deana's friends last night. Piper was there and told us her son was out on bail."

"Anyway," Vince said, "I told Lyle to go ahead with the demolition this morning. We can't take the chance that kids will party there again."

"No, no, no." Ed's voice rose with each syllable. "We have to wait for Raico, the code enforcement officer, to give us the permits. Otherwise we're going to be fined."

April remembered that Ed had tried to get the code enforcement job. The officer was appointed by the borough council. He was given a nice salary for working part-time, making sure building codes were up to snuff. It was usually a reward for pleasing the council members in some other way. A patronage job, but one with authority behind it. A dangerous combination.

Vince said, "I think we should act now and ask for permission later."

"Absolutely not," Ed said.

Vince gave in. "It's your job. But you'd better tell Lyle. Now."

Ed dialed his phone, his face glum. April was struck by how much her father's expression reminded her of the basset hound they'd had when she was little. The same sad eyes, the same forlorn expression.

Worry was his natural state. His parents had settled in northeast Pennsylvania, but they'd never left behind the lingering fears that Depression-era childhoods in the Bronx had fostered. Her grandfather had died before April was born, but her grandmother still lived on the family farm ten miles away. She played bingo seven days a week and cut hair in her one-chair beauty shop in the basement.

Ed said he liked to be prepared for the

worst, but to April it seemed as though the worst rarely happened and in the meantime, he'd driven himself into a complete funk and brought down everyone around him.

Vince didn't seem to be affected by Ed's gloomy outlook on life. He could often cajole Ed into laughing at himself. It was the way April knew they were perfectly suited to each other. She felt bereft when she realized Ken hadn't made her laugh in months.

Today Vince's charms weren't working on his partner. April felt her stomach tighten. There was more to this job than she'd been told.

Ed shook his head. "Damn voice mail." His voice got louder as he left a message. "Hold off, Lyle. I'll talk to the CEO as soon as I'm done with this meeting with Mrs. H. Don't do anything until I call you back."

"Let's get this over with," Vince said, ringing the doorbell. "I've got a half dozen unsupervised men on the Heights job. I need to get up there soon."

Ed fumbled with his phone, dropping it before getting it clipped on his belt. They joined Vince on the porch.

April felt the fluttering of butterflies in her stomach that a new job always brought. She loved going inside homes, seeing how people decorated and assessing the architecture. Especially in older houses. What nineteenth-century artisans had been able to achieve always humbled her.

April heard the clicking of heels. The door opened. From the noise, April had expected to see a maid or a dog, but a tiny, elegant woman was behind the door instead.

She gestured impatiently, shaking the miniature wattles on her arms. "Don't just stand there. Get inside. You're letting all the cool air out."

The heavy door closed behind them, blocking out all sound, and presumably, heat.

Judging by the size of the mansion, she was too rich. Judging from the size of her body, Barbara Harcourt had perfected too thin.

Wearing a navy blue skirt with gold chains across the waist, and a beige silk tank, she looked like a woman who was never without makeup. The silk tank gaped open at the neck showing off a sharp-looking collarbone. Even in this heat, she was wearing stockings with her heels. No one in San Francisco wore pantyhose.

She ushered them through a short hall with built-in cabinets into a kitchen that hadn't been updated since before April was born. The floor was Mexican red tiles, worn thin at the edges, and the appliances were copper. This had been a working kitchen once upon a time.

As they came out of the kitchen, April saw a plastic tarpaulin covering a doorway and relaxed. The construction must be going on in the rest of the house. Her work might be in a bedroom or bath. The mansion had several large wings.

They entered an enormous living room, easily forty feet long. Mrs. H. took a seat on a white linen sofa and indicated that they sit opposite. The lights were dimmed, the shades on the bay windows drawn. April let her eyes adjust to the darkness. After the smoky hot outdoors, the cool air felt good.

Before they sat down, Ed pulled April forward. "Mrs. H, this is the designer I was telling you about. My daughter, April Buchert."

Mrs. H's eyebrows would have shot up if they weren't already penciled in halfway up her forehead. She pursed her lips in a way that pulled every wrinkle into its designated place.

"Daughter?" She looked from her father to Vince and April and back again. "I didn't know you had a daughter. Of course, why would I? I've been living in Europe for the last twenty years."

April was grateful that this woman didn't find her family history interesting. No wonder the Castle meant nothing to her.

The client offered a hand, soft as a cotton ball. She didn't shake April's hand as much as lay her hand in her palm. April was gentle, afraid the arm would break off if she was too vigorous.

Ed was still in full-on grovel mode. "Mrs. H. has had the most amazing ideas for this place."

"Great," April said. "It's a wonderful example of Tudor."

"This house is unique," Mrs. H. corrected. "It was designed by the finest architect in Italy in the late 1800s. Before Tudor became a craze."

"We're doing a total restoration," Ed said.

Mrs. H. said, "My brother nearly ruined the integral beauty of the place. That horrible Castle was just the start." Her tiny shoulders shuddered with revulsion. She reminded April of a hairless dog who was unable to keep itself warm without shaking. "There's flocked wallpaper in the hallway bath," she whispered as though this truth was too horrible to say out loud.

"We'll have her back to her original glory," Ed said with a stiff smile on his face.

"This wing of the house has sixteen rooms. Let's get started in the dining room," she said. "I have a dinner party each August. I want this room finished by then."

Vince and Ed exchanged a look. Was that enough time? April doubted it. Her stomach crawled again.

Mrs. H. led them into an empty formal dining room with paneled wainscoting. The large lead glass windows looked over the expanse of green lawn. April looked again. Not lawn. Fairway. She saw an oval sign that said "Women's Tee. Three."

"The paneling must be restored to its original state." She pointed out places where the wood had been damaged or was missing.

Vince was taking notes. "Don't worry. We've got craftsmen who can duplicate the original molding. You won't be able to tell the difference."

Ed circled the room quietly. April saw a change come over him. He seemed so different now that he was faced with the work that needed to be done. Calm, confident, completely engaged. He was rubbing his hands over the walls, his hands as sensitive as a doctor's, finding flaws and figuring out how to fix them.

The punched tin ceilings were twelve feet

high. The moldings were deep and fluted. The proportions of the room were perfect. Despite its large size, the room felt warm. April felt the buzz she got whenever she was in the room of a master architect.

Mrs. H. ripped a piece of wallpaper with a violent gesture. "No more of this hideousness. In here, I want the walls hand-stamped," Mrs. H said.

Those were the words April was waiting for. "Perfect," she said. "That's my specialty. I have some ideas."

She opened the portfolio and spread her samples on a side table.

Her stamp designs were good. She'd based her designs on woodblock wallpaper with chrysanthemum motifs.

She pictured her design on the walls. The walls looked as though they had been papered and painted over several times. She'd have a lot of prep work to do, but she liked that part of the job. Walls like these were never straight, that was a given, but she could compensate with the size and shape of her stamps.

Lost in mentally measuring the walls and placing her stamps, April didn't hear at first what the client was saying. The sound of her father's voice, however, brought her back to the present. "Sure thing, April can do that," he said. Glancing toward him, April saw that Mrs. H., her father and Vince had moved over to the inside wall. Her portfolio lay open, ignored.

The three of them were studying the wall. April moved behind them, peeking between Ed and Vince to see what it was she could "do."

The wall was covered in a mural. Floor to ceiling, from the end of the wall to the arch leading to the living room; it had to be eight feet by twelve feet. It depicted the local Sioux chief meeting with Benjamin Franklin. Franklin's nose had a major chip, and the colors of the campfire were faded to a pale peach.

"This Refregier mural must be returned to its earlier glory," Mrs. H. said.

"And Retro Reproductions is the right firm for that," Ed said.

April looked at her father in shock. What was he doing? She didn't know anything about restoring murals.

April tugged on her father's elbow and whispered, "Painting? That's not what —"

"No problem, Mrs. H.," her father said over her protests.

She fought to regain control of the conversation. She picked up her sample board and tried to waylay Mrs. H. with it.

"Look," April said, "once my father's team finishes restoring the floors and the paneling, these *other* walls are just right for my expertise. You can see my stamps will work perfectly in here. They are reminiscent of the period without being exact replicas . . ."

The older woman gave one disdainful look at April's work and ignored her pitch as thoroughly as she would a door-to-door vacuum cleaner salesman. "All in good time, my dear. You don't have a problem beginning with the mural, do you? Your brochure says you do all kinds of decorative painting."

Brochure? Mrs. H. patted a bulging loose-leaf notebook that sat on a sideboard. Opening it, April found pages and pages of design ideas, pull sheets of floor coverings, wood choices, paint samples. The woman was a pantheon of organization. Flipping through the neatly bound collection, April soon located her so-called brochure and pulled it out, frowning.

Vince shot her father a told-you-so look. Ed shrugged.

Her father had used predesigned paper and his computer to make the marketing material. The front read "April Buchert Interiors." The address was the barn's and the phone number, her cell. There was something about seeing her name in print like this. She was touched and pissed at the same time.

She started to open her mouth to deny authorship, but her father's pleading look stopped her.

"We need this job," he mouthed. He rubbed his thumb and fingers together in a crude gesture that meant money.

Her indignation faded. Who was she kidding? *She* needed this job if she wanted to eat. She shrugged and tried to remember what she'd learned in art school about touching up paintings.

"I'm thinking I would also like painted built-ins," Mrs. H. said.

"No one is touching any furniture I make," a new voice said. His tone was firm but slightly teasing. Mrs. H.'s eyes widened in anticipation.

"We're in here, darling boy," Mrs. H. trilled.

"Must be Mitch," her father said.

April turned to see the speaker, a tall sandy-haired guy wearing a red baseball cap that read "Winchester Woodworking." He gave Mrs. H. a stern look, but a smile danced on his lips as he leaned in to hug her. She petted his cheek.

"My brother's crowning achievement,"

she said.

Ed snorted.

"Come on, Ed, you know you love me," Mitch said. He pumped Ed's hand and bumped knuckles with Vince.

"I love you as long as you don't get in my way," Ed said. "We're on a tight schedule here."

"You won't even know I'm here," he said cheerily. He turned to April. "Mitch Winchester, carpenter." He held out his hand. So this was Rocky's brother, the table maker.

His forearms were well developed. He smelled of wood and coffee. She fancied she could see shavings clinging to his blue jeans and vintage adidas sneakers. Someone must have told him he looked good with a two-day-old beard. They were right.

April was always attracted to men who worked with their hands. They seemed so competent. And then there was the idea that they'd be good with their hands at other things. Her stomach tingled. She took in a breath to calm down. She was not interested in men. Those that worked with their hands or any other kind.

"I'm April Buchert," she said. "Of April Buchert Interiors. Evidently."

She shot a look at her father to let him

know that they'd talk about her new job title, and the scope of her work, later. He shrugged.

Mitch said, "Oh, Ed's daughter, the girl that makes things pretty. I'm the guy who builds the shelves." He picked up her sample board. "Nice detail. You've really nailed the sensibility."

Vince spoke. "April is a restoration expert, Mitch. Paint and stamps."

"Mostly stamps," she corrected, but she smiled at Vince to let him know she appreciated his plug.

Mitch held up his hands in mock horror. "No stamps on my furniture. No paint, no inks, no faux finishes."

"I do not faux," April said haughtily.

He smiled at her.

Mrs. H. interrupted. "We'll discuss all that later, Mitchell. I have Ed's assurances that April will do whatever we need. For now, I want to show Ed and Vince the drawing room. I'm sure, April, you'll want to study the mural."

The trio walked into the hallway. Immediately, their voices got loud and the tone contentious. April heard them discussing the Castle.

Mrs. H. detailed her difficulties. "Do you know what an attractive nuisance is? Not my nude sunbathing neighbor, no. My lawyer says it's the Castle. A ruin of a building that entices young people to go there. And hang out, playing loud music and doing drugs."

Mrs. H. had never hung out in her life.

Ed murmured something conciliatory.

"Since it's on my property, I'm responsible. I'm the one who will have to pay if someone gets hurt. I could get sued."

Now Mitch was listening, too. He twitched his eyebrows at April.

Most of Ed's words were lost, but April heard him finish. "It's a challenge, Mrs. H. The road to it is completely overgrown. I can't get the bulldozer back there without knocking out trees. And the town tree committee is on me —"

"Not good enough. I can't be responsible if kids get hurt back there. I don't want them to have a place to party here anymore. The Castle is just too much of a lure. Take it down. Immediately."

Mitch had lost interest in the conversation and was looking intensely at April, his gaze as focused as a laser. A scratchy feeling settled in her belly.

"We've met." He tapped his front teeth with a pen. "I'm sure of it. Did you grow up around here?"

She nodded.

"Belong to the club?" Mitch asked.

She shook her head and put a finger to her lips. She should be paying attention to her father's discussion in case he volunteered her for some other chore.

"Go to the club pool?" he persisted.

April nodded. As the daughter of an employee, she had had pool privileges.

The conversation in the other room was just murmurs now. The contentious tone was gone. Vince's deep voice carried, reassuring Mrs. H. that the Castle would be cleared out by the end of the week.

April relaxed. They weren't talking about her. "I don't remember you."

He pointed to his chest. "Picture me with a whistle around my neck and zinc oxide on my nose. Scrawnier."

"The lifeguard? Axl?" The Guns N' Roses song "Sweet Child o' Mine" filled her head. She and Deana had played that song over and over the summer they were twelve.

Mitch groaned. "Oh, God, no. No one has called me that in years. You remember that?"

"Remember that? How could I forget? You played *Appetite for Destruction* at the pool party. Heavy metal at the club. Deana and I thought you were the coolest."

"I've always considered myself more Slash

than Axl." Mitch planted his feet and started playing air guitar. April laughed. He looked so not cool.

He said, "They fired me for that, but it was worth it."

The voices were returning to the dining room. April turned to the mural and pretended to be scrutinizing the paint.

Mrs. H. turned the corner into the room. Vince and Ed were right behind her. The air in the room felt different, as though the molecules had changed. April felt pressure in her ears and she looked to her father. He had a quizzical expression on his face, but she couldn't tell if he was more worried than he'd been.

Suddenly, there was a concussive *boom!*

April grabbed her father's arm. Mitch stood in front of his aunt protectively. Vince and Ed exchanged a glance. Neither looked as surprised as April thought they should.

CHAPTER 4

"What the hell was that?" Mrs. H.'s voice lost its practiced refinement. The dishes in the china cabinet rocked, and the crystals on the chandeliers tinkled daintily. April thought Benjamin Franklin had winked at her.

"Dad?" April said. She knew this wasn't part of the plan. What happened to waiting for the code enforcement guy?

Ed said, "It's okay." He grabbed his phone as though the answers would be found on it.

Vince said, "Apparently, we *are* taking down the Castle today."

"Well, I'm glad of it, but I didn't expect it to rattle my bones," Mrs. H. said. Mitch put an arm around her. April thought, unkindly, that Mrs. H.'s bones probably rattled when she sneezed. There was no fat on them to cushion the blow.

"Sounded like someone went a little

overboard on the dynamite to me," Mitch said. He looked to Vince and Ed. "We shouldn't have been able to feel it all the way over here."

April tried to picture where the Castle was in relation to Mirabella. The last time she'd walked between the two, she'd been a teenager. Maybe a ten-minute walk.

Like a fire alarm, the old-fashioned phone-jangle ring-tone of Ed's cell phone rang out, setting April's teeth on edge.

Ed took his call, walking to the far corner of the room. He was whispering fiercely, his voice rising and falling. April knew that tone of voice. Ed was panicking. She followed him. Vince remained by Mrs. H., reassuring her that the noise was not that unexpected.

He was whispering fiercely. "No, we don't have the permits yet. I told you to hold off."

As he paced, Ed's face reddened until it was the color of the satin drapes in the room, maroon. April thought of the high cholesterol number he'd reported after his last physical. She positioned herself next to a built-in corner cabinet filled with trinkets, pretending to inspect them for damage, keeping a covert eye on her father, trying to remember the signs of a heart attack.

"Yost?" she heard him say.

What was the local cop doing there? She

moved closer.

He clicked off his phone and went back to where Mitch, Mrs. H. and Vince stood.

"That was my foreman," Ed said. "The Castle is down. Just as you requested."

Mrs. H.'s protestations had been trailing off. As a final salvo, she said, "Did you have to blow us all to kingdom come? I think you knocked some fillings out of my head."

Vince said smoothly, "It would take more than a little explosion to upset a woman like you, Mrs. H. Let's get back to work. Show me those lighting fixtures you're interested in."

Mrs. H smiled and seemed mollified by Vince's remarks. She returned to her large notebook, opening to a page on lighting fixtures, tapping with her red nails. Vince looked over her shoulder. It looked as if life was going to go on as usual.

Except for Ed. He'd snapped his phone shut, but instead of returning to Vince's side, he was moving quickly toward the kitchen. And the back door.

"Ed," Mrs. H. called. "I need you here. I have more to go over." She looked to Vince for reinforcements.

Vince looked at his partner and his eyes darkened. He smiled quickly at Mrs. H., the wrinkles next to his eyes not moving.

"We'll be right back," he said.

April asked, "Is there something wrong?"

She got no answer from Vince. As he passed her, April could see a small vein throbbing in his jaw. He was seeing something in her father that disturbed him. Ed wasn't telling Mrs. H. everything he'd heard on the phone call. Something was wrong.

April ran after them, but by the time she'd cleared the back door, Vince and Ed were already in the truck. She could see her father's tight face as they passed. He was in the passenger seat, arms thrown up as he railed at Vince. She couldn't hear him, but he was not happy.

The pickup reversed out of the drive, fishtailing as Vince accelerated toward the road, coffee-colored dirt spewing from the tires.

"That explosion sounded too big," Mitch said in her ear. She whirled, surprised to see him on the porch with her. Mrs. H. was tapping her way through the kitchen.

April felt her voice constrict. "Do you think someone got hurt?"

"Hard to say. Demolition can be tricky," Mitch said.

April twisted her fingers together. Her father had looked so upset. She needed to know what had gone wrong.

81

"I've got to get to the Castle. Where is it from here?" she asked Mitch.

"Come on, I know a shortcut," Mitch said, passing April, fingering his keys. "They have to go all the way around on the main road."

"Don't everyone go off and leave me," Mrs. H. whined through the back door.

Mitch called to her, "No need for all of us to go, Aunt Barbara. We'll report to you in a few minutes."

Mitch threw himself into his small green Jeep, which was open on the sides and top. April climbed in the passenger seat. She'd only just clanged the door shut when Mitch started up the engine, his arm slung over his seat, looking backward. Concentration furrowed his brow, but one dimple showed on his right cheek.

The Jeep followed the dirt road leading out the back of the Mirabella property, into the woods. April's butt left the seat, and she scrambled for the shoulder harness and plugged it in.

"Hang on," Mitch said.

"Duh," April said, unable to let his demand pass. She looked at him. Had he hit that pothole on purpose? He had a slight grin on his face, making the dimple dig deeper in his cheek. She stifled a laugh, feeling silly and scared at the same time. Scared like she was on a roller-coaster ride, but frightened when she thought of Ed's red face.

The dirt road ran on the outskirts of the woods, paralleling the tree line. After a hundred yards or so, Mitch yanked the Jeep to the right, between several towering pine trees. April grabbed the roll bar with one hand and the door handle with the other.

They were deep in the woods now. The canopy of trees met overhead. The sun's rays didn't penetrate the tree cover, and she could barely see where they were going. Birds flew out of the trees in great bursts, like ashes out of the fireplace. Squirrels hurried up tree trunks. April had the impression all the woodland creatures knew Mitch well enough to get out of his way.

She tried to picture where the Castle had been situated. She knew it was close to the main road out of town, the same road that she'd traveled to get to Mirabella. Thick woods hid it from view.

The Jeep burst through the trees into a small clearing, before Vince and Ed arrived, as promised. Mitch pulled the emergency brake and the car jerked to a stop. All heads turned toward them.

There were four men standing in dust,

surveying a pile of rubble. Henry Yost, the local policeman, was easy to spot. He held a rifle in his left hand, low on his leg. He was wearing calf-high black boots, a light gray uniform and a Smokey-the-Bear hat. His badge was bright and shiny and a dead giveaway that he was local and not a state trooper.

Two older men, too old to be workers, stood at Yost's side. They were chattering excitedly to each other: One was completely bald. His face was red with excitement. The other had crew-cut gray hair and was sporting a Members Only jacket over his khakis.

Yost was ignoring them, instead watching a tall man in a yellow hard hat and steel-toed construction boots. He stood with his feet planted wide apart, hands on his hips. His T-shirt read "Retro Reproductions." This had to be Lyle. His long face was unlined. He looked completely at ease.

April got out of the Jeep and walked toward the rubble. Mitch joined her, whistling. "Wow. He did quite a number on the place."

Most of the house had fallen in on itself. The chimney stack was exposed. A raw red pipe stuck out of the ground like a graveyard marker. Pieces of wallboard had been tossed into the trees overhead. The smell of cordite lingered in the air. Smoke hovered.

The rock fireplace in the front of the house was still intact. April could see a panel of a heavy oak door and mangled window frames. Glass glittered in the dirt. A few steps to her right, and April was looking at a cross section of the building. It reminded her of her favorite Richard Scarry books. *How Do Things Work in Busytown* was the best. She'd learned enough about construction from his books to keep her intrigued by her father's work.

Lyle had a phone to his ear, and he nodded as they approached. Mitch lifted his chin in acknowledgment.

"What are you doing here, Mitch?" Yost said. "Coming to see what's left of your legacy?"

April flinched at the officer's tone, but Mitch just smiled. "It's not every family that has its own ruins," Mitch said cheerfully.

Yost was wearing sunglasses, practicing his dead stare. April felt the controlled excitement coming off him, a man who had nothing to police most days of the week but unlicensed dogs.

He looked her over, found her uninteresting and turned back to Mitch.

"Most ruins happen over centuries," Yost said. "Your father managed to run down this place in less than twenty years."

Mitch's eyes darkened, and his tone grew harsh. "Don't pretend you didn't have a role in that," he said to Yost. He moved away, out of Yost's sight line. April followed him, feeling his cop gaze on her.

The gray-haired man caught Mitch's arm. "Too bad your father wasn't here to witness this. I don't know if it would break his heart or cheer him up," the man said.

"The latter, Mo," Mitch said, his forehead furrowed despite his light words. He shook Mo's hand and the hand of the bald man. "You two sidewalk supervising? Doing your part to help out?"

Mo chuckled, his face a wide expanse of wrinkles and grooves. "You know these jobs go smoother when we're here. We watch that these whippersnappers do their job right."

"Not so sure that worked today," Mitch replied, then turning to April, said, "These old fellas have got nothing better to do than hang around watching other people work."

He introduced her to them. "This is April Buchert, Ed's daughter."

The description didn't bother Mo or his friend at all. They watched Yost and Lyle with interest. Yost took a phone call.

The bald man's arms were tattooed with purple age marks. His head bobbed as though the connection between it and his spine was tenuous. He held a hand out to April. "I'm Curly. Your father calls us the Three Stooges."

April looked for a third man. The old man's face fell when he saw her questioning expression. "Guess we're not that anymore," he said quietly. Mo touched his arm.

Mitch said, "Where *is* George?"

"Didn't you hear?" Mo said. "He died last night, man."

Mitch's face fell. "God damn."

"I know what you mean," Curly said, his voice cracking with emotion. April felt her own throat thicken as the old man's eyes filled with tears. He patted Mitch several times on the shoulder, unable to stop.

Mo became animated. "You won't believe this, Mitch. Yost dragged us here this morning, trying to pin George's death on the Castle. He's got some lamebrain idea that George fell down yesterday when the three of us were out here and hit his head, and then died in his bed."

"But if he died in his bed . . . Yost brought you two out here, for what exactly?" Mitch asked. His forehead wrinkled with concern.

Curly said, "He doesn't think George died of old age in his bed. He's trying to pin it on us being here at the job site. He'd like nothing more than to keep us away from the jobs. Says we're a nuisance."

"He wanted to see if we could handle the terrain. You know how hard it is to get to the Castle from the road. He parked up there," Mo said, pointing up and behind them.

April looked. She could barely see the blacktop from here through the brush. The slope was steep, unlike the road through the woods. From their vantage point, the berm of the road had to be at least ten feet over their heads. April searched for her father's pickup but could see nothing. She heard a car go by without stopping.

Mo was still complaining about Yost. "He had us climb down here. We told him George was in better shape than both of us, but Yost wouldn't listen. We didn't know the place was getting blown up today."

"You should've seen Yostie when he saw Lyle setting his charges." Curly chuckled. Yost was disliked by young and old, evidently.

"What did Trocadero use?" Mitch asked. He watched Yost and Lyle conversing.

"Dynamite," Mo said.

Mitch whistled. "That's what I thought it was. No one uses that anymore." He looked worriedly at April. "This could really be a mess if Retro Reproductions didn't have the proper permits," he said.

Curly shrugged. "Lyle's old school. He learned demolition at the quarry his dad worked at. He goes with what's familiar."

A sharp voice broke through their conversation. "Damn it all to hell, Lyle! What happened?" Ed yelled.

Vince and Ed were climbing down the steep embankment. Vince was ahead of Ed, who was hanging on to tree roots to steady himself. Ed's face was mottled red, and his chest was heaving. April felt her own diaphragm tighten and pressed on it.

"Great," Ed muttered as he passed her. "Deputy Dawg is already here."

Vince and Ed skirted April, Mitch and the two old men. Vince nodded at her. Her father made a beeline to Lyle.

Lyle met him at the corner of the clearing, moving aside a piece of insulation with his toe. Yost was right behind him, still talking on his phone. "You told me to go ahead," Lyle said.

Ed said, saliva spraying, "I did no such thing. I told you to wait."

Lyle waggled his hand, middle fingers bent in as though he were talking on the phone. "You called back. I heard you and Mrs. H. She wanted the building down."

He pitched his voice up. " 'Immediately,' she said."

April grinned. His imitation of her upper-crust accent was spot on.

Vince took Ed's phone out of his hands. He read the screen and pointed out some-thing to Ed. Ed's eyes rolled.

Vince said, "You must have hit the redial when we were talking to her. Look, there are two calls to Lyle's number. One at eight fifty and then one a half hour later."

"I hate this damn phone," Ed said, jam-ming it onto his belt holster.

"Damn," Vince said, looking at the scene. "We had a lot of salvage possibility in there."

Mitch whispered to April, "There was a lot of good wood in the Castle. Cherry beams and oak doors. Copper pipe. All worth money."

Ed looked at April as though he'd forgot-ten she was around. He gave a light frown and a shake of the head, indicating she should disappear, fast. He couldn't afford to focus on her. She smiled, trying to let him know she was there to help.

Vince stepped forward, shaking Yost's hand after he'd hung up and stashed the phone on his belt. "Don't think you're go-ing to need that," he said, pointing at the rifle.

Yost tightened his grip and ignored Vince's comment. He looked at Ed. "Eddy, Eddy, what have you done? I'm always cleaning up after you, it seems."

"Look, Yost, don't start with me," Ed said, sputtering.

Vince put a calming hand on Ed's arm and said "Sorry, Officer Yost, but everything is under control now."

Yost continued to speak just to Ed. "You certainly know how to shake things up. That racket was heard all over the valley." He held up his cell phone. "I'm getting reports of mortar fire from the vets, and old Mrs. Billheimer is holed up in her tornado cellar."

Ed said, "Lyle was a little overzealous with the dynamite." He glared at Lyle.

Yost squinted at him from under the brim of his hat. "I'm going to assume you have the necessary permits. I'll leave that to the building inspectors. If not, you'll face a hefty fine."

He sounded as if nothing would make him happier. He took off his sunglasses. The skin on his face had darkened except for the area around his eyes. It was obvious he hadn't thought about the raccoon results his favorite eyewear were causing.

Lyle said, "We were cleared. I had a verbal okay."

Ed looked worried. April knew not having permission in writing was the same as not having permission at all.

Ed tried to sound tough. "No big deal. We were commissioned to take down the Castle, and we did."

His bluster didn't ring true to April.

Vince said, "I hear you've been raiding these woods. Did you find a meth lab? Maybe that's why it blew the way it did."

Yost shook his head. "The Castle was clean. The kids weren't even partying here. They were closer to the main house."

He looked toward Mirabella. Two of the chimneys were visible from here. April wished she was back there, prepping the walls for her stamps. The dance between her father and Yost was tying her stomach in knots. She remembered Officer Yost as a guy who picked on teens. Clearly, he'd moved on. Ed was in his sights now.

Yost said, "Let's take a look at what you've done here. My main concern is safety. Walk with me, you two."

Ed and Vince had no choice but to follow him. Lyle leaned against a tree, marking their progress without seeming to look at them. April suspected he wanted Ed to forget he was there.

"Uh-oh," Mitch said.

On the trail Mitch had used, Barbara Harcourt arrived in a Ralph Lauren golf cart, complete with yellow and white striped, fringed surrey top. Her high heel tapped the brake. She didn't bother to get out but let the cart get to within inches of the clearing and surveyed the damage.

Yost moved to her side, offered her his hand and helped her out of the cart. With his uniform and hat and deferential manner, he looked like a limo driver.

A woman used to being heard, she didn't wait for an explanation. Her voice carried. "Well, that certainly did the trick. I'm sure I'll be hearing from some of my neighbors' lawyers. They don't like to be awakened by sonic booms."

Mitch said to April, "Don't worry. Her neighbors are just like her. They never sue each other. They'll just take their revenge on the golf course. Or force her to pay too much at the next charity auction for the Gstaad ski trip."

Ed began, "Mrs. H. . . ."

"No need to explain, Ed. The Castle is gone. I'm happy about that. Just clean up and get the mess out of here. I don't want any more fuss about this place." She glowered at him. "I'll be gone for the rest of the day. I have a hospital board meeting to attend. When I get back, I expect to see this gone. Understood?"

Ed nodded morosely. "Mrs. H., we will do our best to get rid of the debris from this job as soon as we can. I'll get some men on it right away."

"See that you do, Ed. See that you do." She took one last look, shaking her head as she got back in. Mrs. H. pulled hard on the little steering wheel, nearly causing the cart to tip over. As she drove off, a strong breeze rattled the pine trees. A shower of pink insulation pieces fell down upon the cart, creating the illusion of a sylvan bride being pelted with rose petals.

Yost and Ed and Vince continued to walk the grounds, arguing about the best route to take out the debris. Ed's hands were moving in wide circles. He was getting agitated again. Yost was still going on about safety.

April moved away from Mitch. Curly was telling him a convoluted story about the way the blast had made him deaf for several minutes.

April couldn't watch Yost continue to berate her father, so she took several steps into the shady woods. The trees thickened,

94

a combination of old- and new-growth pines with an underpinning of mountain laurel. The waxy dark green leaves and woody trunks seemed too bulky to hold the delicate pink flowers that were just beginning to bloom.

Somewhere back here was where her father's job trailer had been sited, fifteen years ago. Searching for any sign of it, she thought she saw a faint path, leading away from the Castle. The play of light on the green forest floor attracted her. Shards of glass from the blast captured the sun's rays, making little rainbows on the ground. She bent down to move a branch so she could see the ferns beneath. A startled cardinal flew out of the tree. Tiny fiddleheads curled their way out of the brown leaves mulched under the mountain laurel. April noted their delicate violin shape. She could use that curve in a stamp. She described the shape in the air with her finger, trying to memorize it. This was an image worth preserving. Too bad she hadn't brought her sketchbook. It was in the car, back at Mirabella.

She felt her phone in her pocket and remembered its camera. April balanced herself, squatting, and snapped a shot of the fern. She looked at the picture she'd taken. She snapped several more. The lighting wasn't great, but the fern was there.

She straightened. Immediately she felt a tremor under her feet. She glanced toward the earth. It didn't seem to be rolling. Still, she'd been in enough earthquakes to send her running away from the trees back to the clearing.

"Dad!" she yelled, heart pounding.

Ed was frozen in place, watching the Castle as though it was possessed by an inner demon. When she came into his peripheral vision, he grabbed her and tried to protect her head with his meaty hand. Vince moved closer to her on the other side.

As if one body, everyone took a step back. Mitch was behind her. Lyle looked worried, as though expecting to be blamed for this, too. Yost positioned himself, arms spread wide, in front of the two old men. They peeked around him like kids on Christmas morning trying to get a glimpse of reindeer on the roof.

The rumbling was not coming from a fault in the earth, but from the fireplace as it threatened to disassemble, the mortar crumbling, some inner flaw about to reveal itself. The noise grew louder as the rocks began to slide. The two old men chattered like disturbed blue jays.

Stones dropped from the top first. The

bottom tier began to slide forward. There was a hesitation, and the forest was unnaturally quiet. Then, as though tapped with an invisible mallet, the entire structure tumbled down, stopping just in front of April and her father.

The sigh could be felt as well as heard when the stones finally came to rest. Now nothing of the Castle remained standing.

After a moment, as the dust literally cleared, Ed said to April, "You okay?" His voice was throaty and deep. When she nodded, he asked loudly, "Everybody okay?"

Mo was wheezing. Yost pounded his back as the old man's face turned white.

"Let's get him out of this dust," Yost said. Ed's face grew more concerned as the old man hacked. Vince put a hand on Mo's arm, watching him closely. He led him away and Curly followed.

April could not take her eyes off the fireplace rubble. Something looked out of place. Her artist's eye was always drawn to anomaly. She took a step forward, willing the swirl of dust to stop so she could identify what she was seeing. Amidst the stones were bricks. The fireplace must have had a brick interior.

As she was making sense of what she was seeing, an object tumbled to the foreground.

The words burst out of her mouth. "That's a skull."

Yost heard her and in several long strides was at her side. Ed was right behind him.

"Stand back," Yost yelled. Mo's wheezing lessened, and he and the others moved back to the Castle.

"The Castle gives up its dead," Curly said.

The hair stood up on the back of April's neck.

Ed spoke first, head cocked. "Mitch, do you know where your father is?"

"Bora Bora. Doing missionary work."

"Are you sure?" Ed said.

Officer Yost was quiet, staring at the skull as though it was going to talk.

Mitch threw up his hands. "That is not my dad, for crying out loud. I took my mother and him to the airport last month myself."

"Perhaps it's a friend of his then," Ed persisted.

"This place has been empty for years. You know it was never used."

"Except by partying kids," Ed said.

"It could be anyone." Mitch's voice was not as sure as it had been a moment ago. "The Appalachian Trail's not that far from here. Maybe a hiker took shelter."

Ed finally said, "Maybe it came from a

cemetery grave. Someone's idea of a sick joke."

Mitch shook his head. He picked up a stone and tossed it from hand to hand. "I know these woods. There's an old Polish cemetery on the Upper Mountain Road. There's no other graveyard within a mile of here."

Curly and Mo were watching the exchange, their eyes bright with excitement. "I think they found Judge Crater," Curly said. "Or maybe Amelia Earhart."

Yost was quiet. He squatted down next to the skull and studied it. He seemed to be impervious to the speculation buzzing around him.

"A homeless person?" April suggested.

"This ain't no big city," Ed said. "We take care of our own here."

She looked to her father. Ed was mopping his face in earnest now, his large hand starting at his forehead and down to his chin over and over, distorting his features alarmingly. April wanted to stop him, grab him and hold him still. Vince touched his elbow gently. Ed shuddered once and stopped. Worries about Ed's health reentered April's consciousness.

Ed was a guy who could have written the worst-case scenario books, but even in his worst nightmare, he couldn't have imagined this. A skull floating out of his job site.

April peered over his shoulder. The skull was tipped on its side, presenting just one vast open eye socket. She felt a shudder rush through her body. The idea that this had been a live person — walking, talking, arguing — washed over her. A son, brother, sister, daughter. Someone must be missing this person.

Yost was gathering up the two old men, insisting that they leave. "Go wait for me in the cruiser."

"Are you nuts, Yostie? We're not going to miss this," Curly said.

Mo's mouth worked without noise for a moment. Finally he said, "I was here when this job was built. I want to be in on this now." He coughed violently.

Yost barked, "I'll arrest both of you for obstruction if you don't get out of here."

The two men grumbled.

Yost said, "Somebody drive them home."

He was watching as Mo bent over double, unable to maneuver the steep path. Ed walked up behind him, taking his arm, then opened his mouth, but Yost cut him off. "Not you. I need you and Mitch to stay here. And Lyle. I'm going to want to take statements from you three."

"I can't drive them. My car is back at Mirabella," April said.

Vince volunteered. Yost and Ed joined in to help the men walk up the steep embankment to the road where the car was parked. Mo's coughing grew fainter as the men moved out of view. April turned back to look at the site.

"What do you think?" she asked Mitch.

Mitch was on all fours, staring at the skull. "It's definitely human. I've been digging in these woods all my life." He pointed through the woods, toward the base of the mountain that rose up behind them. "The Sugarloaf Massacre site is just over there. I've found plenty of arrowheads, even bullet fragments. I've come across the occasional deer carcass and once a bobcat skeleton, but never anything like this."

Deana, too, had a collection of arrowheads. Maybe this was a historical artifact. She would want to see this, April thought. She pulled her phone out of her pocket and flipped it to camera mode. She didn't want to seem like a voyeur. Holding it low on her leg, out of Mitch's line of vision, she snapped a shot of the skull.

She turned away and looked at the picture. Not bad. The three planes of the head were visible, and she was surprised at how dis-

101

tinctly the stitching lines showed up.

Mitch's cell rang and he stepped away for some privacy.

April took advantage of his distraction to snap two more pictures of the skull. She circled the object, getting pictures from all angles. The skull was the color of a tea-stained mug. She could see a broken indentation in the side just above the hole where the ear would have been. It was cracked like an egg that'd been dropped.

She moved the camera closer and snapped a few more pictures.

Lyle caught her just before Ed and Yost returned. Mitch was still on the phone. She heard him talking about measurements and wood grain.

"What's the idea? Need a few pictures for your scrapbook?" he asked.

She stuck her camera in her pocket, guiltily, then looked up, but he was smiling.

He said, "I know how you stampers are. My wife is always making me stop on the side of the road to take a picture of tiger lilies or some decrepit corn crib."

April wondered how he knew about her stamping, then remembered the man who'd dropped his wife off last night at the barn. "Tammy is your wife?" April asked. Certainly there couldn't be more than one Lyle in this small burg.

"Fifteen years," he said proudly.

"That's nice," April said, but she was thinking Tammy was awfully young to have been married that long. Lyle looked to be at least forty, so maybe ten years older than she was. Tammy must have been one of those girls that had married right after graduation.

"Have you worked for my dad long?" she asked him.

He took off his hard hat and put a hand through his hair. It was surprisingly thick, and long, coming past his collar. "Since I was an apprentice carpenter. Twenty years."

"So you worked for his old company?" She'd spent some time on her father's jobs when she was a kid, but she didn't really remember any of the guys who worked back then.

Raised voices came from the other side of the clearing. Ed and Yost were arguing, on their way back down from the road.

"This is a job site, Henry," Ed said.

Yost's voice was strong. He carried a roll of yellow tape in his hand. "Not anymore. No one falls in a fireplace on their own. Until I figure out what happened, this is my site. A crime scene."

CHAPTER 5

April looked to Lyle. His face had shuttered. She felt bad for him. She was sure
that when he'd woken up this morning he'd
had no intention of unearthing human
remains. And his wife certainly had her own
problems, with people dying at the nursing
home.

Ed followed Yost as he walked the perim-
eter. "You've got to be kidding me, Henry.
You heard Mrs. H. She wants this area
cleaned up. Today."

"Not going to happen. Mitch, your father
never used this place, right?"

Mitch shook his head. "It was never finished."

"So someone could have died in here,
decomposed and no one would have been
the wiser," Yost said as he tied yellow tape
around a small tree and walked toward the
west.

"I would have known if someone died,"

Ed replied pointedly. "We were building the place. I was practically living on the premises."

Yost said, "Exactly. And when you left?"

Ed shrugged. "We never came back."

Mitch said, "The place was boarded up the day after Rocky's graduation party."

Yost looked at Mitch. "Would it surprise *you* that someone died that night?"

Mitch's mouth was set in a straight line. "Didn't you do enough to my family back then? Do you have to keep it going by trying to tie this in?"

"I'll take this wherever it leads me," Yost said. "I'm not out to protect anyone's family. But I don't think it was a random kid from the party. That parent would have reported their precious Jimmy or Connie missing."

Mitch shrugged. "For all we know, it was a hiker."

"More likely it was one of Ed's men," Yost said. "You hire a lot of transients, don't you?"

Ed stared at Yost, clearly irritated by the officer's phrasing. "I wouldn't call them transients. I hire union guys out of the hall. They work for as long as I need them, and then they move on to other jobs."

"That's the point. One of your workers

could have died on the job, and you never would have known. If you weren't so busy in your job trailer, doing God knows what to who knows who . . ."

"Officer Yost . . ." Ed warned.

April felt her heart fall in her chest. They could only be talking about one night.

The night of Rocky's graduation party. April had gone to the job trailer to find her father. He hadn't been home much that spring . . .

Ed was seated on the couch at the end of the trailer. Only it had been opened up and was heaped with bed pillows and blankets. A brass lamp screwed into the wall lit the paperback he was reading.

When April pulled open the door of the job trailer, he looked up, startled. No, more than startled. Scared. He pulled off his glasses and sat up. His feet were bare.

She wasn't scared, she was angry. Angrier than she ever remembered being in her sixteen years alive. Her father had disappointed her for the last time.

"April? What's wrong?" her father asked. "It's late. You shouldn't be out at eleven o'clock. How did you get here? You didn't ride your bike, did you?"

April let the door slam behind her. She

saw him wince as it banged shut. But he stopped talking.

She cocked a hip, her hands resting on her jutting hipbones. "What good is having a father if he can't even bother to come to see my concert?" She bit back the tears that threatened to ruin her tirade. She really wanted him to know how much he'd let her down tonight.

Her father was bewildered. She could see the wheels turning. He flipped over the pages on his day-to-day calendar. It had been behind a day, on June 12.

Ed clapped his hand to his forehead. "Oh, don't tell me I missed graduation."

April's eyes flashed. "Yes, and in case you've forgotten, I was the only junior to take over a first chair. Deana's mother said it was so beautiful, she cried. But no one from my family was there." She was trying not to sound juvenile and pouty, but she felt like stamping her foot. She was determined not to cry.

"You know your mother had to cook for the Women's League Golf Tournament at the country club . . ."

April nodded. She was used to Bonnie working nights. That was okay. It was her father that she'd wanted there.

In two steps, Ed was in front of her, trying to hug her. She crossed her arms over her chest and held herself stiffly.

"I'm so sorry, hon," he said into her hair. "Work. You know I've been staying at the job trailer because of the vandalism. Officer Yost is on my case about the wild parties being held out here, but this is the last night, I promise. After tonight, all the troubles will be going away."

She looked around the job trailer. Ed's familiar blue pajamas were laid out on a chair. Over the sink were his toothbrush and the Waterpik he used to floss his teeth. She realized with a jolt what was going on.

"You're not working late. You're living here."

"Apey, please."

"Why are you here? Why aren't you home?"

In the garbage can were the remnants of his microwave dinner.

Outside, a girl giggled and a guy made loud smacking noises. April remembered the couple she'd seen in a tight embrace in the woods as she'd biked in. People were out there having fun.

Loud noises spilled through the open jalousie window. Ed frowned and picked up the phone.

"I've been calling and calling Yost. He promised to come out and put an end to the partying going on at the Castle. It's getting out of hand."

April didn't care what was going on outside. She had another terrible thought.

"You're cheating on Mom. You've got another woman. That's why you're here."

She didn't stop to listen to her father's excuses. She pushed her way out of the trailer and ran toward the party.

"Officer Yost, my father was with me that night," April said, but the two men weren't listening to her.

"Why would I kill one of my men?" Ed asked wearily.

Yost leaned in. "You were pretty far in the closet back then. Maybe someone found out . . ."

"No you don't," April yelled at Yost. She put herself right in front of him and shook her finger at him as if she was a babushka-wearing woman from the old country. "That's not fair —"

Ed took April's arm and moved her away from Yost. He looked worried that she might strike the police officer.

Mitch took a step away from Yost, as if he didn't trust himself, either.

Ed's voice was low. "April, I need you to go up to the mansion. Now."

"No, Dad. I should stay here. You and Officer Yost —"

"Yost and I will settle things. I don't need you to help."

"Dad . . ."

He closed his eyes and rubbed them. When he spoke again, his voice was strained. "The most important thing now is to keep Mrs. H. happy. April, can I count on you?"

She gave Yost another glare. "I just want you to know, Officer Yost, I will do whatever it takes to keep you from railroading my father."

Yost smirked. He turned his attention to Lyle. "Trocadero, don't go anywhere."

Ed took her by the hand, taking her away from Yost. "Forget him."

"Dad, you can't let him walk all over you like that."

"April, please. I've been living in this town a lot longer than you have. Let me handle Yost my way. I need your help with something else."

She felt her anger simmer down. He was right. She was the outsider here.

Ed said, "I've got a crew working at the mansion that Lyle was supposed to be supervising." He glanced at Lyle, who was

110

being led by Yost away from the skull. Lyle was listening to Yost, head tilted, hands in his pockets. Ed looked at his watch. "It's eleven now. They're probably breaking for lunch. I can't afford to have them lollygagging. I need you to go check up on them."

"I think I should stay here with you." She glanced back. Yost was watching them carefully over his pad of paper. He wasn't finished with her father yet. "Won't Vince be back soon? He could go." A shaft of light came through the trees, lighting up the skull eerily.

Ed shook his head mournfully. "He's got the Heights job. He's going there right after he drops off Curly and Mo."

April crossed her arms across her chest, hugging herself. She was adding to her father's stress level by not doing as he asked. "All right."

"That's a good girl. Talk to Mike, my foreman. I called him earlier and told him the blast was no big deal. I need you to tell them what's going on."

"About the skull?" she asked. She wasn't sure how far she should go.

"Tell them what you need to. They're in the north wing."

Mitch jangled his car keys. "Come on, I'll take you back to Mirabella."

111

April looked at him. He couldn't take his eyes off the ruins. She decided he was only being polite.

"No, thanks," she said. "I can walk back the way we came."

He didn't protest. April could see he really wanted to stay here and find out what would happen next.

She started to walk to the mansion, but her father called her back.

"April," Ed said, "please make sure they're not using the inside toilet."

She started to laugh, but her father's serious expression stopped her. She waved and left.

April entered Mirabella through the open kitchen door. No locking of the doors on this side of town. Surrounded by the country club, Mirabella was in a cocoon of safety and security.

She would make sure Ed's men were working, fill them in on what had happened at the Castle and then get back to Ed. He needed someone to shield him from Yost's venom.

She went through the plastic-draped door she'd seen earlier and followed a long hallway. The walls were covered in what looked like suede. She touched the surface.

It wasn't a paint treatment; it was fabric. She started to mentally calculate the square yardage. This had to be thousands of dollars of fabric. It would be a shame to pull it all down.

She heard laughter and turned into a sunny room at the back of the house. It was long, probably some kind of ballroom in the original plan, with a wall of windows overlooking the slope of the yard into the woods. She tried to get her bearings. The garage wasn't visible from here, but it was over to the right. The Castle site was to the left, out of view.

Three guys in Retro Reproductions shirts were on a window seat. Another was seated on the floor, leaning against the wall. Next to them was a large yellow Igloo cooler with a red lid. White bags from the deli were tossed on the floor, and each of the guys had a hoagie in hand. She smelled the greasy sweetness of salami and Italian dressing.

Their comfortable chatter died out as she came in the doorway. All eyes scrutinized her as she crossed the wide room. She kept a smile plastered on her face and strode as fast as she could, faking a confidence she didn't feel.

"Can we help you? Are you looking for

Mrs. H.?" a man with chubby cheeks asked, coming out of the shadows. He was carrying a clipboard. The front of his shirt had a fresh stain. He must have finished his lunch already.

"No, I'm April Buchert, Ed's daughter?" she said, falling into the local cadence of speech, ending a statement with a question mark.

"I'm Mike McCarty," the chubby-cheeked guy said. He came forward and shook her hand, giving her a nice smile that put her at ease.

A barrel-chested man squinted at her. "Holy smokes, I thought that was Bonnie coming through the door. You look just like her when she was younger."

April struggled not to blush. Her mother had been Miss Alfalfa at the Bloomsburg Fair in high school. She'd never thought she'd made the grade.

"The spitting image," another guy said.

"Don't mind these galoots," Mike said. "This here is Butch, that's John, and Carlos and Bernie."

Butch wasn't finished. "You the daughter in Californ-i-a?"

April nodded. Living in San Francisco to these people was akin to settling on Mars, except the Martians were considered less alien.

"Good thing you got out before the Big One," the second guy, maybe John, said gravely. "It's only a matter of time before Arizona is beachfront."

April smiled slightly. People in Aldenville pretended they wouldn't want to live in California because of its tectonic shifts, but the truth was they were afraid that they were missing out on a big adventure. Convincing themselves California was full of loonies protected them from that realization.

"What's going on at the Castle?" the guy on the floor asked. "We heard the blast. Lyle make a big mess?"

"Not that that would be anything new," John said.

A dark-skinned man crossed himself and kissed his knuckles, raising his eyes to heaven. *"Dios mío,"* he muttered. Surely this was Carlos.

April knew construction workers could be a superstitious lot. They didn't like it when things went haywire. People got killed on the job from a stray hammer blow or broken scaffolding far too often. The deaths usually seemed random and unpredictable, happening despite the best efforts at safety. For some guys, a job curse explained the unexplainable.

She also knew that men would walk off a job rather than work under dicey circumstances. Her job was to keep them all here.

She decided not to say anything about the skull. They'd find out soon enough. She didn't want them too distracted to work. Instead she said, "Things are fine over there. Ed just wants you to keep doing what you're doing."

John said, "So why are you here?"

She shrugged her shoulders apologetically. "I know you're not slacking off, but my dad —"

"We know your dad, April," Mike said. "He's a nervine of the highest order."

She laughed. "So you know he sent me over here because he needed me to check, not because you needed checking up on."

"Exactly. Here's the report. We've spent the morning ripping down the east and west walls of bookshelves. We've piled the salvageable lumber outside the French doors for Lyle to pick up. We're right on schedule."

April was impressed. "You do know my dad. You've covered all the bases."

The barrel-chested guy stood and stretched out his back. "And we haven't used Mrs. H.'s bathroom once."

April laughed again. "My father must be

116

pretty predictable."

Butch said, "Someday I'm going to retire and open a porta-potty business. I'll get the exclusive on your father's jobs and just rake in the dough."

The men laughed, then started gathering up their sandwich wrappers. One of them held his fist to his chest and burped loudly. April ignored his bid for attention.

"Well, I'll tell my dad all is well here. In the meantime, you've got plenty to keep you busy?" she asked.

McCarty nodded again. "Oh, yeah. You going to stick around? I've got some boards that need the nails pulled out," he said.

April could see he was only half kidding. "No, thanks," she said. "I've got to get back to the Castle."

"What about the cleanup over there?" Mike said. "Ed said I needed to schedule that for this afternoon."

The cleanup. She'd forgotten Mrs. H.'s demand that it be done today. There was no way Yost was going to let that happen.

"Probably not today. Ed'll call you when he's ready." She said her good-byes and quickly left. She hadn't done a great job of answering his questions, but it would have to be enough. For now.

She walked back through the house, hoping not to bump into Mrs. H. She didn't want to be the one to break the news of the skull to her. After all, if Mrs. H. wanted to, she could shut down the Mirabella job.

Outside once more, April yanked the car door open. Hot air flooded out. She felt her thighs burn when they hit the upholstery. In San Francisco, she'd never needed one of those ugly windshield screens. Summer meant fog, cold fog. Here a screen was a necessity. Even though it was only early June, the heat and humidity built up in a closed car. The black interior felt hot enough to boil water.

April rubbed her hands, touching the wheel now and again to see if it had cooled off enough for her to drive. Her phone rang. Ken's ring. She threw the phone on the passenger seat. The day had been frustrating enough without adding to it.

Bankruptcy. The word sent a chill down her spine. She'd done everything she could not to repeat the family history. In California, she'd paid off every creditor she'd had. It had taken all of her money, but it was worth it. The stigma of bankruptcy was hard to overcome. It had taken Ed years to build his business back up again.

April pointed her car to the right, to return to the Castle.

About a quarter mile up the road, a man in a real Smokey-the-Bear hat stopped her. Up ahead was a large white truck with "Forensics Van" written on the side, just under the Pennsylvania State Trooper insignia.

The trooper leaned in. "Sorry, ma'am, but the road is closed. Are you a local resident?"

She thought about lying, but he'd probably check the registration and find out she didn't live on this road.

She shook her head. "I work with Retro Reproductions, the contractor on the Castle job."

"Sorry, there's an investigation in progress. You'll have to turn around."

April hesitated. Her father was in there. The stony-faced trooper stood in the middle of the road, directing her three-point turn so she didn't end up in the roadside ditch. She turned the car back toward the barn, trying to figure out how best to protect her father. Ed was going to be no help. She would have to do this herself. If she could prove to Yost that all her father's employees were alive and well, he'd have to leave her father alone. No missing employee would mean that the skull belonged to some other unfortunate, and that her father was not involved.

■ ■ ■ ■

Back at the barn, April scanned the file boxes neatly stacked next to her father's desk and pulled out the one marked "The Castle." File folders slumped in the bottom, so she carefully set them on the kitchen table. Her father's desk was littered with papers. She didn't dare touch anything. He'd flip out if she disturbed his work method.

Inside the bulging folders, April found invoices, bills of lading and statements from the various supply houses that Buchert Construction used. The old Castle job had generated a lot of paperwork.

She leafed through the invoices. She found one for kitchen cabinetry — custom, from the looks of it. The invoice, clearly marked "The Castle" on the upper right-hand side, had been sent to the old business address, which was the house where Bonnie now lived alone. Red check marks were placed along the margin, indicating that the cabinets had been received. She saw a note in her mother's handwriting. Back then, the offices had been in the garage and Bonnie had helped out.

April set aside that folder. It was fascinating to see the raw materials that made up a job, but she was looking for people. She could get Yost off her father's back if she could just show him that all of Ed's men were accounted for.

She found a folder marked "Payroll." Ed used a payroll system with ledger entries attached to each check he wrote. Each payroll check had its own sheet, with the man's name, the hours worked, the deductions taken: SSI, state tax, union dues.

April started at the end. There was no payroll after the second week in June. The job had come to an end right after the party. She hadn't made the connection until Yost said it earlier.

Of course, she'd known that Buchert Construction had gone bankrupt. Her senior year in high school was one of no new clothes and no gas money. She'd been forced to sell candy to the neighbors to pay for her band uniform. She'd taken a part-time job at the IGA.

She had escaped as soon as she could. With enough credits to graduate in January, she did that and left for college in San Francisco. And stayed there.

Her father had found work with other contractors until he and Vince opened Retro Reproductions about ten years later. After a few lean years, they were just starting to make a profit.

She went back to the file box. There were piles of change orders. The job had been started nearly three years before the graduation party. It seemed that Warren Winchester had changed his mind on a monthly basis.

Red-striped code violations were mixed in with the papers. She pulled out one to read. The initials at the bottom were "GW." George Weber. He had taken exception to the addition of an air-conditioning unit that had not been in the original plans. There was no sign of how Ed had fixed the problem.

Nearly at the bottom, April found a rubber-banded group of time cards. The men used yellow time cards, gridded by day of the week. There were columns for jobs worked, in case a man worked on two different jobs on the same day.

She flipped through the timeworn cards. There were six. She recognized a couple of names: Lyle Trocadero, Mike McCarty. The other four were Clyde Reiser, Danny Whitlock, Frankie Imperiale and Martin Festler.

She walked over to her father's desk. Were any of those four guys still working with her dad? Lyle and Mike had come back to work for Ed. Maybe there were others.

She found the Retro Reproductions checkbook and pulled it out. Last week, Ed had paid ten guys. Excluding Lyle and Mike, she compared the list to the names of those who had worked on the Castle. One matched. Clyde Reiser.

That left three.

She turned on her father's computer and clicked on the Internet icon. She'd go the easy route and see if anyone was listed in the online white pages. Bingo. Martin Festler lived in Moosic, thirty miles or so up north.

She was two-for-four and feeling pretty good. If all the guys were still alive, her father would be in the clear.

Where else would these former employees be listed? Her father had a cup on his desk, full of bright blue pencils with a gold insignia. Carpenters Union Local 76. The phone number was right below. Buchert Construction had been a union shop. Unions kept records. There were pensions and health care plans.

April called the hall. "This is April Buchert, from Retro Reproductions. Can you tell me if Frankie Imperiale and Danny Whitlock are still members of Local 76?" she asked in her best businesslike manner.

"I'm sorry," a nasal voice whined. "We don't give out information on our current members."

April thought fast. "That's a shame because I've got a paycheck to send to them. I just need current addresses."

The phone went silent, and then April heard the dulcet tones of Johnny Mercer. She pushed the speakerphone function on her end, and waited.

"Ed? Is that you?" a booming, hearty voice came through the tiny speaker. "It's Danny O'Malley."

April's heart sank. She wasn't a member of the good-old-boy network that was so fundamental to doing business here. "No, this is his daughter."

"Cripes, I thought Ed was pulling my leg. Send a check to Danny Whitlock? He knows Danny disappeared. What, eight, nine years ago?"

April's heart pounded. "Disappeared?" What if it was more like fifteen years ago?

"You know, moved to Florida. Those guys always say they'll stay in touch, but then they disappear."

April let out a sigh of relief, then said, "Sorry. My dad isn't here right now, and I was just trying to track down some of his old employees."

"Planning some kind of a surprise party, are you? Is the old geezer getting ready to retire?"

"Something like that," April lied. "What about Frankie Imperiale? That name ring any bells?"

"Sorry, sweetie, no. But you know how it is. Workers come and go. Some guys don't have what it takes, you know."

"I suppose." April quickly realized she wasn't going to get any more information from this source. She thanked him and signed off.

She tapped the time cards. Frankie Imperiale was the only one not accounted for. That didn't mean anything, she told herself, trying to resolve the niggling feeling she had that it might. He could have dropped out of the union or moved out of the county.

She found her father's local phone book. It was at least five years old. There was an Imperiale in Butler Township. She called the number, but there was no answer and no machine to take her message. She saved the number in her cell to try again later.

She closed up the box and stashed it back in its place among the others by her father's desk. A set of blueprints was rolled up in the corner. Written in blue ink on the light blue page, she saw the word "Winchester."

She pulled them out. The rubber band was so thinned with age, it broke as soon as she touched it.

April spread the prints out on the kitchen table. They were dated September 1991. These must be the prints for the Castle, April thought, but the building didn't resemble anything remotely regal. It was a simple design. No towers, no turrets, no crenellations. Just three rooms. One half was a large living space. The other contained a kitchen and a bath and a bedroom. A modest fireplace. Nothing like the stone façade that had come tumbling down earlier.

The plans were initialed by GW. George Weber, Code Enforcement.

She hadn't really found exactly what she was looking for, but she was getting closer. She needed more details before she went back to Yost, though. Then she thought about the skull. Yost had no real reason to suspect the skull was only fifteen years old. Maybe it was much older, dropped there by an animal after the site had been abandoned.

She looked at the pictures of the skull on her phone again, wishing she could decipher what it had to tell her. How long had the skull been there? Was it a male or female? How had it come to be inside the fireplace of the Castle?

Suddenly she realized she knew someone who could help her.

CHAPTER 6

Since Deana's place was only a few miles from the barn, April decided to take a chance and drive by the funeral home.

The Hudock Family Funeral Home and Mortuary was out the Sugarloaf Road. She turned off Route 93 and headed south. Once she was past the new elementary school, farms took up most of the available acreage. Now and again a cookie-cutter Harris rancher would appear at the end of a long driveway. She drove slowly, remembering how the deer liked to amble from field to field using the road as a cut-through.

At the top of a long rise, she saw the funeral home. The sign was discreet, carved wood with gold accents. Billboards announcing its location were unnecessary. The Hudocks had been in the same spot for over fifty years. Only the building had changed. Deana's parents had built the new place, a sprawling red brick Colonial, in the eighties. A colonnaded front porch spanned the length of the building. White wicker furniture was grouped in several seating areas. Large pots of geraniums graced the top steps.

April pulled into the farthest spot of a large black asphalt lot. A line of Normandy poplars blocked the view of the back door. April got out, leaving her car window open, hoping the car wouldn't get so overheated again. She headed toward the hidden path she knew was there. This route, through the trees into the rose garden to the family entrance, more than all the places she'd been since returning to Aldenville, felt like home. As a child, she'd ridden her bike to Deana's house every day during summer vacations. She felt herself relax.

At the back door April admired Deana's décor. She'd done everything she could to distinguish it from the formal front, the business end of the house. A peeling faded blue wheelbarrow held a dozen pansies. Deana had arranged a bright yellow rain slicker over a distressed wooden bench and placed a pair of green rain boots alongside. The resulting vignette was homey and inviting.

When there was no answer to her knock, April's disappointment was sharp. She couldn't stand the idea of going back to the empty barn, with its unanswerable questions about Ed, just yet. It was only four thirty. Dinner at Bonnie's was always at six. Going there early was not an option. Her mother was not very social in the throes of cooking.

Reluctant to leave the backyard, she wandered through the roses. Deana's mother had planted most of them. The tiny red buds promised a good show later. From the back corner of the garden, April noticed a new trail, a path of colorful flagstones with hues of subtle pinks and reds and purples leading away from the parking lot. The path turned through some trees, and following it, April came to a pond.

The water was rimmed with tall grasses, reeds and cattails instead of the pampas that April was used to seeing. Bushes clustered along the bank — mock orange, forsythia. The leaves from a low-reaching weeping willow dappled the light on the water's surface. A rustic wooden bench had been placed facing away from the house, with a pretty view of the geometric cornfields beyond.

There'd never been a pond here before. This had to be one of Mark's projects. An oval stone sign read "Sanctuary." What a beautiful place to see the sunrise, April thought. There was silence except for the occasional splash from a fish or the rustle of the wind through the grass. She could see for miles. Quiet spaces with wide-open views had been too rare in her busy San Francisco life. Too often, her view had been the inside of her car or the paint store, or a customer's wall.

This day had been a crazy one. April scratched her chin. Trying to keep Mrs. H. happy was looking as though it would be a full-time job. Add to that, trying to keep Yost away from her father, and she felt close to a breaking point. But being here was helping her to relax. April breathed in and watched a mallard serenely paddling. The sunlight changed the green iridescence on his feathers until they looked translucent. The duck was unaware of the beauty on its back. She thought about going back to the car for her sketchbook, but the sun on her face felt too good.

She heard a car pull in, and as she came part way up the hill from the pond and saw Deana exiting her car, April waved.

"Stay there," Deana called. She was wearing tan slacks and a crisp button-down pink shirt. With her blonde hair, which would get even lighter as the summer went on, she looked more like a California girl than a funeral director.

April waited, watching a goldfish with a speckled back surface to catch a fly and go back under the water.

Deana arrived, slightly out of breath from racing downhill. She hugged April and sat next to her, patting her on the knee. "This is a nice surprise."

"So is this," April said, pointing to the view. "You must love it out here."

Deana squinted, looking over the pond. "I never sit out here. Mark built it for the clients. See that forsythia over there? Planted by a family that lost a kid in an ATV accident. The willow was put in by the Kenner grandkids for their nana. The place has evolved into a living memorial. We didn't plan it that way."

April looked at the pond with fresh eyes. She could imagine someone grieving, finding solace out here. It would be a lovely place to regain your equilibrium. Or start to.

April sighed.

Deana asked, "So you were out at the Castle when the remains were found?"

"Geez, I thought for sure I could be the first to tell you."

Deana shook her head. "The state police called to see if we had room for body parts if need be."

April didn't want to think about where Deana might have room. She pulled out her phone and flipped it to the pictures. "I was thinking of you," she said, showing Deana the skull.

"Cool," Deana said, taking the phone from her. "You're the best."

"It was creepy at first, but the funniest thing happened. While I was taking pictures, the skull just became another object. I got caught up in the light and getting the best angle." April felt sheepish, but she knew Deana would understand.

Deana twisted and turned the camera, studying the skull. "Don't be ashamed. You got some great shots. You have to detach. If I didn't, I'd never get anything done."

"Can you tell how long it's been there?" April asked.

Deana shook her head. "Can I? No, but the forensics lab in Harrisburg surely can. Usually they would do soil samples from around the ground. Was any of that preserved?"

April shrugged. "Not sure. How long would it take for the body to decompose?"

"Depends on the time of year. Summertime, decay happens pretty fast if we're having one of our hundred-degree spells."

"Yost thinks it was probably a murder."

Deana shrugged. "Officer Yost is just eager to have something to do besides escort drunks home from Cousin Joe's."

"Well, he's sinking his teeth into this."

"There are plenty of missing people in this country. Yost has a long list at the police station. We're right at the crossroads on the two most heavily traveled interstates in the country. Chances are some poor soul wandered in there and died."

April wanted to believe her friend. It could have been a homeless person, despite what her father said. Or a hiker like Mitch suggested. "It just seems a little nuts that someone could die at the Castle and no one would notice."

"Even around here," Deana said, "where everyone knows everyone else's business, people's lives sometimes fly under the radar. It's not that difficult to disappear."

April considered that, but her experience had been completely different. When she had to return to high school after her father had left her mother, she'd tried to make herself invisible, but it seemed that overnight everyone knew who she was. She'd hated the attention. And now she was going to be branded again. Daughter of a murderer. A bankrupt murderer.

She picked at her thumbnail, making it ragged.

Deana stopped on the shot that showed the skull's fracture and pointed to it. "Someone got bonked pretty hard," she said.

"Bonked? Is that a technical term?" April teased, grateful for any lightheartedness. "Did you learn that in college?"

Deana said, "Forensics 212, I believe. See that crack?"

"Couldn't the blast have done that?" April asked.

Deana shook her head. "The jagged edges are all the same color. A newer crack would look whiter. This guy definitely took a blow to the head back then."

"Or girl," April suggested.

"No, most likely a guy. See here?" Deana said, pointing at the image. "That's pretty clearly male. Women don't have such broad foreheads."

April's heart sunk. Yost was right about that, at least. It was a man.

"And a fairly young man," Deana continued. "See the stitches along the skull plates? Those fade in older people, after sixty or so. His are very visible."

Worse news. A young man. April gnawed on her cuticle.

Deana closed the phone and looked at her

friend. "What are you really worried about, April?"

April leaned back on the bench and sighed. Deana knew her well. "Two things. I'm afraid that it's one of my father's workers and he'll be accused of murder, and I'm scared to death Mrs. H. will shut the job down and I'll have nowhere to work." Tears pricked the corners of her eyes and she fought them back. "I can't go back to California," she added quietly.

Deana put an arm around her shoulder and hugged her. "Ken?"

April took a breath and shaded her eyes. A heron skidded to a graceful stop on the edge of the pond, flapped his wings once and settled down to watch the water.

April turned toward Deana. "I've left him. He stole a Biedermeier vase from a client. I found the pawn ticket in his pants pockets. When I went to the shop, the vase wasn't there. My engagement ring was."

"The one you thought you lost down the drain?" Deana was shocked.

"Yup. That rat let me think I'd been careless. Even insinuated that I lost it to get him in trouble with his family. It had been his mother's. Meanwhile, he'd swiped it out of the little dish on the sink."

Deana's face was a mask of empathy, her

mouth turned down in frustration. "What did you do?"

"When Dad called about work at Mirabella, I said yes. I promised to pay the client back for the vase, and got in the car and drove here." Broke.

Deana hugged her friend again, hard. "I'm glad you did. You've been taking care of Ken for too long. You've completely neglected yourself. Let me and your mother take care of you for a while."

"You, yes. My mother, not so much."

They laughed. Both of them had been at the receiving end of Bonnie's smothering attention.

"Seriously, Deana, my mother doesn't know about Ken. Please don't tell her."

"Of course not."

"Good. I need a little time to prepare her. She's going to be really upset. She loves the bum."

They sat quietly for a few moments. April soaked up the affection she felt from her friend. She wanted Deana to know everything. "Ken robbed from other customers, too. He's been doing it for years. The vase was just the last humiliation. My jobs were drying up. The dot-com money was mostly gone, and with Ken driving away my customers, it got so no one would hire me. He trashed my reputation."

Deana knew how important a pristine reputation was. She treasured her good name and worked hard to keep the Hudock integrity in all of her dealings.

Deana caught her hand. "I'm really sorry, honey. I feel a little selfish saying this, but I'm glad you're home. I just wish you hadn't had to go through all that to get here."

April felt the muscles in her throat relax. She felt her burden lift. She could always count on Deana.

She tried for a lighter tone. "But I went from the frying pan into the fire, I'm afraid. I didn't even tell you about the Mirabella job. It's a disaster. Mrs. H. has this ginormous mural in her living room depicting Benjamin Franklin and the Indians signing a peace treaty."

"Hold on. Benjamin Franklin and the Indians never signed —" Deana said.

April held up a restraining hand. "I know, I know. It's awful, not to mention borderline racist. But it's some kind of freakin' family heirloom. Thanks to my father, I have the job of restoring it."

Deana hid her mouth behind her hand, a sure sign she was going to lose it. "Can you talk her out of it? Or how about this: spill a bucket of red paint right down the middle?"

April started to laugh, too. "She'd probably make me remove it with a toothbrush and paint remover. I'll die from turpentine inhalation poisoning and you'll have to bury me."

Deana was laughing so hard now, she snorted. "You don't want to be buried. You always said you want to be cremated. And tossed off Ocean Beach."

"Yup, in San Francisco. Which means you'll have to get on a plane and take me there."

Deana hadn't flown since September 11. "I can drive," she said quickly.

"Three days cross country with me on the passenger seat beside you? You'll flip out."

"At least you won't eat my Snickers. Or yell at me for going through yellow lights. You won't even care if I play Bob Seger night and day."

"Oh, I don't know about that. Two days of 'Like a Rock' might make me mad enough to haunt you."

Deana squeezed April's hand. "I'm going to love having you back in town."

April felt better for just having talked to her friend. "Me, too."

"I better get inside. Mark's ice cream is going to be mush," Deana said, standing and stretching. "Do you want to stay for dinner?"

"No, I promised Mom she could feed me. After that, I've got to go home and brush up on my painting techniques."

"Brush up, funny." Deana smiled.

"Well, I better do something or I'll be run out of town on a rail. I think those Winchesters have done that before."

"Not on my watch. I'd hire you. You can be a Stamping Sister dealer. You'd be a big hit."

April's face reddened. That was another humiliation. "Not after last night. I didn't sell a thing and the party broke up early. And Mary Lou didn't pay me for the stuff her daughter took. I wouldn't last two minutes as a salesperson."

Deana said, "I heard all about it. The stampers are coming here tonight, for a makeup session."

April groaned. Her friend didn't sound upset, but it was her fault that the party was such a bust. "Oh crap, now I feel even worse."

Deana looked at her askance. "Not to worry. They'll spend enough tonight to make up for any lost commissions. Guilt is a wonderful thing."

Deana and April made their way back to the parking lot. "I've got your supplies in my car," April said as they reached the asphalt. "I'll help you unload the groceries and bring that stuff in."

The pair worked together to get Deana's fabric grocery bags out of the car. She'd stamped images of fruits and vegetables along the top.

April carried the box of Stamping Sister items. Deana pulled the slider door open and led April into the cheery kitchen. The white bead-board paneling, yellow gingham curtains and bright rag rugs screamed country, a style not found much in San Francisco. Deana's tastes weren't April's, but April admired the sunny colors and rooster theme.

They dropped the bags on the counter, and Deana put the ice cream in the freezer.

"You haven't seen my new studio. Follow me," Deana said, leading the way down the hall to a familiar door.

"This is your old bedroom," April said.

"Plus the room next door. Mark has my father's old study, and we still have one room for Dad when he comes up from Florida, so I took two rooms and combined them. Isn't it decadent?" she said. Her grin told April Deana felt entitled to every inch.

She indicated a shelving unit straight ahead. "You can put the box over there. All my Stamping Sister stuff is stored in bins on that wall."

A waist-high, L-shaped countertop ran the length of two walls. On it were racks of colored and patterned paper, boxes and boxes of inks, and a die-cut machine.

Deana opened the door to the closet. April gasped. Floor-to-ceiling wire baskets were filled with stamps.

"I have nearly three thousand stamps," Deana said proudly.

"I thought I was bad," April said. She thought of her extensive collection of antique stamps and her vast array of inks. Nothing like this.

"Well, I don't smoke or drink. Got to have a vice of some kind."

"Mark doesn't mind?"

"Mind? He's got more lures than I have stamps. Fishing is far more expensive. In a race to see who spends the most on a hobby, I'd say we're even."

April saw the time on a wall clock made from recycled metal. She was due at Bonnie's in just a few minutes.

"I've got to scoot," she said.

"Come back after you have dinner with Bonnie. You're going to need to talk after you see your mother."

"I always do."

"More than usual," Deana said cryptically.

"What's that supposed to mean?" April remembered her mother said something yesterday about a surprise. Deana obviously knew what it was.

Deana said, "You'll find out. Trust me. You're going to want to talk."

CHAPTER 7

The surprise Bonnie had promised had gone out of April's head with all the other events of the day. As she drove the familiar route between Deana's and her mother's, April wondered what it could be. Other surprises from Bonnie had included a trip to the orthodontist that resulted in a three-year stint with braces, a bunny that got out of its hutch in the first week never to be seen again, and under-wire bras brought home from a Philadelphia shopping trip. All of them memorable, none of them exactly welcome.

Once she'd pulled into her mother's driveway, April stopped to call Ed. He wasn't answering, so she left a false cheery message for him. She hadn't figured out a way to clear him with Yost yet. Deana's news about the skull had not helped her cause. She called the Imperiale number again, too. If this *was* Frankie Imperiale, and he called back, she'd tell Yost he could go pound sand. She wanted to do that, badly.

Hanging up, she leaned across the steering wheel, peering out the windshield, looking for changes in the house she'd grown up in. Everything looked the same except that the margarine yellow aluminum siding had faded another hue to a soft buttery color. If Ed hadn't moved out, he would have torn off that siding long ago. Any surprise her mother had for her was not on the exterior.

The house that Ed had built as a wedding present for Bonnie was a long rancher with three bedrooms and a full basement. A bay window with nine large panes defined the living room. A vine of pink climbing roses just starting to bloom surrounded the red front door. Next to it was the double-hung window of April's childhood bedroom. Bonnie had turned it into a sewing and craft room years ago when it became apparent that April wasn't coming home for more than a week at a time.

She sent up a silent thanks for the barn. She wouldn't have to spend the night in the fussy guest room where she and Ken had always slept on their visits. Her mother's display of her Marie Osmond line of porcelain dolls always caused Ken to erupt in a

145

naughty rendition of "I'm a Little Bit Country, I'm a Little Bit Rock 'n' Roll." She'd laughed every time. It was too hard to remember the connection they'd once had, now gone. She turned away from the sad feeling.

Trips home had always been tightly choreographed. They usually stayed at Bonnie's but made sure to spend days with her father. Her itinerary was negotiated minute by minute so that each parent got equal time. Thankfully, now the barn gave her a place to live independent of them. If she was going to stay in this town, even for only a few short months, she needed a place of her own.

Being an only child, she'd had no one to help her navigate through the minefield of divorced parents. But she'd learned quickly that the key to having a good evening with Bonnie was to avoid talking about Ed. April had determined, through much trial and error, that a Don't Ask, Don't Tell policy was best. Tonight, despite the skull at the job site, she was hoping to keep the conversation clear of Ed. That wasn't going to be easy.

April climbed out of the car. She couldn't be late. Her mother's dinners were works of art, and timing was everything. Bonnie had probably spent the morning shopping for food, maybe even going all the way to Wegmans in Wilkes-Barre for the good Pugliese bread and real Pecorino.

Expecting her mom to be in the kitchen, April walked to the side door and went in.

Just inside the door, half of the kitchen space was taken up with a bright orange diner-style banquette that April had always hated. In the wintertime the faux Naugahyde was cold and clammy, in the summer, hot and sticky. The plastic made a horrible farting noise that was a constant source of embarrassment.

She was surprised to see that the kitchen was empty. April dropped her purse on the cushion, skirted the table and went through to the U-shaped food preparation area, which was anchored by a copper stove, refrigerator and stained porcelain sink.

April could hear a TV on in the next room. "Mom?" she said loudly.

"In here, April. We're in the living room."

We? She searched the kitchen for any sign that her mother had gotten a dog or a cat. No water dish or cat-food bowl. She sniffed the air. Nothing but the smell of garlic and basil.

She was waylaid by her stomach, growling in protest as she passed the stove. The oven light was on, and she could see a bubbling casserole inside. She'd missed getting the cooking gene. Her idea of cooking was microwaving whatever Trader Joe's had on special. So the wonderful smells of her mother's cooking caused her stomach to rumble. She grabbed a piece of tomato off the salad on the counter.

Insistent theme music of the local news came from the living room. April walked toward it.

"Hello," Bonnie said. She was sitting in her favorite chair, an upholstered recliner, a knitting project in her lap, frowning at the television. The news had gone to commercial. Bonnie muted the volume. April kissed her cheek and was surprised to realize Bonnie's skin was getting papery, older.

Bonnie sighed dramatically. "Leave it to your father to make the news." She pointed with the remote. "After the commercial, there's going to be a story about the skull," she said sharply.

"It's not exactly Dad's fault." April felt herself reverting to her default position, defending her father. Old patterns were hard to break. She tried to access her more mature nature so as not to object to every word her mother uttered.

"I didn't say that it was," Bonnie said. She

148

looked wounded.

April fought the urge to head back out to her car. She took a breath. "Mom, I just meant that Dad had nothing to do with the fact that someone died at the Castle long ago . . ."

"Just his luck," Bonnie said. "His rotten luck."

It was hard to disagree with that, so April tried a smile. Bonnie's face was shuttered. "Okay, Mom, I'm sorry . . ." she began.

She was interrupted by the noise of a toilet flushing down the hall. She stopped in midsentence and flashed a questioning look at her mother. Her mother's face, to her surprise, had turned pink. She was blushing.

"Who's . . . ?" April didn't get to finish that thought, either.

A gravelly voice, with a British accent, came from the hall that led to the bedrooms. "Don't mind your mother. She's just taking the piss."

April turned to see a man in the doorway, zipping his fly. April took a step back. She couldn't have been more surprised if a leprechaun had come out of her mother's bathroom. Which, with his slight build and wild hair, this man did resemble.

He had one hand stuffed down his Wranglers, tucking in an olive green T-shirt that said, "All My Good Ideas Land Me in Hot Water." On his feet were brown corduroy slippers with broken down heels. He finished his dressing and made a beeline for April, looking as though he was going to hug her. She backed up into the coffee table. Her mother watched April's reaction.

"Mom?" April said, begging for an explanation.

Bonnie stood and gestured the man to her side, and he obliged. She took his hand and reached for April's. April gave her her hand reluctantly. Bonnie brought the two hands together and smiled.

"Clive, this is my daughter, April," Bonnie said. "April, this is the surprise I was telling you about."

Surprise? That was an understatement. April searched her mother's face, but she seemed determined to treat this as nothing out of the ordinary. Yet it was monumental. Her mother had never had a boyfriend. Oh boy, Deana was going to pay for not preparing her.

The man bowed in front of April. "Clive Pierce," he said with a flourish, his British accent clipping off his words. "Bonnie has told me so much."

Feeling unsettled, she gave him a quick

smile. "That makes one of us," April said.

Bonnie frowned, and April cast her a look. Come on, Mom, she thought. You could have told me. Her mother gave a tiny head tilt.

April noticed now that the living room looked different. There was a huge leather recliner in one corner and a pile of *Rolling Stone* magazines on the table. A new picture on the wall seemed to be of the Queen of England.

The shifting image on the television caught April's eye. Next to the perfectly coiffed newscaster, a graphic read, "Aldenville Mystery."

The television went black.

"Mom!" April caught the remote in her mother's hand. Bonnie pulled it out of reach.

The Ed embargo was on. April let her hand drift. If there was any more news out of the Castle, surely her father would call. She'd let Bonnie have this victory.

"That's enough of that. Dinner's ready," Bonnie said. "I've got to get the chicken Parm out of the oven before it dries out. Go sit down."

April followed Bonnie into the kitchen. Bonnie donned bright blue oven mitts and opened the oven door, letting the tantaliz-

151

ing smell of melting cheese waft out. April felt her hunger again. She stepped out of the way as Bonnie set the casserole dish on the tile countertop.

"Can I help?" April asked.

Bonnie glanced at the table. "Just sit. Clive! I thought you already set the table," Bonnie said. She was only slightly irritated.

April said, "That's my job. I can do it."

Bonnie shook her head. "You're a guest tonight. *Our* guest."

Clive called, "Coming, Mummy."

April flinched at the endearment. She was not *his* mother. She tried to imagine Vince calling Ed "Daddy." Yuk.

Bonnie caught her reaction and set her straight. "He thinks he's being funny. If I boss him around too much, that's what I get."

Clive winked at April and patted Bonnie's derriere as he crossed behind her, opening the cupboard door over the refrigerator, taking out placemats and napkins. April felt her eyebrows rise at the fanny pat. Bonnie was unfazed.

Bonnie whisked balsamic vinegar into olive oil. She handed April the wooden bowl. "You can toss," she said.

April took the bowl and the tongs and settled in at the built-in banquette. She watched as Clive opened the silverware drawer next to where Bonnie was standing. Bonnie didn't even protest this encroachment. She simply shifted her hips to give him better access to the forks. April was amazed.

She'd never seen anyone in Bonnie's kitchen before. Even Ken, who Bonnie thought charming, had never been given such access. Of course, April couldn't remember Ken offering to set the table or touching a knife or fork except to eat.

Clive Pierce. The name rang a bell, but she didn't know why it sounded familiar. She was sure Bonnie had never mentioned him. In fact, Bonnie had never talked about any men since the divorce. And, April had to admit, she hadn't asked.

The man's accent was familiar, too. And not just because she liked to watch the BBC America channel.

Clive efficiently laid down the straw placemats, lining up the edges of the fork and knife, folding the watermelon-print cloth napkins, laying them to the left of the plate as Bonnie required. He hummed cheerfully as he filled water glasses from the Brita pitcher in the refrigerator.

As he poured, Clive said, "You were there when they found the skull? How very Hamlet. Tell me everything. Nothing this exciting has happened in this burg since I landed my car in the Nescopeck Creek. That resulted in my license being suspended. Tell us all. I'd love to hear a good tale that doesn't have me as the punch line."

Before April had a chance to answer, Bonnie paused in her bread slicing. She pointed the long serrated blade at Clive. "Can't we talk about something else? Dead bodies aren't my idea of dinner conversation, Clive."

Clive turned so Bonnie couldn't see him and pulled a face that made April giggle. He returned her smile before moving to the glass-fronted cabinets that separated the built-in banquette from the kitchen. He opened one of the doors and began to rummage through the delicate contents.

"Clive," April hissed. She tried to get his attention, to tell him to get out of that cupboard, but he ignored her. She held her breath, waiting for Bonnie to react.

Home to her mother's prized salt and pepper shakers, these shelves had always been off-limits to April. Bonnie's collection numbered well over two hundred pairs. Shakers made of ceramic, wood, metal. Shaped like grapefruit, lighthouses, cocker spaniels. Any shape that could be dreamed

154

up and have holes put in the top. No one but Bonnie touched the shakers.

But Bonnie hadn't flinched. Clive pulled out a black-and-white striped set of ceramic prisoners with tiny leg irons. April had bought the pair on Alcatraz.

"We'll use these, in your honor," Clive said. To April's amazement, Bonnie smiled at him as he set the pair on the table.

"That's perfect," Bonnie said. "I love those little guys."

Something was definitely going on here. This had to be serious. Clive was too much at home.

April sat down at the table, expecting Clive to do the same. Instead he snapped his fingers, said, "Pickles!" then flung open the cellar door and disappeared.

April looked to her mother. Was this some kind of code word? Maybe the two of them had given up cursing, saying "pickles" instead. Or perhaps it was their alternative to saying grace. The thought of a secret language between them made April shudder.

April didn't wait for the door to finish closing. He would be back upstairs in a moment. She asked, "Why didn't you tell me you were dating someone?"

Her mother took off her apron and hung

155

it on a hook by the broom closet.

Bonnie didn't look up. "What am I, in high school? I don't think 'dating' is part of my vocabulary."

"He's practically moved in. He certainly knows where everything is," April said.

"I don't think it's any of your business."

"I can almost understand why you didn't tell me over the phone," April said, fully aware that she hadn't talked to her mother about anything substantial for a year. "But yesterday? We were together for the whole day and you said nothing."

Bonnie shrugged.

She was getting angry at her mother's passive-aggressive approach. "Mom, come on. What's the big deal? I don't care if you're dating Clive. I'm just a little hurt that you didn't tell me."

"Date, schmate, April. We started spending time together. He likes my cooking. He's lonely, I'm lonely. What's the harm?"

Lonely. April hated that word. The last six months with Ken in San Francisco had been the loneliest time she'd ever spent. She could understand if her mother didn't want to be that unhappy.

Clive clattered back up the stairs, a jar of pickles in hand. He used his fingers to slop some into a dish. April looked at her mother to see if she was still breathing. She'd have stabbed Ed with her paring knife if he'd neglected to use the pickle spearer. Her mother had it bad for this guy.

Bonnie bumped April's hip. "Shove in."

April hesitated. If she moved in, she'd be flanked by her mother and her boyfriend. She'd be in the dreaded middle, a place she knew was a dead zone. She hated this diner seating that Ed had installed. She'd spent too much of her childhood trapped between parents who were unwilling to let her go until she'd answered all their probing questions.

Maybe Clive would settle next to her mother, leaving April a clear way out.

He dropped the Depression glass dish full of homemade pickles on the table and sat next to April. Her heart sank. She was outnumbered again. She felt as though she were twelve years old.

The only way out was through. She asked Clive to pass the chicken Parmesan. The faster they ate, the faster she'd be out of here. The three of them passed dishes and filled their plates.

Clive tucked his napkin under his chin and said, "So how long are you in town?"

Bonnie's eyes flashed at her daughter. April had been deliberately vague with her mother about her future plans. "Do tell," Bonnie said.

"I'm not sure. It was kind of a spur-of-the-moment thing. Dad had this job for me, and my work in San Francisco was at a lull, so I decided to come home for a while."

"And your husband?" Clive asked. "Bonnie tells me you're married."

April winced. "I am."

"Yes," Bonnie said testily. "How does Ken feel about all this?"

April studied the plate in front of her. Her mother wouldn't understand why she'd left Ken. To her mother, being left was the worst thing in the world. She knew her relationship with Ken was over, but she didn't have the words to explain that to her mother yet.

"He's okay with it," April said simply. She closed her face, hoping her mother would recognize this topic as off-limits.

Silence reigned. Clive reached for a piece of bread and sopped up his plate. He popped the crust in his mouth.

"What do you do, Clive?" April asked, determined to get the conversation off her. Besides, she still had the niggling feeling she knew this guy.

"I'm retired," he said simply. "I used to be an entertainer."

"How long have you been in Aldenville?"

April asked. Bonnie shot her a look, but she ignored it. She could vet her mother's boyfriends. It was payback for all the grief her mother had given her in high school.

"Just a few years. I passed through years ago and thought it looked like a good place to live."

"You must have been looking for a complete change of pace," April said with a slight snicker. "Nothing ever happens here."

He pointed a finger at her. "Are you having a laugh? Take today, for example. A body in the ruins. Did you see the skull?" he asked, tossing a quick look at Bonnie. She shook her head, but he persisted.

April nodded. She nearly pulled out her phone to show him the pictures, but she knew her mother would never tolerate that.

"Did you touch it?" he asked.

She shook her head. "The state police took over the site pretty quickly. They were keeping spectators far away."

"Were there more bones? Are they going to excavate?" he asked.

Bonnie said, "That's got to cost a pretty penny. With the never-ending complaints about rising taxes in this state, I sincerely hope the state police don't spend a lot of money on this. It can't be cheap."

"I'm not sure what the police will do," she

said. "Yost seems to think it could have been murder."

Clive's eyes widened comically, and April was reminded again how familiar he looked. But then, she often had that sensation when she was visiting Aldenville. She'd see a kid pumping gas and realize it was the younger brother of a neighbor or a girl she'd gone to school with. But Clive was not a part of this town's gene pool.

Bonnie sighed. "The Castle has always been bad luck."

"For the Winchesters?" April asked.

"For the Bucherts," Bonnie said. "And George. I heard today that was the last place he was seen, before he went back to the nursing home. That place has bad karma."

"I've got to try and sneak a peek," Clive said. He rubbed his hands together. "I know where I'll be tomorrow."

Bonnie pointed her fork at him. "You're a little too young to become a supervisor. Don't get too involved. Either one of you."

April kept quiet. Her mother didn't need to know how involved she already was.

Once dinner was over, Clive cleared the dishes, insisting that April and Bonnie remain seated. He sang softly as he scraped the remains of dinner into the garbage, his voice pleasant in a boy-band way.

160

Bonnie said, "Just because you're working for your dad doesn't mean you can't spend time with me, you know."

Bonnie liked to keep score, April knew that. But how was she going to manage to spend as much time with Bonnie as Ed? She'd be working every day with him.

"Mom, please, don't make my life difficult."

Bonnie pouted. "You'll see him every day. How about coming here for meals?"

April flinched.

"You've got to eat," Bonnie pointed out.

"Mom, most nights I'm happy with a scrambled egg or a protein shake."

Clive watched the exchange from the refrigerator where he was putting away the leftovers. "I hope we'll see a lot more of you," Clive said pleasantly to April.

April caught his eye. His expression pleaded with her to be nice to her mother.

Bonnie shook her head. "You can't keep eating like you're in college. You need a real meal once in a while. One that requires actual chewing."

April knew her mother would never let this rest. "You can feed me once a week," April said, in the spirit of compromise.

"Only one night?" Bonnie asked, disappointed.

April didn't speak, determined to hold her ground. Bonnie relented and they agreed on Wednesdays. April was pleased with herself, proud that she'd put up a boundary.

"I'll see you tomorrow, right? At George Weber's wake?" Bonnie asked.

April's heart sank. She knew her mother had given in too easily. "Why would I want to go to that?"

The wake was just the kind of small-town stuff that April didn't want to be sucked back into. She said, "Don't you people ever get sick of each other? I mean, you see half the town at the club every day. You see the rest in church on Sunday, Bible class on Wednesday, Eastern Star on Thursday."

"There's book club and the sewing circle, too," Clive put in, earning a dirty look from Bonnie.

April shook her head. "I can't imagine what you have to say to each other every day."

"Wakes are not about talking to your neighbors. They're about helping the living say good-bye to the dead. Deana knows that."

The old comparison-to-Deana gambit. April had never scored well in that. "If I'm not too busy, I'll be there," April said, worn down.

Bonnie said, "Wait here. I bought you some towels that were on sale at Boscov's. I'll go get them."

Bonnie's bedroom closet was a repository for all things discounted.

As her mother left the room, Clive winked at April, a broad wink. In that instance, April knew why he looked familiar. This was *that* Clive Pierce, the lead singer of the most popular band of the seventies, as recognizable, if not as respected, as the Beatles.

The Kickapoos were a band with their own television show in the early seventies. She and Deana had discovered it on *Nick at Nite.* When the band had gone on a reunion tour, Bonnie had taken ten-year-old April. April had been hooked. Now she was in the same room as their lead singer. He looked the same, only tinier and more wrinkled.

The song he'd been singing as he cleared the dishes had been the Kickapoos number one hit.

He caught April staring at him and smiled. She lowered her eyes and then snuck another look at the man putting out cookies and the sugar bowl. Clive's eyes were red-rimmed, and his once-luxurious brown locks had gone gray, but she recognized the smile, and the twinkle in his eyes had not faded.

On TV, he'd been the zany one of the foursome. He was always causing a ruckus with his misunderstandings and his mala-propisms that the other boys would have to rectify. Each show ended with him apologizing to his mates for getting them in trouble. Then the camera came in for a close-up of his smile, enhanced with a fake starburst of bright light.

What on earth was Clive Pierce doing with her mother? The woman to whom life was an endurance test, a race that couldn't be beat. She'd often told April that the most you could hope for was not to get kicked in the teeth each day. What was she doing with a guy who never took anything seriously? Who found life to be an adventure.

Clive took out the garbage. April marched down the hall to her mother's bedroom. Bonnie had dumped the contents of a large bag on her bed.

"Mom! Is that who I think he is? Clive Pierce from the Kickapoos? What's he doing in Aldenville?" April said. She couldn't keep the wonder from her voice. This little town's only brush with fame had been Jack Palance's farm up the road several miles. Not exactly paparazzi material.

"He fell in love with the place when the band came for a concert at the Grove twenty years ago."

"You took me to that concert," April cried.

"No need to shout, dear. I remember. We had a wonderful time."

April remembered it that way, too. She'd been young enough to like hanging out with her mother. For a mother and daughter about to enter the rending teen years, it had been a wonderful day. One of the best days of her childhood.

And now. Ewww.

"What's he doing with you?" April said.

Bonnie's eyes flashed. "Is there some reason he shouldn't be with me?" she said crustily.

"That's not what I meant," April said, even though that was exactly what she'd meant. "It's just that . . ." April paused to look at her mother. She softened. Her mother looked young and pretty, tiny tendrils of hair stuck to her ruddy cheeks.

"Mom, he was a megastar."

"Yeah, well, superstars need to eat, too."

"Is that all you do for him?" April regretted the words as soon as they left her mouth. Bonnie frowned deeply.

April was trying to figure out how old he was. He had to be older than Bonnie, who was fifty-eight. April remembered finding an original Kickapoos record in her mother's collection. What about that fashion rule? If you wore bell bottoms the first time they were fashionable, you couldn't wear them the next time they were popular. Did that apply to your pop icons? If you had a crush on them once, when you were a teenager, weren't you forbidden from dating them forever?

Bonnie shrugged. "He's just a man, April. Nothing special."

April knew her mother well enough to know that this was a lie. He was something special to her, not because of his superstardom, but despite it. He had given her reason to smile again, and for that April was glad.

Plus it meant her mother would leave her alone more.

She followed Bonnie back into the kitchen, where the towels were pressed on her, and she gathered up her purse. "I'm glad you've got someone in your life," April said.

"Don't be a stranger," her mother said, bussing her cheek and brushing a hair from her face. "I like having you in town.

April pulled at the door. It opened easily, as Clive was coming through from the breezeway. He grinned at her, his teeth bright white in the fading sunlight.

"Who's up for a game of cribbage?"

April begged off. She wasn't yet ready for a family game night with Bonnie and her new beau.

CHAPTER 8

After leaving her mother's, April sped over to Deana's, slowing down when she realized she was doing forty-five miles per hour in a thirty zone. Yost had often lingered just beyond the curve to catch speeders. She let out a breath when no red lights materialized behind her. Yost should be off duty.

Through the door, April saw Deana's husband, Mark, get up from the kitchen table in answer to her knock. Deana had met her husband the first year of mortuary college. April remembered the calls she'd gotten about the cute redhead in her embalming class. Mark had turned out to be a keeper. Gregarious and empathetic, he had no trouble fitting into the community.

Mark greeted her with a friendly hug. He was one of the good guys. When the world seemed too full of Ken-type man-boys, April clung to the belief that Mark was more representative of his gender.

"Good to see you," he said. "Are you glad to be back in town?"

April laughed. "Considering the day I had, I'm reserving judgment, for now. I just got out of playing cribbage with the old folks."

"Better cribbage than canasta," Mark said in the manner of someone who'd experienced both.

"The best part of being back is being this close to Deana. I hope you don't mind me dropping in. Often," she warned.

Mark smiled. "I'll console myself with the nonexistent phone bill."

Mark led her down the hall, past the bedrooms, opening a door at the end. "They're in the reception hall."

The hall was used for postfuneral luncheons and dinners. People in Aldenville liked to eat while mourning their dead. The walls were painted a serene moss green, with an oak wainscoting that ran around the room. The industrial carpet had been replaced since she and Deana had practiced their handstands and round-offs, and was now a gleaming hardwood floor. Racks of folding chairs and piles of collapsed tables sat in the far corner, waiting for the next big event, which, according to her mother, was George's wake tomorrow.

As she entered the room she saw two of

the eight-foot banquet tables had been set up in the middle of the floor, and the stampers from last night were seated at them. She recognized Rocky, Mitch's sister, sitting next to Tammy. Mary Lou, the realtor, and Suzi, the gardener, had their heads together. Mary Lou's pregnant daughter was not here tonight. That was too bad. She liked Kit. There was no sign of Piper.

Deana waved her over.

Papers, ink pads and fancy-edged scissors littered the tabletop. April smelled the heat gun as a small piece of metal in front of Mary Lou shriveled away from the high temperature as if it were alive.

"Look who's here, everybody," Deana said as she pushed away from the table and put an arm around April. The group said hello. April thought she heard a warning in her friend's voice. The kind of warning given when the subject of today's gossip walked into the room. She knew the skull would be on everyone's mind. Even in San Francisco, where the weird and bizarre were the norm, the appearance of a human skull was likely to garner some attention.

She glanced at Rocky. After all, the skull had been found on her family property. But Rocky looked nonplussed. The Winchesters had more experience with family scandals than she did. April only had Ed.

"How are you?" Tammy asked, her eyes searching for an answer in her face. April felt her empathy. Tammy probably made a great nurse's aide.

April decided to ignore the elephant in the room. For now.

"Bewildered," April said, hitching a hand on her hip. "I've just come from dinner with my mother." She let her voice rise dramatically.

She looked to Deana for commiseration, but Deana had crossed the room to fetch a chair for her. It was Rocky who figured out why April was so frazzled.

"I take it you met Clive?" Rocky said.

The group giggled as one. April caught some smiles and an exchange of knowing glances. Everyone knew about her mother's boyfriend.

"Guess I was the last to find out about my mother and the rock star," she said, still keeping her tone light. She accepted a chair from Deana. "Why didn't you tell me?" she said to Deana.

Suzi said, "He's had a crush on your mother ever since he moved here. It's only lately that we've seen them together."

"Honestly, your mother should have better sense," Rocky said.

Now what, April thought.

"I mean, when your name is Bonnie," Rocky said with a grin that gave April pause, "you really shouldn't date someone named Clive. People will mistake you for bank robbers."

Everyone laughed. The gentle teasing helped. April was beginning to feel at home. Deana winked at her twice, their secret signal. April felt the tightness in her chest ease. She winked back.

"He's the sweetest guy," Tammy said. "I did private duty nursing for him when he got out of rehab the last time."

"Rehab?" April's mood shifted as her stomach plummeted. A new worry.

"He's doing great," Tammy hastened to add. "He's been clean and sober for months now. Your mother insisted."

Mary Lou cleared the table next to her. "Come, sit, you need to get your hands dirty. Have some glue, shake out a few sparkles, and breathe in the ink fumes. That'll set you right. You've had a shock."

April obliged. Creative clutter usually did make her feel better. She fingered a floral rice paper. The pastels were soothing, a balm to her soul. She took in a breath.

"I don't have a project with me. Deana insisted I stop by."

"You can help me," Tammy said. "Deana and I are working on funeral cards for George."

"Funeral cards?" April asked. Tammy handed her what looked like a book mark.

Printed on ivory-colored heavy linen stock were the words, "Friend, husband, father." A black-and-white picture of a fresh-faced World War II sailor was at the top of the paper. Below, "George Weber, April 2, 1925–June 13, 2008."

April remembered him. In addition to being a code enforcement inspector for the town, George had been an insurance agent — *her family's* insurance agent. He'd come to the house when she was younger, scaring her silly about the winter driving, telling her more about the pitfalls of black ice than she'd ever wanted to know. *In*-surance, he'd called it, like a southerner, although he'd told her, twice, that he'd lived in the valley his whole life.

Ed had not been living at home for months by the time she'd passed her driver's test. She missed him and did not appreciate George's attempts at fatherly heartiness. Bonnie had not been happy with her when April had interrupted George's story about a trucker stranded during a massive snowstorm and left the room in a teenage huff before he'd even finished the Boston cream pie Bonnie had made.

Deana said, "We're embellishing three hundred memorial cards for George."

"Three hundred?" April asked, thinking she'd heard her wrong. Did George know that many people?

Deana nodded. "That probably won't be enough. George was an elder in his church, a Rotarian with a gold pin . . ."

"Do you do this for all your customers, Deana?" April asked.

Deana laughed. "No. We did it once before, when Suzi's aunt died. She was a quilter so we did a beautiful card with buttons and antique lace. I was vacuuming up the sequins for weeks. George's will be a little less three-dimensional."

Tammy handed her a finished card. It looked nothing like the dull mass-printed one that they'd started with. A blue ribbon had been threaded through an eyelet in the top, and the card had been stamped with a typewriter, desk and mug. She had even used Angelina fibers to represent steam.

Tammy said, "George was kind of special. We're using images that remind us of him. He was a hunter and fisherman. Bow and arrow. He loved his coffee. Ate at the Sunlite Diner every morning for the past thirty years." Each time she mentioned a hobby or interest, she showed April the appropriate stamp.

Rocky held up a card and blew the excess embossing powder off it onto a clean piece of paper. "Yeah, we're leaving out the bits about how he pinched every girl's fanny on the way up to the choir loft."

Mary Lou said, "Oh yeah, you never wanted to be walking in front of him going up the stairs. No-oh. Bastard had six hands, I swear."

"Only George could combine piety and pervy and get away with it," Rocky said.

"You'd better be careful he doesn't come back from the dead and grab you," Suzi cautioned.

Deana said, "There'll be no talking of people rising from the dead in my house."

"Bad for business," April muttered. The group laughed, and April felt a little more accepted. She liked this group of women.

"April, you should remember him. George was always at your dad's job sites," Tammy said. "He was code enforcement officer back in the day."

Rocky said, "That's always been a patronage job. Useless people with not enough to do with their lives, so they muck up someone else's plans."

April understood Rocky's vitriol. She remembered the code violation forms she'd seen in the file. The violations had only been part of the reason the Castle job took so long, though.

"He would have been hanging out at the Castle yesterday except . . ." Tammy began.

"He was dead," Mary Lou finished.

"Mary Lou, please." Tammy suddenly sounded very defensive. Her eyes flashed angrily, and she waved an X-Acto knife in the air. "He shouldn't have died. He was doing well in the nursing home, just being rehabbed after hernia surgery last week. He was expected to go home in a day or two. But he up and died. Right at the end of my shift."

Rocky rubbed Tammy's back. "She's got such a soft heart," she said to April. "She takes all the deaths out there personally."

'Soft' was not a word April would use to describe Tammy right now. Brittle, yes. The group fell silent, hands busy but each with her own thoughts.

"Where's Piper? Is she coming?" April asked.

Deana answered. "Celebrating Jesse's birthday."

Tammy reached for a grommet tool. She stood and leaned hard on the tool, pushing the tiny metal eyelet into place. When she finished, she looked to Rocky as though for approval. Rocky nodded slightly.

"Friday night," Tammy said. "We're having our annual Stamp Til Dawn party at the club. Why don't you come?"

April looked again to Deana for explanation, and she obliged. "We stay up all night and stamp. The club provides food and coffee, and we stamp until sunup."

"Oh, I don't know," April said. "I'll probably need to work on Saturday, and I shouldn't skip that much sleep."

"You'd really miss out," Rocky drawled. "It's fun. Not like new-boyfriend kind of fun, but it's the most fun you can have with your clothes on."

"Do you usually do things with a stamp pad and your clothes off?" Mary Lou wanted to know.

"Thanks for putting that image in my head," Suzi said.

"Hey, Mary Lou, you were looking for an inspiration for a new project," Tammy said. "How about a naked body?"

Mary Lou waved her off. "Honey, I don't even look at my own husband without his clothes if I can help it," she said.

Rocky stopped what she was doing, threw her hands up, and drawled, "Well then, how on are earth do you shave his back?" she asked.

Mary Lou led the laughter. April liked how easy they were with each other, able to poke fun and laugh. She needed to laugh.

April felt her heart soothe and the anxiety in her chest loosen as her own fingers combined stamps and inks and torn tissue paper. The card under her fingers started to take shape. She didn't remember George well, but she knew about good design.

"So, April, tell us what you know about the explosion at the Castle," Suzi said.

"Yeah, what happened?" Mary Lou asked. "Tammy's not telling."

Tammy protested, "I haven't spoken to my husband since he left for work this morning. I came straight here from the nursing home."

"I guess the place was already falling down," April said, looking to Rocky to step in and clarify. When she didn't, she went on. "The owner was worried about kids throwing parties out there, so she wanted it leveled. My father and his crew took it down, and found the skull."

Rocky said, "My Aunt Barbara must have flipped out. She never approved of my father's projects. The two of them have been fighting over that piece of property for years.

She finally made him an offer that he thought was acceptable."

Mary Lou's eyes widened and she whistled. "That land is worth a lot."

"My father was holding out for his price." Rocky turned to April. "You should know before you get involved with my brother that there are plenty of other skeletons in my family's closet. Not the real kind, but still. Unwanted babies, undesirable spouses, philandering husbands. Murderous wives. It's Shakespearean, I tell you. Before you start dating my brother, you should think twice."

April's stomach flipped. "Dating? Mitch?"

Deana said sternly, "April's married. She's not looking for a man."

Tammy laughed. "Just because Mitch is the best-looking and most eligible man in this valley, doesn't mean every woman is after him, Rocky."

"I didn't say every woman. I just said April." Rocky's eyes were cold, and April wasn't sure if she was kidding or not.

She forced herself to sound calm. "I don't know what you heard, Rocky, but I'm not interested in Mitch. We're just working together, that's all."

Mary Lou and Suzi exchanged a look. April wondered if Rocky was this territorial all the time or if it was something she brought out in her. She would keep her distance from Mitch, just in case.

The stamping went on until just after eleven. Deana walked people out while April picked up. She stacked George's memorial cards in a box. She liked the way they looked.

Deana came back in. "Thanks. Those cards mean a lot to Tammy."

"Oh, did she pay for them? I mean, I didn't think this was part of the service."

Deana laughed. "Not really, no. It was just something Tammy needed to do."

"Isn't it kind of expensive providing all the supplies to decorate the cards?"

Deana shrugged. "I guess."

April changed the topic. She asked Deana if she could stay and watch the news. "I don't have a TV in the barn. Do you mind? I'm afraid . . ." April stopped. She feared her father would be on TV again.

Deana put an arm around her. "Of course you can. Mark always watches the eleven o'clock news before he comes to bed. Let's go into the study."

She followed Deana down the hall. The first room on the right had been Deana's father's sanctuary for as long as April could remember.

"It looks exactly the same," April said as they entered. The walls were painted dark green and covered with dark wood shelves running from the floor to the ceiling. A large desk sat in the middle of the room facing the door. Mark was seated there. A small television was hanging from a wall bracket in the corner of the room. Mark waved them in, and they sat on a leather-tufted couch. The news wasn't on yet.

April looked to see if Mr. Hudock's collection of Aldenville High memorabilia was still on display. She was not disappointed. Mr. Hudock had always tried to temper his role as funeral director with something more fun. He didn't want to be known in the community just as the man who buried their relatives. He'd coached Pop Warner football and sponsored ads at the Little League field. She still had a softball jersey with the Hudock logo on the back.

She pointed to the glass-fronted cabinet where his trophies, plaques and flags resided. "Still the number one booster, eh?" she asked.

Deana looked at her husband. "Mark's nice enough to leave him that intact."

Mark laughed. "As if I have a choice. I can take his precious daughter, I can run his business, but Ron Hudock would kill

181

me if I touched his pennants."

They all laughed as it was obvious Mark didn't really care.

"Dad comes back from Florida for football season. He hasn't missed a home game in over fifty years."

Mark pointed the remote at the TV. "Quiet now, the news is on."

The Castle was the lead story. A solemn newscaster faced them, her blonde hair frosted and highlighted and cut into a helmet that didn't move. She tried to convey how serious this story was without frowning and causing wrinkles. She looked constipated. April winced as a picture of Mirabella came on the screen.

"Retro Reproductions got more than they bargained for this morning while demolishing a ramshackle building on the property of Winchester heiress Barbara Harcourt," the newscaster began.

"Mrs. H. is not going to like being on TV," Deana said. "She doesn't like publicity."

"No one needs this kind of exposure," Mark said.

April's heart sank a little deeper. Now she was sorry she'd watched.

"A skull was found in the rubble. The state police say that the skull is human but will not speculate as to how it came to be at the Castle job site. Mr. Buchert and his partner, Vincent Campbell, owners of the company, have been renovating high-end homes in the Aldenville area for ten years now."

The news anchor managed to make "partner" sound sordid. April cringed. Deana patted her hand.

"NewsTrack Eleven will be following this story and keep you informed of any new developments. A house fire in Sugarloaf has left a family of five out in the cold . . ."

Mark flipped to another channel, which was telling Ed's story also.

April had had enough. She stood up. "I'm going to go home."

Deana led her to the back door. At April's car, she hugged her and April stayed in her friend's arms, drawing comfort and solace from the woman who had grown used to this as part of her profession. It didn't feel professional, though; it felt very personal.

"My homecoming is not what I thought it would be," April said quietly.

Deana patted her back solicitously. "I know, I know."

"My father is up to his eyeballs in a messy job, the messiest. And my mother. My mother has a boyfriend. A boyfriend."

Deana pulled back and looked at her. The

parking lot was lit with old-fashioned street lamps. "I know it sounds cliché, April, but you never know how much time you have with someone. Your mother could be gone tomorrow."

"Please, Deana, don't lay the life-is-short thing on me. I know you see it all the time in your job, but come on. What if life's too short to hang out with people who want too much from you?"

CHAPTER 9

When she pulled in the barn's driveway a few minutes later, April was surprised to see light leaking from the clerestory windows over the sliding barn doors. The barn didn't have many windows facing the drive, as Vince and Ed had been more interested in preserving the original façade. During the drive home, April had been regretting that she hadn't left a light on. Of course, she hadn't expected to be gone until after dark when she'd left the house early this morning.

Skirting the cumbersome sliding doors, April entered through the small kitchen door and flipped on a light. The vast emptiness of the space, highlighted by her lack of furniture, glared back at her. Empty except for her father.

In the far corner of the room that served as Retro Reproductions' office, Ed was seated at his desk, a small circle of light coming from the desk lamp, illuminating the sheaf of papers in front of him. White banker boxes were stacked at his feet. The top one looked empty and the contents strewn on the desk.

April tossed her purse on the kitchen counter and crossed the main room. "I didn't know you'd be here," she said. Her voice echoed and she lowered it.

At least if he was here, he hadn't seen the latest news report. There was no television.

"Paperwork," he said, rubbing his hands together as though he were trying to start a fire. The barn was cool but not cold. As she got closer, April could feel the exhaustion emanating off him. The usual bags under his eyes looked darker, bruised and painful. She felt her heart soften.

She kissed the top of his head and rubbed his shoulders. He sighed. After a moment, he shrugged her off. Her father could never stand too much relaxation.

"What's all this?" April gestured toward the top of the desk. Three standing files were lined up. They were labeled — the Castle, Mirabella, Heights.

Ed tapped his pen on his teeth and pointed. "We're running three jobs right now. This is how I keep the job costs straight. All the workers' hours, the invoices for supplies, the bills of lading go in the appropriate file. Once a week or so, I go through and allocate the costs to the right job. I usually do it on Tuesday, but since today was such a mess, I'm trying to catch up."

"It must be tough, keeping track of three jobs." Especially by hand. April used project management software.

"Three jobs, ten employees, two subcontractors. A total of four hundred thousand in contracts," Ed said wearily. "So far this year."

April widened her eyes. She hadn't realized her father's business had grown so big. "Can I help?"

Anyone else would be proud of their accomplishments, but Ed looked stressed. "I can't finish. Some bills are missing. Lyle must have paperwork in his truck that he hasn't turned in yet. I always have to hound him to turn in the invoices when he gets a shipment or buys something." He sighed heavily. "I was just getting ready to go home."

"The state police done at the Castle?" April asked.

He shook his head. "Not by a long shot. They might be there for days, depending on what they find. They're sifting through the rubble with sandbox toys."

She laughed at the image. Ed frowned. "Sorry," she said. "I was picturing a big yellow shovel."

"This is serious, Ape. They're looking for more bones. That body was inside that house," Ed said, gnawing on a knuckle. "Inside that house that I'd boarded up years ago."

April felt scared. This sounded like more than his usual alarmist folderol. "That's just Yost's bullshit, isn't it?" she asked.

Ed shook his head sadly. "I heard the medical examiner tell the staties that the bones hadn't been exposed to the elements. There are no animal bites, and something about the color makes him think that skull has been inside for at least fifteen years, maybe longer."

April's scalp tightened. She didn't like the time line. Deana had said the same thing.

"So they're searching for the rest of the bones?" she asked.

Ed rubbed his face, hard. He got to the real problem on his mind. "There is no way I'm going to get paid for the Castle demolition until they're finished and we can get in and truck away all that debris."

"Mitch said you'd been hoping to salvage some of the stone and wood," she said.

"The blast took care of that. Nothing is going the way I'd planned. But then, things never do, do they?" he said sadly.

"What about the Mirabella job?" April asked. Any stoppage would mean a delay in her paycheck that she could not afford. "The remodeling will go on, won't it? I mean, the Castle is really an outbuilding, and —" April had her arguments lined up.

He waved her off and she felt her jaw unclench. "Over there, it's business as usual. The mansion is far enough away that the cops are not considering it part of their scene."

"Now what?"

Ed put the lid on the box. "Now, I spend the next couple of days with the state police. Vince won't be able to handle the other jobs we have by himself, and business falls off horribly. Mrs. H. doesn't pay the final installment on the work we've already done . . ."

April put her hand over his mouth. "Dad, please. Stop."

He looked at her warily. "This could happen. I'm not being overly dramatic."

Ed's cell rang. The vibrate function was on, too, making the phone skip across the desktop. April could see it was Vince, so she walked away to give them some privacy.

Ed did have a point. If this body wasn't identified quickly, Mrs. H. might get antsy and shut down the Mirabella job. Bonnie had been right: the Castle was bad luck for the Bucherts. April had to make sure this wasn't a repeat of the last debacle. She would do whatever she could to keep Retro Reproductions on the job, doing their work and earning their paychecks.

Listening to her father's murmurings to Vince, she was comforted by his change in tone. Vince could always calm her father down.

She didn't want to go back to California just yet. It had taken her years to forgive her father after he'd moved out of the house and into the loft over the garage. Not until she was graduated from college did they begin the process of repairing their relationship.

San Francisco had been a big factor in that. Out of the constricting bounds of the small town, each of them flourished. He'd visited her, sleeping on the futon in her living room. Exploring the city with him, April had learned who her father was. She'd found out about his passion for Janis Joplin while they shared drinks at the bars in the Mission. They'd cheered for his Yankees at an intraleague game at the new ballpark. At

City Lights Bookstore, he'd introduced her to the poems of Ferlinghetti. With great seats at *Beach Blanket Babylon,* she'd recognized her own offbeat sense of humor in his guffaws. She gradually came to love him for who he was.

About five years ago, he'd brought Vince to San Francisco. April had been leery, not ready to face this part of her father's life, but Ed with Vince was a revelation. He had a buoyancy that she'd never seen before. She recognized what had been missing in his relationship with Bonnie. Ed liked Bonnie, she'd been his best friend, but he loved Vince with a depth and spirituality that touched April's heart.

In fact, seeing Vince and Ed together had showed her what was wrong with her and Ken. They didn't have that sense of being soul mates. She'd never been happy in her marriage after that. She'd seen what could be and was not willing to put up with anything less.

Ed hung up. "Vince says I should come home and go to bed."

April tugged on the back of his chair until he pushed away from the desk. "He's right," she said.

Ed stood and stretched. He yawned. "I'll get out of your way so you can get some sleep. Tomorrow's going to be a bear. Where have you been anyhow? It's late."

She ignored his attempt to parent and told him about having dinner with Bonnie and visiting Deana and the stampers. While she talked, he put a few folders in his briefcase and zipped it closed.

He tried a smile, but it didn't reach his eyes, which remained glazed. He hadn't let go of his work problems. "Don't forget to check in on the men again tomorrow. Lyle's got to go with Vince on the Heights job. I'll need you to be my eyes and ears again."

"But I'll be nowhere near them," April said. The warm and fuzzy feeling she'd been generating disappeared in an instant.

The mansion was huge. How could she keep an eye on her father's employees when she couldn't see them? There was five thousand square feet of house between the dining room and the north wing. She wondered if they'd even be in the same zip code.

His take of her responsibility on this job and hers were miles apart. She thought she was there to stamp on the walls. First the mural, now this. She felt resentment flare.

She needed to sit her father down and explain to him how she worked. This morning her reaction had been cut short by the blast. She needed to be sure Ed understood she was not a painter. Or a babysitter.

She looked at him. "Don't forget, thanks to you, I'm working in the dining room," April said. "Trying to clean a mural. I have no idea how I'm going to do that."

Ed's looked at her with puppy-dog eyes, wide and beseeching for forgiveness. "Please, April, not now. Do what you can with that wall."

"Dad, you need to treat me as a professional. I'm not your gofer."

"Come on, things are different today. I messed up, I admit. But I need your help."

She straightened her shoulders and took in a deep breath. She was tired, the day's events catching up with her and weighing her down. But she knew better than to add on to her dad's worry pile.

He saw her giving in and reached in his briefcase. He pulled out a black radio. "I'll give you my walkie-talkie. Just use that to stay in touch with the guys and drop in on them once in a while."

She was about to suggest that he could use the walkie-talkie himself to keep in touch with the boys from the Castle site, but her father's deep sigh cut her to the quick. Ed's jowls shook on the exhale. She hated to see him so stressed.

His voice was even quieter. "We've got to

keep Mrs. H. satisfied, whatever it takes. She's not going to be happy that I'm not on-site. I can't afford to lose this job. She has yet to pay the final payment on the first phase of the job."

April needed this job as much as her father did. More. She had the money she'd gotten from the stampers to last her until the next paycheck, but she needed a steady income. She said, "Don't give it another thought. I'll make sure everything goes smoothly tomorrow."

He kissed her on the cheek, and she hugged him tight. He broke away and headed for the door. Suddenly exhausted, April felt a physical need to lie down. The desire to be off her feet was overpowering. Before Ed even reached the doorway, she put a foot on the ladder that led to the sleeping loft. The mattress that had seemed kind of lumpy last night was calling to her. Her research would have to wait until morning.

Ed stopped and saw her about to climb up. His hand on the doorknob, he was suddenly animated. "Did I tell you about that ladder? State-of-the-art. Light enough to be handled by one person. Weighs only eight pounds."

Ed loved his gadgets. The lightweight ladder, the remote-control blinds on the sky-light, the faucets that came on without touching.

The sleeping loft was bigger than many San Francisco bungalows. In fact, loft was a misnomer, as the ceiling soared twelve feet above the built-in bed. The only thing loft-like was the ladder entrance. If a permanent staircase had been installed, it would have been considered the second floor. April wondered if the real reason Ed and Vince had left the barn was because they were tired of climbing. Their egos wouldn't let them admit they were getting too old.

Ed continued. "In case of a home invasion, you can pull that ladder up and hunker down. There's a phone jack up there, too."

"Dad. Really? Home invasion? Who's going to break in here? A black bear, maybe."

She stepped off the ladder and held up a hand to stop him from coming any closer. He might get a charge out of his high-tech toys, but she was too tired for a lecture.

Ed said, "A bear is a possibility, you know. Make sure you double wrap your garbage. Between the bears and the skunks, it's better to be prepared."

She'd heard those words all through her childhood. Of course, there'd been no way to prepare for the one thing that changed her life forever.

"Go home," April said.

Ed hesitated in the door, looking back at her. "Sleep tight, bug."

"Don't worry, Dad."

She knew telling him not to worry was like telling the tide not to come in, but she couldn't resist. She loved this man, but her private fear was that she was just like him, always fretting about the smallest thing. She felt her anxiety level rise whenever she was around him, but tonight she forced herself to look on the bright side.

"Everything will work out just fine." April wasn't known for her optimism, but next to Ed, she looked like Pollyanna. It was going to take her some time to get used to having her parents around on a daily basis. She fell right into roles she'd have sworn were long gone.

"Lock the door," Ed said.

"Yes, Dad." How could she ever have survived living in San Francisco for the past fourteen years without his constant reminders? Of course, he had called her once a month to remind her to change the batteries in the smoke alarm.

She washed her face, brushed her teeth, changed into her softest T-shirt and shorts and scampered up the ladder.

In the loft, her sketch pad was next to her pillow. She turned on the light over the bed and fluffed up the pillows so she could sit up. She moved the pencil across the page. Images started to appear. She felt herself relax. The stress of the day faded as she drew.

She turned the pages quickly, filling them with images. She stopped when she realized she'd drawn pages of skulls.

The sketch pad looked like a Day of the Dead poster. Obviously, her psyche had been disturbed to see the skull, stirred in ways that her conscious mind hadn't absorbed. She'd drawn grotesque eye sockets, gaping and wide, no life anywhere. Cavernous mouths. The proportions were all wrong, but she never doubted what her hand drew. Her mind worked with her fingers, in ways she often didn't understand, recording images she hadn't realized she'd seen.

She went back down for the scissors. Last Halloween she'd seen a string of skulls like paper dolls, cut from one piece of paper, and she wanted to see if she could duplicate it. She got her sharpest pair and a heavy-duty paper, and climbed back into the loft. April looked at the image and let her fingers do the cutting. The first one looked misshapen, but the more she worked at it, the more familiar the shape looked. She didn't stop until she had twenty skulls connected. A deadly garland.

The activity had awakened her. She climbed out of the loft. Her brain was reeling with thoughts about the body. She decided to do her Internet research now and booted up her father's computer.

While she waited for the booting to finish, she fished her cell phone out of her purse. It needed recharging. She plugged it in and saw the call she'd made to the Imperiale residence. No one had ever called her back.

She realized she hadn't told her father what she'd found out about his employees. Three of four accounted for. Not a bad average. Chances were she'd find the fourth guy alive and kicking.

CHAPTER 10

"Do I smell lunch?"

April turned her head, one hand still working the cut onion into the mural. She sponged with her left hand, using a rag dipped in lemon juice.

She'd been working on an area behind the massive carved oak door for the past two hours. She'd tried this method on an inconspicuous spot first and had been surprised by the results. Apparently the Internet could be right sometimes. It hadn't taken her too long last night to find an article about cleaning artwork. She'd been in bed by one.

Mitch leaned around the doorjamb, grinning at her.

She leaned back on her haunches and wiped the sweat from her eyes. Lemon juice dribbled down her arm to her elbow, finding a small cut and settling in. She blinked away the pain, noticing as she did her less-than-impressive work site. Half an onion lay on a paper towel at her knee, garnished with the squeezed hull of a lemon. A baguette was sticking out of the grocery bag nearby.

Mitch said, "I thought the poem was about a loaf of bread, cheese, wine and thou. I don't remember one about onion, a lemon and what's that — Italian bread?" Mitch's eyes were dancing, his forehead well creased with laugh wrinkles. April had to admit this was her favorite kind of guy, one who noticed the comical side of life. But she wasn't in the market for a man. No matter what Rocky thought.

"That's right," he continued. "You're from San Francisco, it must be sourdough."

She said, "According to this article I read, the enzymes in the onion break down the dirt and the lemon collects it. I think it's working, don't you?"

Mitch moved in to get a closer look. She stood and backed into the corner, feeling pleasantly trapped as he squinted at the mural. His clean, slightly woodsy smell fought with the noxious lemon-onion combination she'd been breathing in, and she felt slightly dizzy.

His khakis were crisp. He was wearing a matching safari-type shirt, the kind favored by news anchors on location in a war zone or presidents trying to look intrepid. The look suited him. His braided belt was real leather and matched his soft loafers. No steel-toed work boots for him. He managed to look fresh out of an Abercrombie and Fitch catalog. The old ones, before the teen set latched on. Casual, well-fitted, expensive.

Whatever crispness she'd possessed was long gone after spending the morning in the stuffy dining room. She'd dressed to look professional but comfortable. Her good jeans were stained with lemon juice that was forever changing the color of the denim. Maybe she could pass them off as designer jeans now.

Mitch squinted at the wall. "I see a difference."

April was vindicated. "You do?" She looked where he was pointing.

"Right there," he said. "Isn't that moccasin brighter?"

"Damn," she said, frowning at him. "I haven't touched that part of the mural yet."

"Oops, sorry." Mitch looked penitent. He avoided catching her eye, studying the mural instead.

She ignored his critique. If he couldn't see how much cleaner the mural looked, he was blind.

"What are you doing here today?" she

asked him.

"More measuring — this time for the closet cabinetry. Have you seen the plans? My aunt's powder room is the size of my living room. She's putting in drawers and shelves that would put most kitchens to shame. About fifty thousand in wood alone. For a closet." He sounded amazed. "All sustainable lumber, though. I'm insisting that she go green."

"Good for you." April was impressed. Most of what she'd seen in this house had been built with woods that were no longer available. She suspected the paneling was ebony.

"Measuring'll take me most of the day. Do you want to meet up for lunch?"

April blushed. She shouldn't be ashamed of brown bagging her mother's leftovers, but she was.

"I brought my lunch," she said.

"Me, too. I'm not suggesting we go out, just meet out back about noon."

He was smiling at her invitingly. She didn't want to lead him on, letting him think she was available or interested in dating.

"What about Mrs. H.? Does she approve of lunch breaks?" That was another concern — April couldn't afford even the look of impropriety. Picnicking with the owner's nephew might fall into that category.

Mitch said, "It's Wednesday. Women's golf league at the club. She'll be gone all day. I'll come back in an hour or so. What do you say?"

"Okay," April agreed. What was the harm? Just having lunch with a coworker.

But why did he want to have lunch with her? She pushed a hand self-consciously through her hair. She must look like a mess. She'd sweated through her clothes, and the hair at her temples and neck was damp with perspiration. And she smelled like an Italian deli.

He didn't seem to notice. He smiled. "All right then," Mitch said. "Carry on." He walked away, and she watched his cute butt disappear around a corner.

Why did the good guys always appear at the wrong time? Hold on a minute. She didn't know if Mitch was one of the good guys. She reminded herself that Ken had been adorable once upon a time, too. The first time she'd met him, he'd been attentive, insistent and charming. Over time, she'd learned to distrust such charm.

Before going back to the mural, she tried her dad's cell. No answer. That was the third time this morning she'd called with no result. She didn't leave a message.

Detouring into the study, she heard the men talking before she got there. There were only four of them. She greeted them.

"No John today?" she asked Mike.

"Out sick," he said.

At the same time, Butch said, "He's on Lyle's job today."

Mike jerked his head toward Butch. April caught the look between them.

"My bad," he said, shrugging. "Yesterday he said he was coming down with something."

April waited a beat but no one said anything else. She wanted to ask which was it, out sick or on another job, but she'd leave it to Ed to sort out.

She asked, "Everything going well back here? Got everything you need?"

Mike said, "I've got a list for the supply house. Things we'll need for tomorrow. Do you want to look it over?"

April took the list from him, reading the items on it. Nails, brads, just the small stuff that every job required. She said, "How does it usually work? Don't you just charge what you need? Does my dad or Vince approve everything?"

He shook his head. "I usually run my needs by them. If it's something we have in the shop, then I just get it there. But I broke the last drill bit this morning."

April considered. She couldn't run to her father with every small problem. This seemed innocuous. "Just go ahead and pick up another."

He put the list in his breast pocket. "I'll go get it after lunch."

"Well, okay, call me on the walkie-talkie if you need me. I'm in the dining room."

True to his word, Mitch came back an hour later. She felt as though she'd made progress, the onion doing its magic. The area she'd worked, small though it was, was definitely cleaner. She took heart. She might be able to accomplish this task after all. The work was tedious beyond belief, but at least it was paying off. She rubbed the small of her back, feeling the workload in her tired muscles.

She deserved a break. And she was hungry.

Mitch led her outside. "It's a great day, not too hot. There's a nice spot under the sycamore tree out back."

The sun was shining, and the air was warm but not humid. Clouds, soft and white, so unlike San Francisco's gray fog, punctuated a picturesque blue sky. She'd forgotten how perfect an early summer day could be in this part of the world. There was a lush greenness that existed only for a few weeks, after the rainy, too-cold spring and before the too-hot summer.

Mitch led her across a large expanse of green lawn to a gazebo. Clematis vine climbed up the wood supports. Inside the octagonal-shaped middle was a glass-topped table with six wicker chairs. The paint was well-worn along the arms and she could see that the wicker had been repaired several times, but it was obviously the real stuff. She could picture it on an English Colonial house porch.

April sat down, feeling a little uneasy being on Mrs. H.'s lawn furniture. She looked around to make sure there was no sign of her golf cart. Pennsylvania was so different from San Francisco. The class wars were still being fought here. Was it improper to sit at the mansion owner's picnic table?

She decided she didn't care. She'd been on her knees all morning, stooped over a bucket of foul-smelling concoction, scrubbing. Besides, Mitch had invited her. This had been his place. He was her ticket to the show.

Mitch and April unpacked their lunch. Mitch had a reusable sandwich container and a peanut butter and jelly on rye inside.

He unpacked a bag of Sun Chips. He offered her iced tea from his thermos, producing two paper cups.

"Thanks," April said.

Mitch nodded his head in the direction of the Castle. "What do you hear from over there?" he asked.

"Not much," April said. "My dad's not answering his phone. I'd like to go over there and talk to him."

Mitch took a bite of his sandwich and washed it down with iced tea. "Don't bother. I tried but the staties turned me away."

April felt the futility in their actions. She wished her dad had never heard of this job.

"What's the story? What happened to the Castle? Why was it never finished?" April asked.

Mitch leaned back in his chair, taking the bag of chips with him, and ripping it open. "You'd have to know my dad. He was not a happy man when I was growing up. He was never challenged by his job. So he'd have these projects going on all the time. The Castle was supposed to be an apartment for my sister and me."

"An apartment?" It was as big as a California bungalow in her San Francisco neighborhood that had sold for over a million dollars.

"Dad's idea was that once we were out of the house, we were out for good. He'd give us a roof over our heads but no more." Mitch continued. "My dad was a hippie. You know, one of those privileged kids with no reasonable thing to rebel against. He hit the sixties with a vengeance. At the beginning of the decade, he was a crew-cut ROTC jock at Penn. By the end of the decade, he was a long-haired dude living on a commune in Colorado, growing pot and spending money like he'd made it. In the early seventies, his father made him come home, marry my mother and go to work in the family business."

"Which was?"

"Banking," Mitch said.

April knew about unhappy fathers. She wondered if they were like unhappy families: all the same.

He stood abruptly. "Sit tight. I have a surprise for you." He wiped his hands on the napkin he'd brought. He shook off the memories.

Mitch bounded across the lawn to where his Jeep was parked. He was like a dog, a golden retriever, full of curiosity and pleased by everything he encountered. The talk about the Castle was seemingly forgotten.

She wasn't interested in a relationship, but she wasn't going to lie, it was nice to have a man's attention. He was charming, funny and easy to look at. The consideration felt good, balm to her Ken-battered feminine psyche.

A surprise might be nice. It had to be better than Bonnie's surprises, anyway.

Mitch reached over the open top of his Jeep parked next to her car. He pulled a leather portfolio out of the back seat. He was untwirling the small orange tie as he walked, and smiling at her.

"I brought pictures of the main house in its heyday to show you," he said. "I thought you might get inspired."

April smiled at his thoughtfulness. Seeing the house in its original décor could help her devise her wall coverings. He pulled out a large black scrapbook.

"Any baby pictures?" she teased.

"Not mine, my dad maybe," he said, opening to the first page. "I brought the oldest album I could find. I figured you wanted the history."

"Mirabella has always been in your family?" she asked.

He nodded and laid the book on the table and leafed through the pages. April saw posed families for whom smiling was not an option. One showed a quartet of women in the gazebo she was sitting in right now.

In the third or fourth picture, April caught sight of the dining room. She brought the book in for closer scrutiny.

The table was set for fourteen, six on each side and two on the short ends. The damask tablecloth was hand-embroidered with entwined flowered vines, and the matching napkins were folded so that a fancy "W" was in view. Each place setting had three crystal glasses and rows of forks. The china had to be Meissen. A tiny rosebud vase held a place card, the gold lettering ornate.

The shot was taken from the adjoining living room. April said, "I can't see the mural."

"It's on this side." Mitch pointed to where the wall would be. "The wall in the living room used to have access to the dining room. Your father unearthed those pocket doors. They'd been covered with wallboard sometime in the seventies. My parents didn't use this room much. Our dinner parties ran more to hot dogs than haute cuisine."

April said, "Darn. Even in this picture, the walls of the dining room have been painted. I would love to see what was on the walls before that."

Mitch closed the scrapbook. "Maybe I can unearth older pictures. My mother dumped all the family photos in my spare room when they hit the road. If you want to come by my house, I'll dig them out."

April hesitated.

He sensed her reluctance. "Or I could bring them by the job tomorrow."

She agreed to that. April finished her iced tea and gave the cup to Mitch. She should get on with work, but she was enjoying being outdoors so much, she didn't want to go back in just yet. She breathed in the fragrances of the grass and flowers. She looked around to make sure Mrs. H. wasn't watching them.

April remembered Ed asking about Mitch's dad yesterday. Carefully asking. So she said lightly, "So your father is, um, traveling?"

Mitch laughed. "Yes. My parents went into the Peace Corps on his sixty-fifth birthday. That was four years ago. He sold Mirabella to his sister, Aunt Barbara, who always loved it, and put his money in trust and took off. He and Mom come home every six months or so, to drop off more swag and continue round the world. According to the e-mail I got yesterday, they're building straw yurts in the Gobi desert right now."

"Do you mind that he didn't leave you the house?"

"God, no. It's a money pit. I don't have the kind of fortune that Aunt Barbara has. She married a superrich guy and has no kids. She can afford to dump a million dollars into fixing it up."

A million dollars? Was Mitch exaggerating? He said it so casually, as though she knew. Ed hadn't told her this job was so big.

No wonder Ed was worried about getting paid. He must have a huge outstanding bill at the supply house. On any job, the contractor had to buy the supplies he needed before he got paid. Usually, that wasn't a problem, but on a renovation this size, if Mrs. H. got behind in paying Ed, he could end up overextended.

April felt herself begin to sweat. She didn't want to think about that. She turned a page in the album and exclaimed over a baby in an elaborate christening gown.

On the next page, Mitch pointed to a picture of his parents in wedding garb, and chuckled. "Finally. After thirty-five years of marriage, now they're perfectly matched."

April looked at the picture. His father was

a younger version of Mitch. "That's a nice story."

"You think? I guess it is kind of a reverse love story. I had to live with them through the years when they were working things out. It wasn't always pretty. They fought like hell when we were little. Suddenly, all the kids are out of the house, and they discover that they like each other. Hell, they fall in love with each other."

April said, "At least it has a happy ending."

"What about you? You have siblings?"

April shook her head and gathered up the garbage from her lunch. She didn't want to get into her home life. She started back toward the house. "Well, thanks for the conversation."

"Same time tomorrow?" Mitch asked, catching her.

April shrugged. "Sure."

No harm in a little lunch, she told herself. Even Rocky couldn't object to that. Even if April was looking forward to noon tomorrow more than she had any meal in a long, long time.

Several hours later, April windmilled her arms. They ached from staying too long in one position. She cracked her knuckles and

213

massaged her fingers. Her back was sore, too. She stretched, loosening the kinks in her body, and let her attention wander around the room. The stamps she had in mind would be layered, giving shadow and dimension. She'd use at least a half dozen shades of blue and gray to get the effect she wanted. When she was finished, the walls would look like they'd been covered with expensive, hand-drawn wallpaper. She couldn't wait to get started. At the rate the mural was going, she would be able to begin in a day or so.

A tapping across the tile kitchen floor, changing timbre on the hardwood floor, brought April out of her reverie. She stopped in midstretch to see Mrs. H. enter, wearing fringed two-tone golf shoes. Pink and white to match her pom-pommed socks. Her birdlike legs were white as bond paper. She was wearing a visor that made her look like a poker dealer in a ladies-only club. Or a country club golfer.

"Miss Buchert," Mrs. H. said curtly, "why does my dining room smell like an Italian deli?"

April offered up the cut onion and lemon. "I'm cleaning the paint. This is a wonderful method for removing —"

"Is this how they do things in San Francisco?" Her voice dripped with disdain, as if San Francisco were akin to Bedlam, the home for lunatics. "Do you think it's appropriate to smash food on my wall?"

"No," April began, but Mrs. H. wasn't interested in hearing how her method worked.

"I don't see any progress." She moved closer, bumping into the wall and knocking her visor sideways. She straightened, scowling.

April pointed to the section she'd been working on. "You can see right here. I've gotten rid of the surface dirt, and now I'm getting to the deeper encrusted gunk."

Mrs. H.'s face screwed up in disgust at the characterization of her dust as "gunk." April mentally kicked herself, wishing she had chosen a better descriptor. She knew how to handle high-end customers. She'd convinced the richest woman in the Presidio that she'd been the right person to design the wall coverings for her breakfast nook. She just had to sound as though she knew what she was doing. Even if she wasn't sure. Especially if she wasn't sure.

April took a deep breath. "The mural is much cleaner. Brighter."

Mrs. H. stepped in front of April. April felt her disapproval in her gut as the metronome of her foot tapping signaled her displeasure.

April said, "The enzymes in the onion break down —"

Mrs. H. cut her off with a wave of her hand. "Unacceptable. Your father told me this was your area of expertise. I'm not seeing expert results." She bit off each word sharply.

April felt a surge of anger at her father, and at Mrs. H. She hated justifying her work. Of course she was no good at restoring murals.

"I did the best job I know how," April said, but she was interrupted again.

Mrs. H. pulled a white leather glove out of her pocket and stuffed her right hand into it, skinny gold bangles escaping up her arm. "I'm off to the club championship. My tee time is at 2 p.m. It's a shotgun start so I don't know which hole I'm teeing off on, but when I'm on the third hole, the one right outside the living room, I will look back in on your work. And I want to see a difference. I suggest you use alcohol. A little elbow grease wouldn't hurt either."

April's temper flared, but she bit her tongue. She knew the client was always right. She could only hope that Mrs. H. teed off on the fourth hole so it would be hours before she got near the house again.

April had no choice but to make a trip to the local hardware store. Ernst Hardware Emporium was only two minutes away, out on Route 93. She had fond memories of accompanying Ed to the cluttered place Saturday mornings. Luckily for her, nothing had changed. She found the things she needed, in the same place they'd been when she was a kid. She picked out a mask, heavy-duty rubber gloves, alcohol and a bag of rags. She piled her purchases on the counter.

"Put these on the Retro Reproductions' account," she told the teenager working the register.

"What is your name?" he asked. She told him.

The teenager dutifully wrote up the purchases but frowned when he got to the computer. "You're not authorized to charge things to this account," he said, positioning the screen so she could see who was. Ed, Vince, and Lyle.

"It's okay," April said. "I'm Ed's daughter. I just started working for him. He hasn't had time to put me on there. But I need these supplies. Now."

The boy looked at her dumbly. He held up his hands. "There's nothing I can do, ma'am."

Ma'am? Was he kidding her? Did she suddenly look eighty years old? "Look, kid. I'm not old enough to be your mother, but —" She stopped herself. This kid wasn't the problem. "Let me talk to the owner."

"Mr. Ernst," he yelled without moving away. April flinched as spittle flew from his mouth.

Mr. Ernst came out of his office, wearing his familiar gray cardigan despite the warm June weather. She took a peak at his elbows. Sure enough, leather patches.

"Hi, Mr. Ernst, do you remember me?" She prayed he did — she didn't have enough money to pay for her purchases.

But Mr. Ernst smiled and pulled her in for a hug. "April. Your dad said you were coming to work for him. Pleased as punch, he was. Robbie, write her up and let her be on her way."

April untangled from his long arms. One crisis averted. "Thanks, Mr. Ernst."

Back at the house, she put on the gloves and the mask. She did not want to inhale the fumes of the alcohol. She layered several rags and decided she would try this new technique someplace inconspicuous first. On her hands and knees, she took in a deep breath and poured alcohol on the rag. She touched the thick cloth tentatively to the toe of Benjamin Franklin's buckled shoe.

She wanted to go slowly. She couldn't be sure what kind of reaction she would get. She'd assumed these were oil paints on the wall, but she could be wrong. She daubed the painting gently and sat back.

Nothing. The paint hadn't bubbled or cracked, but the shoe didn't look any cleaner, either. April poured more solvent and rubbed harder.

The shoe brightened a bit. That was better. April rubbed more enthusiastically. Brighter. Good. Emboldened, she widened the area she was working on. The shoe was looking good.

The walkie-talkie crackled to life, startling her. Her world had shrunk to the buckle of Benjamin Franklin's shoe, so her heart pounded at the noise. Alcohol dripped randomly as she reached to answer. She'd nearly forgotten about Ed's crew since she'd checked on them before lunch.

It was Butch, but she didn't catch what he was saying. The transmission broke up. She pushed the return button and responded.

"Try again," she said.

". . . tomorrow . . . plumbing . . ." was all she heard.

She hit her button again and got nothing

but static. She rose, figuring she'd have to talk to him face-to-face.

A big truck was pulled up to the north wing. To April's surprise, Lyle was standing alongside, supervising the unloading of lumber and pipe coming off the truck.

"Hey, little lady," he said, taking off his baseball cap gallantly.

"What are you doing here?" April asked.

Butch passed her, shouldering a length of copper pipe. "That's what I'd like to know," he said under his breath before disappearing into the house.

Lyle ignored him. "This delivery had to come today. The schedule is all fu— screwed up," he said. "I got a call so I came down. Mike didn't think it should be unloaded. His crew is ready to go home."

April looked at her watch. "It's nearly four." She felt her heart rate quicken. "We can't afford overtime, Lyle. Why can't we take the delivery in the morning?"

Lyle shrugged. "These guys" — he indicated the "Corcoran Supply House" name on the panel truck — "they insisted on getting it off the truck tonight. They were going to charge us a restocking fee, so I figured it was cheaper to pay the men."

That wasn't much better. "All right, I guess."

"It won't take long, I promise. Besides, we need this stuff first thing in the morning." The truck driver approached, bill of lading in hand. She tried without success to decipher the computer printout of jumbled numbers. "Sign right here." He pointed and produced a pen from behind his ear.

She signed and pocketed the invoice to put on Ed's desk later. "I need to get back to my project. You'll be done soon and send the guys home?"

Lyle nodded. April walked back to the main house. Butch might be unhappy about staying late, but at least the supplies were on hand now.

In the dining room, the light had changed, now slanting through the long windows directly on the mural. April closed the heavy door and inspected the shoe she'd been concentrating on. To her horror, she saw the shoe had turned a funky yellow color instead of the deep brown it should have been. This was not good.

She rubbed harder with a clean rag, then looked at the rag. It was getting black. The paint was wiping away.

Her heart thumped, and she looked around to see if she was alone. She changed cloths and dabbed softly, just lifting the cloth gently up and down. But it was too late. The solvent had sat on the paint too long, and the layers of oil paint were dissolving along with the grime.

"Shit!"

"Miss Buchert?" That was not the walkie-talkie. She glanced up. The doors remained closed.

Mrs. H. came around the corner from the living room. Dang. April hadn't considered she could get in the dining room another way.

"Problem?" She must have entered through the French doors overlooking the golf course. April could see a triangular flag with the number three on it.

April put the offending rag behind her back and stood in front of the ruined portion of the mural, even though she knew she couldn't hide the mustard-colored stain. Mrs. H. pushed her aside, using her golf club.

"What have you done?" Mrs. H. shrieked. "You incompetent . . ."

Mrs. H.'s compressed lips turned white as her face grew dangerously red. A vein pulsed unattractively on her forehead.

Her words came out stiffly, with shrill undertones. April fought the urge to cover her ears from the onslaught.

"You've ruined my heritage. My family's legacy."

April considered trying the baguette. The bread might soak up the worst of the alcohol. But one look at Mrs. H. told her that option was out.

Mrs. H. pointed with her golf club. "Get that out of my sight. I want you out of here."

April pleaded, "I'll fix it."

"Get out," Mrs. H. said. "And don't come back."

"But —"

"Take the rest of your father's crew with you. Buchert Construction is off this job. For good."

CHAPTER 11

"For your information, it's not Buchert Construction anymore. It's Retro Reproductions," April muttered as she walked out the kitchen door. She ripped off her rubber gloves and stuffed them in the back pocket of her jeans. She was too mad to see straight.

She paused at the top of the back steps, afraid she'd topple right down if she kept going. Ed was going to flip out when she told him.

"Say again? Are you talking to me?" Mitch was standing next to his Jeep, a few feet away. Without responding, April clomped down the steps and headed toward her car. She turned to see the kitchen curtain flicker and fought the urge to stick out her tongue. "Witch," she said to the now-empty window.

Mitch looked bewildered, his eyes tracking to the house and back to her. "Aunt Barbara do something to you?"

She took in a deep breath and began. "She

kicked me, us, off the job. I've got to go tell my father that his men have nowhere to work tomorrow. Dad won't get paid and Retro Reproductions will go belly up."

April's words tumbled out of her, one after the other, like a collapsing Jenga tower. She saw by Mitch's puzzled look that she wasn't making sense. Like Ed. If she stuck around here too long, she'd be just like him.

He put his phone in his back pocket. "Slow down. Tell me what happened."

She laid it out for Mitch. "I ruined a very small spot on the mural trying to clean it. Mrs. H. fired me. Not just me, the whole company."

"Oh," Mitch said. His face said everything. She was in big trouble. His aunt Barbara was not the forgive-and-forget type. April's heart sank even lower.

She brought a finger to her lip to chew on the cuticle and yanked it away. It tasted like rotting onion. The taste was so vile, she spat on the ground. She wiped her hand across her mouth, hoping to get rid of the lingering ickiness.

Mitch took a step away. From the crazy lady. Not that she blamed him.

April hugged herself. A late-afternoon breeze had kicked up, and she felt cold although she'd been sweating earlier.

"Every day we're off the job, we're losing money. How am I going to tell my father?" she said.

Mitch laid a hand on her arm. "You're doing it again. Stop a minute."

She felt a flare of resentment. He didn't know her well enough to tell her she was doing "it" again. She pulled her arm away roughly. Why was this guy always hanging around? Didn't he have any real business to attend to?

She knew Mitch's type and she was done with them. Been there, done that, got the credit card debt to prove it. No more rich boys for her. Trust-fund babies were not to be trusted.

She shot him a dirty look full of misplaced resentment, but he wasn't looking at her. He was thumbing through the contact list on his phone.

She reached for her own phone to call her father, then changed her mind. She could not deliver this news over the phone. She took out her keys, but her hands were shaking. She was too angry to drive all the way around on the main road. She knew the quickest way was through the woods.

She'd walk. That would give her time to rehearse giving her dad the bad news.

April started up the path, feet slapping

the ground resolutely. She was going to face the music. Tiny Johnny-jump-ups were blooming in the shady undergrowth. She admired their intrepidness, popping out in purple blooms under the worst circumstances. Usually. Today, she trampled one underfoot.

She was about halfway back to the Castle when the sunlight came through the trees and glinted off something in the mulchy undergrowth. She leaned down, curious. It was a brass piece, as big as April's palm. A belt buckle. April felt the heft of it. The brass had dulled to an antique gold hue. When she was a kid, it seemed as if every adult had one of these huge buckles on their Wranglers. They were available at kiosks in the mall, in the shapes of ships or bears or a beer company logo. This one was shaped like the side of a panel truck. An embossed logo was written across the truck.

The lettering read "Buchert Construction." Ed's old company.

One of Dad's workers must have dropped it when they'd worked on the Castle, April thought. What a find after all these years. She pocketed it. April felt her heart lighten. She would surprise her father with it, later, after this had all blown over. He'd get a kick out of it, she was sure. Maybe she'd go to

Boscov's and get him a belt to go with it.

"Hold on," Mitch yelled. He was panting, running to catch up with her. "I've got an idea on how we can repair the mural. If we fix it, Aunt Barbara will be okay. The only thing she cares about is that silly mural. If it's not ruined, she'll be cool."

"Fix it? How?" April said. "Believe me, it's beyond help."

"Come on. Trust me," Mitch said, nudging her off the path, onto a smaller trail that was headed into the woods to the north of the mansion. The Castle was to the east.

April planted her feet on the dusty trail. "Why should I?"

Mitch said, "You can't do this to Ed. Not without trying to fix it first."

She stopped. Her father's face, devastated from the news, came into her mind's eye. "How?" she asked.

"I know an artist. She'll know what to do."

He was right. She had to try.

"Where is she? Is it far?" she asked. She was torn between the comfort of putting off telling Ed and the need to get it over with.

Mitch shook his head. "Nope, right up the hill. If she can't help, you can go tell your father. Right now, what he doesn't know won't hurt him. From what I've seen of your dad, ignorance is bliss."

That was true. Right now, her father had no idea that he'd lost the Mirabella job. If she redeemed herself in Mrs. H.'s eyes, she wouldn't ever have to tell him. Ten years from now, they could have a good laugh. *Gee, Dad, it was so funny. Mrs. H. tried to throw us off that job.* It would be a memory about that summer they worked together. Before she went on to New York, and fame and fortune.

Mitch said, "I'm guaranteeing that she will be able to help."

April felt a glimmer of hope. And with that came the overwhelming sense that she could do nothing right. She felt tears sting the back of her eyes.

Mitch slowed. He looked at her closely. "You okay?" he finally asked.

His kind, caring tone caught her by surprise and released the tears. To her horror, she felt a sob catch in her throat. She turned away, but he patted her shoulder awkwardly. She felt herself lean his way, his warmth attracting her like a moth to a flame. She hadn't been held by a man in forever. She'd been angry with Ken for so long that being close to him hadn't been an option. The need to be held took her by surprise.

When he pulled her in, the tears came freely. April was mortified, but each time she started to move away from him, the waterworks began again. The tussle with Mrs. H., the uncertainty of her job situation, the cross-country flight from her husband, all the frustration of the last few days came pouring out of her. Finally she stopped and leaned back on an oak tree. She pressed on her forehead with the heel of her hand. She didn't want to look at Mitch. She'd already allowed him to do too much for her.

She wiped her tears with the back of her hand. "I'm ready to go," April said. She straightened her spine. A stream bubbled nearby, probably the same one that went by the Castle. She knelt and splashed the icy cold water on her face. It stung but felt good. She didn't look at Mitch but motioned for him to lead the way.

She followed Mitch across the stream and through a dense copse of ash trees. The sun dappled the ground. She longed to have a pencil and her sketchbook in her hands. She wanted to remember the patterns the sun was making on the forest floor. She wanted to create her own art, so different from the mural.

After a few minutes' walk, Mitch moved a low-hanging branch out of the way and said, "We're here."

April looked through the canopy of trees. She ducked behind the nearest one. "Na-uh. This is the club. I don't want to go in there. Your aunt is there."

She recognized the low-slung, one-story building, the roofline interrupted by the blue and white striped awnings that sheltered the windows. The huge south lawn was the perfect site for a garden wedding.

Mitch was already heading up the slight hill, hands in his pockets. Could he be any more like Opie? If he started whistling, she was going to hit him.

She hissed at him from her hiding place behind the tree. "The club? Why are we here?"

Mitch stopped and looked back as though surprised she hadn't moved. He took several steps back. "I told you I'd get you help. Well, help is inside."

"I can't go in there. I'm a mess." She patted at her face and dragged her hand through her hair. Her clothes smelled of lemon, and her T-shirt and jeans were wrinkled and stained. She knew her face would be red from crying despite the stop at the stream.

Mitch looked at her. "You don't look any worse than most of the teenagers that come here in their ripped jeans and holey T-shirts.

Your pants could pass for that designer, whatsis, Losing My Religion."

"It's True Religion, dork."

Mitch reared back at her insult, then laughed. She smiled despite her misgivings. The insult had just come out. She wiped her face on her sleeve and tucked in her T-shirt.

"It'll be fine," Mitch said. His deep-rooted sense of belonging would not allow him to believe she might be unwelcome. "Besides, you'll be with me. The dork."

April still hesitated. Mrs. H. was on that golf course somewhere. The last person she wanted to see.

But Mitch was already moving quickly on a slate path she knew led to the front entrance. If they were going in there, they'd have to do it her way.

"Hang on," she said, catching up to him. "Follow me." She'd explored every inch of this place as a kid. She could show him some places he'd never been before.

She steered him away from the main entrance, through a nondescript side door that led to a dark storeroom. She paused, waiting for her eyes to adjust. Weird shapes began to coalesce into recognizable objects. A row of portable gas heaters were lined up, ready to warm the outdoor patios. A forest of Christmas trees, with the lights already strung, leaned in a corner. She saw a scarecrow, a disco ball. Everything needed to turn the club into a winter wonderland or a haunted house or the June bride's fantasy.

Mitch said over her shoulder, "You told me you used to come here as a kid. I didn't realize you meant backstage."

"You're about to find out what makes the club run so smoothly."

She shuddered as she felt his warm breath on her neck. She walked faster, eyes adjusted now so she could make out a clear path.

She said, "I was here all the time. They let me use the pool because my mom worked in the kitchen. Still does. Now she's the head chef."

"Oh man, the food is the best. That's your mom? When I was a kid, I would have starved without the club. My mother was a terrible cook."

She wasn't about to admit it to Mitch, but her attitude toward her mother's employment at the club had been ever changing. The fact that her mother worked for the country club had been a source of pride when she was a little kid, then embarrassment in her early teens. Torture by the time

Ed had left home. She was ashamed to admit to him how often she'd ignored her mother when she'd been here.

She opened a door at the far end of the room. April heard the rattling of dishes. She stopped to make sure the coast was clear. Dinner prep would be in full swing, and she knew better than to get in a prep cook's way.

"Stand close to me," she whispered, and Mitch obliged. Holding on to her waist, he was too close, but she couldn't object.

She waited as someone whizzed past, carrying a pan of sizzling butter. She motioned Mitch to move forward. They looked through the round window in the door together. April ducked as her mother strode past and into the walk-in. Now was the time to move.

April thought for a moment. "Where do we need to be?"

"Get us to the restaurant."

April conjured up the layout. Just beyond the walk-in refrigerator was a small butler's pantry. The pantry held all the dishes and glasses needed for service. From the other end, it was accessible to the bar. The bar was in The Greens, the restaurant that overlooked the eighteenth hole.

"Follow me," April said.

"Lead on, Nancy Drew. I haven't had this

much fun since I helped my date for the winter formal find an earring in the cloakroom. Turned out she'd dropped it into her bra."

"I'm glad you're having a good time," she hissed. "My dad's about to lose his business, and my mother won't appreciate me barreling through her workplace."

April ignored the looks of the cooks who were chopping vegetables and chattering in Spanish. She kept an eye on the door. There was no way of knowing if Bonnie would be in there for one minute or ten, gathering up the produce and protein she needed for tonight's menu. Her heart was pounding, but Mitch was right. This was fun. She pulled him into the butler's pantry just as the door to the refrigerator opened. She stopped, breathing hard, leaning on a shelving unit full of glassware of all shapes and sizes.

"Hey, look at this," Mitch said, grabbing a wooden bowl off a high shelf. "This is Brazilian hardwood. Zebra wood. Completely extinct."

"Put it down," April said. "Let's get out of here before one of the staff decides they need a soup tureen or highball glass."

"Where's this door lead?" Mitch said, moving in front of her and pulling it open.

April jumped back. A startled bartender took a step away from them. He'd been filling a glass with soda and held the nozzle up, ready to shoot.

Mitch flung an arm over her chest, as if she were his passenger and he'd had to stop short. She stumbled and he caught her.

"Idiot," April said. "The other door leads to the hallway. We would have been home free."

"Oops," he said. There was no turning back. He leaned in and smiled at the bartender. The bartender lowered the soda trigger and smiled. To her amazement, he turned away and placed the drink in front of the customer at the far end of the bar.

She looked to Mitch for an explanation.

"What?" he said. "The bartenders around here are used to far weirder behavior, believe me. That's what big tips are for — to encourage memory loss."

They hustled through the bar, ignoring the stares of the patrons, mostly middle-aged women drinking Trix-colored drinks. April pretended that if she didn't look at them, they couldn't see her. Mitch kept his smile pasted on.

They were across the restaurant in a few short strides. He threw open the French doors that led onto a wooden deck overlooking the tee. Large trees shaded the lush grounds. Rhododendrons and azaleas dotted a water hazard, their color the only break in the expanse of green. A flag, designating the hole as number eighteen, snapped in the wind. A bevy of golf carts sat under a wooden portico. Mitch jumped into one and started the engine. An attendant in a blue vest started toward him, but Mitch waved him off.

"Get in," he said to April. "He's going to call the ranger. We've got to move fast. Golfers don't like extra people on their fairway."

"What are you doing?" April hissed. She was still in the doorway. The young man in charge of carts looked unhappy. "Not the golf course," she pleaded.

Mitch grinned and pulled up to her. "My expert is on the fifteenth green. She's got a putt to sink and then we can talk to her."

April sat down, and he took off with too much force. She clutched the side and heard herself gasp as they bounced down the paved path.

Luckily, after the abrupt start, the golf cart wouldn't go more than ten miles an hour. April's breathing steadied, and the breeze cooled her skin. She felt the tension in her belly ease as they moved away from the club. Then her stomach retightened at the sight of a fringe-topped golf cart. She shaded her eyes from the late-afternoon sun and saw that the fringe was not yellow. This better not take too long. Mrs. H. was on this golf course somewhere.

"Where's the third hole from here? Mrs. H. had been on the third hole when she came in and fired me," April said. "I don't want to go anywhere near there."

Mitch flapped his hand in the direction to his left. "Way over there. She's like a mile away. Don't worry."

Mitch steered around a curve, then braked suddenly. April managed to keep her balance, but barely, her butt leaving the seat. She braced her feet on the floor.

April looked for the cause of the abrupt stop, expecting to see a squirrel or possum in the path. Instead, twenty feet ahead, Rocky was standing alongside a cart, putting her putter in a golden leather golf bag. She pulled out a driver. Her hair was pulled into a ponytail that was threaded through the back of her navy visor. Her long tan legs looked great in the crisp white skort. A tan like that in June meant winter vacations somewhere tropical.

"There she is," Mitch said, pleased with himself.

April asked, "That's your expert? I know

her. That's Rocky."

Mitch raised his eyebrows. "Rocky is a painter. A very good painter."

April protested. "She told me she was a collage artist."

"She does that to make a living. But she is a serious artist. Very serious. Studied at the Sorbonne, spent a year in Venice, the whole enchilada."

The whole enchilada that had not been available to April. She'd worked her way through San Francisco State, taking six years so she could work part-time and minimize her student loans.

She swallowed her resentment. Chances were Rocky knew more about paints than she did. Besides, what choice did she have? She had to fix the mural today. "Lead on," she said.

Mitch let the cart drift until he was just about touching Rocky's foot.

"Nice, bro. Back it up," she said, giving the cart a push on the hood with her golf shoe, her long legs graceful. She looked at April significantly, glancing at Mitch and back at April. April rolled her eyes. Did this count as some sort of tryst?

Mitch dutifully put it in reverse and moved back several inches. He jumped out of the cart. April followed. Another cart was parked in front of Rocky's on the asphalt cart path. Next to the cart, three golfers huddled over a scorecard. April recognized them as the stampers Piper, Mary Lou and Tammy. They waved to April and Mitch.

"I got a six on that hole," Piper said. She was dressed in faded plaid shorts and a white polo trimmed in matching madras.

"If you're counting by twos," Rocky put in, leaning on her club. "You took at least twelve strokes. Of course after three Long Island iced teas, I'm sure you're seeing double."

Piper scowled. "Why do you have the last word on the score?"

"Hey, Mitch. Hi, April," Mary Lou called. She wore a shirt and ball cap that advertised her business, Rosen Realty. She waved them over. They returned the waves but didn't move any closer. April didn't have time for niceties. Mrs. H.'s golf cart might turn the corner at any moment. April's scalp tingled as though she sensed the woman's presence. She didn't want to see her until she had repaired the damage she'd done to her wall.

Mary Lou said, "Rocky, I think you're going to win longest drive today."

Rocky shrugged, her competency not an issue. April was sure she was good at everything she tried. She felt a ray of hope.

Maybe her talents extended to fixing wall murals.

"What's the art emergency?" Rocky said, keeping her tone light.

April was grateful for her interest. She gave Rocky the lowdown on what she'd done to the wall and how the paint had reacted. As she listened, Rocky moved her club in a small arc, clipping the grass under her feet. The stampers remained at the other cart, still huddled over the scorecard.

"Are we talking about that horrible mural in the dining room? Was there still color on the wall?" Rocky asked.

April nodded and said, "The shoe seemed to change from brown to a mustardy color."

Rocky took a full swing, her bracelet jangling. She held her follow-through, arms in the air, watching her imaginary shot. April felt the breeze as the club's trajectory ruffled the air, uncomfortably close. She backed away.

"Mustard, huh?" Rocky said. "You're screwed."

April blanched, and Mitch said, "Come on, Rocky. You must know something she can do."

Rocky leaned on her club. "My advice is to paint over it. Black."

"Not helping," Mitch said, his big-brother

tone a clue for her to get serious.

Rocky made a face. "Well, I don't know what you want from me, Mitchell. It's paint, and if the paint is gone . . ." She shrugged her shoulders.

April stepped in. "Wait. You can't really tell how bad it is without taking a look at the wall. Can you come over there with me? Mrs. H. won't be there right now. She would never have to know I was there."

Rocky looked as though she'd forgotten April was part of the conversation. "Not now. I've got four more holes to play. My club championship is at stake here."

April bit the inside of her lip. Her mind raced. She said quickly, "Can we get Mrs. H. out of the house tomorrow? I could see if my dad could take her to the supply house to pick out fixtures." She hit her forehead. "That won't work. I don't want to tell my dad yet."

Mitch held up a hand. "Not to worry. It's wash-and-set day."

April stared at him. Rocky let out a barking laugh.

"Brother," she said, "you've been neutered. What do you know about wash-and-set?"

Mitch defended himself. "I've been working in that house for the past five months.

Friday is beauty parlor day. Every week at 9 a.m. Pardon me for noticing."

Rocky grinned at him. "Eunuch!"

"Tomorrow, then," April said, eager to nail Rocky down. "I'll meet you there at nine."

A cart careened off the path, barely missing running over them. April, Mitch and Rocky scattered. April felt her heart pound, and not just from the near miss.

The driver jumped out. Her feet were bare and she looked as though she'd just gotten out of the shower. April was relieved. This was not Mrs. H.

"Where's Piper?" she asked, her eyes wild.

Rocky said, "Yo, Suzi, chill. You nearly ran us over."

This was Suzi? April looked closer. She hadn't recognized the stamper, whose short hair was plastered against her skull.

Suzi pushed a wet strand off her face. "Piper!" she called. "Come here."

Tammy, Piper and Mary Lou walked over. Piper looked concerned at her friend's state.

"Not all of you. Just Piper needs to hear this," Suzi said, out of breath, her face flushed. She stopped to catch her breath, pushing on her chest with the flat of her hand.

"Hear what?" Rocky asked. She'd stopped

swinging her club, all her attention on Suzi now.

Suzi looked from Piper to the group and back again. "Look, you guys, this doesn't really concern you. I just need to tell Piper something. I'm not even supposed to know."

"Know what?" Piper said.

"Spit it out," Rocky said. "We're not going anywhere until you tell us." She looked around the group. "All of us."

Suzi looked to Piper for permission. Piper nodded.

Suzi took in a breath. "Mitzi Parkhurst is in the dressing room telling everyone. Her husband is Dr. Parkhurst?" Suzi's voice went up at the end in a question.

Everyone stilled. Rocky was the only one who kept moving, sliding the club into her golf bag. The club banged into the others with a noisy clang.

The moment stretched. April didn't understand what was going on. A bullfrog croaked deeply in the water hazard, a barking noise that sounded human and sent a chill through April. A hawk soared overhead. The breeze ruffled through the willow tree. Giggles from the foursome on the next hole filtered back to them.

"So?" Rocky said. She sounded casual, as though she didn't care what Suzi had to say.

But April detected a vein throbbing in her forehead and found her actions a little too studied. Her gaze kept slipping over to Tammy.

Suzi said, "Dr. Parkhurst, the *dentist*."

"We know he's a dentist, Suzi. Get to the point," Rocky said.

"The Castle. The skull," Suzi said, stuttering. "He had a patient that matched the dental records of the skull. Mitzi's not supposed to tell anyone, but she's in there, blabbing . . ."

April froze. The identity of the dead man was about to be revealed.

Rocky roared, "Who is it, dammit?"

Suzi's eyes searched for Piper, who was standing still as though she'd taken root to the sawgrass beneath her feet. Suzi's gaze didn't leave Piper's face. "It's Frankie. Frankie Imperiale."

Piper's eyes grew wide, and she brought her hand up over her open mouth. She made a groaning noise, and she bit down on the soft space between her thumb and finger.

Frankie Imperiale was the body in the Castle. Dots floated in front of April's eyes. She blinked to clear her vision. The sun was too bright.

Frankie Imperiale. Now April knew where

her father's last employee from 1993 was. Buried in the Castle wall.

Her throat closed as though she was trying to swallow golf balls. She had to get to her father. Did he know? What would Yost do if he knew? Had the cops already arrested him?

April was surprised to hear Mitch speak first. "For sure?" he asked. He was frowning, arms tightly across his chest. He glanced at his sister. April heard recognition in his voice. How would he know this guy? He wasn't home that summer. Was the name someone their father knew?

Rocky shook her head at her brother slightly. He took a step toward her, as though to protect her. The memory of Frankie was between them. April didn't know what their connection was, but it was palpable.

The group of golfers was quiet, each of them taking in the information that Frankie Imperiale's skull had been found in the Castle ruins. Mary Lou cleared her throat.

Piper finally broke the silence. "He's dead? The son of a bitch is dead? For how long?" Her voice trailed off, as if the effort of talking was more than she could handle.

Suzi went to her, smoothing her hair, murmuring.

"Who is this guy?" Mary Lou asked.

April was confused, too, but no one answered her question. Piper stared straight ahead. Rocky, Mitch and Tammy formed a tight knot.

A splash broke the reverie. In the nearby water hazard, a mallard dove, showing his tail feathers. When he righted himself, the sun glinted off his iridescent coat.

"What's Frankie Imperiale got to do with you, Piper?" Rocky said, the driver in her hand finally still.

Piper's response was lost in a strangled sob.

Suzi explained, "Frankie is Jesse's father."

CHAPTER 12

Piper glared at Suzi, who shook her head slowly. "I promised I would never tell and I never did," she said. Piper's cries grew more desperate.

Suzi hustled the now shaking Piper into their golf cart and took off.

April exchanged a glance with Mary Lou, who shrugged dramatically.

"That explains why none of us were invited to that wedding," Mary Lou said.

Rocky put an arm around Tammy, who'd gone pale. "She invented a husband who never existed. And we all bought it." Rocky's tone was almost admiring.

Tammy said, "I can't picture her with Frankie. I never remember even seeing them together."

Mary Lou said, "You can never be sure why some people fall for each other. It looks like Piper always thought Frankie was coming back to her someday."

Mitch was scowling. He didn't look as attractive when he was mad. April preferred his smiling countenance. She wondered what his relationship to Frankie was. It was clear it had something to do with Rocky, but what?

He started for his cart, but April headed him off. She grabbed the keys out of his hand.

"What are you doing?"

"Going to my father. Frankie Imperiale was his apprentice. He needs to know he's dead."

She left him, his frown growing deeper.

Ed had found her in the woods almost to Mirabella. The partying kids were spreading, getting closer to the Castle. Ed was uneasy. April wanted to disappear into the crowds.

"April, please. Come back to the trailer. I need to wait for Yost. I promised him I would stay there until he got free."

"No, Dad, let me go. I don't want to go back to that place. You're practically living there. Your crossword puzzle, your Far Side mug." Her voice broke. Her Father's Day present.

He drove her home instead. They sat at the kitchen table. April on one side of the banquette, Ed across from her. He reached for her hand, but she snatched it away.

He sighed heavily. "You're right, bug. I have been spending my nights at the Castle job. And you're right to suspect it's not about work."

To her surprise, she saw tears in his eyes. Ed could be a sentimental guy, crying at movies and at birthdays, but she saw real pain on his face. He looked past her into the kitchen, his eyes taking in the room as though for the first time. Or the last. April shivered and rubbed her arms.

Ed sniffed and turned back to her. Tears lingered in his eyes, and he wiped them away hard with the back of his hand.

"I'm struggling, sweetie. I love your mother, but —"

"I knew it. You've got a girlfriend," April said, but she couldn't sustain her anger. She only wanted him to end the affair. To come home. She wanted Ed to go back to living at home. Living with her.

Ed shook his head ponderously. His shoulders hunched, he looked more miserable than April had ever seen him. "No affair. I've been feeling not right for some time."

April's heart froze. She felt her hands

get clammy. "Are you sick? Dying?" She tried to picture life without her father. Tears filled her eyes. He had a terrible disease and didn't want to tell her.

He sat up straight. "God, no, honey. No. I'm fine. Really. Healthy as a horse."

Her plea to him was a silent one.

His face contorted. "Honey, I'm gay."

Ed told Bonnie as soon as she got home from work that he wanted to leave the marriage. Bonnie was angrier than April had ever seen her, but it was Ed April worried about. His sadness about breaking up the family seemed overwhelming. She stayed by his side, helping him set up a bed in the office over the garage, moving his clothes out of the master bedroom. And watching him until he fell asleep.

The next day, she snuck out, hiking back to the job trailer at midday to get her bike and his favorite mug. When she got there, she saw that the Castle had been completely boarded up.

April's heart was thumping, her foot pounding the spongy accelerator into the floor of the cart. She seemed to be standing still, but she went around a curve and down a slight hill and was soon out of sight of Rocky and her golf cart.

She found the fork where she and Mitch had switched directions and putted over the bumpy trail.

As April approached the Castle site, a state policeman watched her approach. He put his palm up for her to stop. Beyond him, she could see stakes and string gridding the rubble. A man with thick rubber gloves was running a metal detector over the ground. A woman was squatted over a pile, picking through the sifted earth carefully.

"You can't go any farther," he told her. His trooper hat obscured his looks. She wasn't sure if this was the same trooper she'd met yesterday.

"I just need to talk to my dad," she said, pointing out Ed, who was standing on the far side, near the path that led up the embankment.

"Wait here," the trooper said. He conferred with another trooper, who nodded his assent. She saluted her thanks before blushing with the inanity of the gesture. What an idiot.

"Leave the cart, and watch where you're walking. Stay out of the site."

She nodded that she understood and jumped out of the cart. She skirted the yellow tape and walked to where her father stood, clicking his phone shut. She bussed his cheek. He gave her a half frown at her greeting.

"That was Vince," he said. "Our clients watch entirely too much HGTV. They think all of our work should be done in two days." He sighed. "What are you doing here? Why aren't you at the mansion?"

Her news about Frankie was forgotten. April didn't like her father's grayish tone and the way his skin seemed to be sagging. "Did you eat at all today?" she asked.

Ed shrugged. "I don't remember. Yes, yes, one of the staties went out and brought back hoagies. I had a half of an Italian sub."

April looked for Yost. He was talking to several state policemen who were watching the technicians working inside the gridded area. They moved deliberately, like the astronauts in tapes she'd seen of men on the moon.

"Okay," she said. Her response was drowned out as Yost raised his voice. She couldn't make out the words, but the tone seemed combative.

"Dad," she began.

Ed interrupted, focused on the problems at hand.

"Friggin' Yost," her father said. Ed's brow furrowed, the lines cutting across his fore-head so deeply that April wanted to smooth them out. She knew he wouldn't let her and so kept her fingers to herself.

"He's trying to tell the staties what to do. Thinks he knows everything. He's not even on duty. It's his day off."

"Dad, I heard they identified the body," April said. "Frankie Imperiale."

"Where'd you hear that?" Ed asked.

"It's all over the club."

"What were you doing at the club?" he asked, rubbing his face hard. He moved his hands over his cheeks again and again. Was it the identification or the fact that it was being talked about at the club that was bothering him? April couldn't tell.

"Why weren't you at Mirabella?" He looked more worried than he had a moment ago. April's stomach flipped. "I was with Mitch," she said. At his renewed interest, she said, "Had you heard?"

"That it was Frankie? Yeah." He shrugged. "Not that they fill me in," he said, pointing at the police. "You think they'd tell a guy. I mean, this is my job site."

April put a hand on his shoulder, trying to stop him from winding up into a full-blown whine. He sighed, blowing his lips out.

"Did you know him?"

"Frankie? The name's familiar."

"Dad, Frankie Imperiale used to work for you," April said.

Ed's lips pursed. "No, he didn't. I don't remember him," he said.

"I found the payroll records from the Castle. He might have been an apprentice."

"I've had a lot of apprentices over the years . . ." Ed said, trailing off, his eyes squinting as though he could see into the past.

April stuffed her hands in her back pockets. She looked to see if Yost was done yet. He had to be interested to know that the dead man worked for Ed.

Her fingers closed on the belt buckle in her pocket. She looked at her father, his face gray around the edges from the stress he was under. He needed a little relief.

She pulled out the buckle.

"Hey, Dad, check this out." She opened her palm. "Look what I found in the woods," she said, offering up the belt buckle. As she'd hoped, a large smile creased his face. These wrinkles were not as deep as the ones on his forehead. He didn't smile often enough. When he did, April felt the joy in his heart. She smiled back, glad to have given him some happiness.

"Is that what I think it is?" he asked.

She pushed her hand closer. "Take it."

He lifted it from her outstretched hand. "Well, I'll be dipped in cow manure. I haven't seen one of these in years." He held up the buckle and examined it. He ran his finger over the raised lettering on the embossed panel truck. "Where did you find this?"

"Out there." She pointed into the trees. "Can you believe it? It must have been out in the woods for a long time."

"How about that?" Ed said, wonder in his voice. "I'd forgotten all about these. Your mother had them made, for Christmas gifts for the men. I think there were only about twenty of them. Mine is long gone. Man, I wore that thing all the time."

"I remember, especially the time you wore it to my Christmas band recital." All the other fathers had been in suits, and Ed had shown up in his favorite jeans, proudly displaying his leather belt and large brass buckle.

They laughed. Ed said, "Those other parents were so stuck up. Just because their kids played violin."

"Remember the cello player's dad, always carting around her instrument?"

He laughed. "Of course, she wasn't even five feet tall."

"Still," she said. "What was she going to

do when she went off to college?"

"Yeah, a girl can't remain a daddy's girl forever," Ed said wistfully. He thrust an arm around her. "I'm glad you've come back to me."

April's eyes filled. He pulled her in for a hug and kissed her hair. No one else kissed her hair. The feeling was sublime.

Ed's smile turned down. "You say Frankie worked for me, huh? Yost is going to love that."

April wondered if Frankie had a belt buckle like this. "He had to have died the night of the party. The next day the Castle was boarded up. I saw it. He had to have been in the Castle before it was boarded up."

"I inspected the building that night before the party. No one was inside."

"But the party?" April asked.

"Kids stayed outside. The doors and windows were all locked. I checked."

Her father was underestimating the determination of partying kids. Frankie had gotten in. And died inside.

He was turning the buckle over his knuckles in the same way he used to make a quarter disappear when she was a kid. She was glad to see this had lightened his heart somewhat. Because her news about getting kicked out of Mirabella would crush him. She fought back tears.

Ed wasn't listening to her. He was lost in reminiscing. "I wonder if any of the other men still have theirs. Lyle probably has his, still. He doesn't throw anything out."

He looked up and smiled at April. "It was the last Christmas we worked on the Castle. Your mother found some guy who worked in metal and had them made up. Had to be ridiculously expensive. I didn't really have the money, but that job had been such a bear, I wanted to thank the men for working hard."

He gestured toward the Castle rubble and shook his head. "Man, I sweated over that job. The stone for the fireplace never arrived, and then when it did it was stolen off the loading dock at the train depot. We had to wait for another shipment. I never had a job like that before or since. Stuff went missing, shipments were lost in transit. And Winchester changed his mind every two minutes. What a mess."

The state troopers wrapped up their work for the day and headed for the white van. Yost made his way over to where she and Ed were standing.

"Ms. Buchert," he said, nodding to her.

"I heard there is a tentative identification,"

258

she began.

Yost remained stony faced. "You did? Where?"

"At the club," April said. "The dentist's wife."

An annoyed expression flitted across Yost's face. "We're waiting on official confirmation."

"That it's Frankie Imperiale?" April asked.

"I wish I could place him," Ed said, his eyes unfocused, looking into the past.

Yost moved in on her father, planting himself in front of Ed. "You don't remember Frankie?" Officer Yost asked, widening his stance and holding his hands on his belt.

"Not really," Ed said. He didn't notice Yost's attitude had changed. "But then, good carpenters follow the work. Wilkes-Barre, Scranton, Harrisburg, Binghamton. They go where the jobs are."

Yost smirked. He obviously thought Ed was lying. "I can't believe you've forgotten this guy," Yost said. "Cocky son of a gun. He worked on the Castle job. I was looking at him as the ringleader of the druggies that summer. And he worked for you."

Ed shrugged. "If you say so." He looked at Yost and attempted a joke. "They say the mind is the first thing to go."

April could see Yost getting angry. He

thought Ed was making fun of him. She tried to step in.

"Officer Yost?" April said. "I told you before, my father was with me that night. All night, and all the next day."

Her words didn't seem to register. Yost was watching her father's fingers. He snatched the buckle out of Ed's grasp.

"What do you have there?" he asked.

Ed smiled and said, "How do you like that? April found this for me, in the woods."

"When did you find this?" His voice sounded official and he looked at her suspiciously.

"About an hour ago," she answered slowly.

"Ever dawn on you that this might be part of the crime scene?" he asked sarcastically.

April protested, "It was well away from the Castle."

Yost frowned.

"What's the crime anyway?" April asked. "For all we know, Frankie could have died of a drug overdose or exposure."

Yost smirked. "That wouldn't explain the bullet fragment we found."

April's skin went cold. Ed's head was hanging low, one hand washing the other over and over. She grabbed his wrist to make him stop. He squeezed her hand but didn't look up.

Yost turned the buckle over. His eyes widened. He slipped his pen through the metal loops that fastened the buckle to the belt, and held it high, looking at all sides. His gaze lingered on the back of the buckle. April moved closer so she could see what he saw. There were scratches on the back.

"Well, how do you like that?" Yost said. "This buckle is personalized."

He held it out for them to see. April crowded in. She could see a word etched into the back of the buckle. No, not a word. Initials.

A messy job, but someone had scratched his initials into the metal.

F.I. Frankie Imperiale.

"Ed Buchert, you're under arrest," Yost said.

"He couldn't have killed anyone," April said, her voice near panic. "He was with me."

Yost sneered. "So I should take the word of a woman who's already told me she'd do anything to save her father? I don't think so."

"You're coming with me, Ed. Ms. Buchert, you might want to call Vince and tell him his *partner* is with me."

CHAPTER 13

"Go on home, sweetie," Vince said, rubbing her shoulders as he stood behind her. "It's late. Yost can hold him for hours."

"And he will," April replied.

Vince agreed. "There's no point in both of us being here."

It was nearly six o'clock. Vince and April stood outside the police station on Main Street. She stretched, her back tight from tension.

Vince wiped the sweat from his forehead. The small building had no windows and an old air conditioner that couldn't keep up with the day's heat. Ed had to be so uncomfortable in there.

He lowered his voice. "Please, April, your father really doesn't want you to see him now."

She could hear the worry in his tone. "You've been talking to a lawyer, right?"

Vince sighed. "Your dad doesn't want one

right now. He wants to talk to the state police and get this cleared up."

"What about the bullet?" April asked. "Aren't you concerned about that? That has me a little freaked out. It means Frankie was definitely murdered."

Vince shrugged. "Unless they find a bone with a bullet hole in it, it's just Yost blowing smoke. There's nothing to connect it to the body."

April wasn't as sure. She needed to find the evidence that would give Yost someone else to focus on.

She hugged Vince. He held her tight. She stayed in the circle of his arms. The vision of her father being led down the hall in handcuffs was not one she'd forget for a while.

Vince pulled back and, holding her by her upper arms, looked into her eyes. "Listen, we both know he's innocent. This will sort itself out."

They walked to where she'd parked her car, in the bank parking lot across the street.

Vince had such a steadiness to him, she believed him. Ed was lucky. Someday, she'd like to find a man like Vince. For now, it was enough that he could take care of her dad, leaving her free to find out what happened to Frankie Imperiale.

And she knew where to start. George Weber had been the code enforcement officer when the Castle was being built. He would have known Frankie. Someone at his wake might be able to tell her the connections between the two. Maybe they knew each other through church. This was a small town. Most people's lives intersected somewhere. She just needed to find out where.

She glanced at her watch. It was just after seven. "I promised my mother I'd go to George's wake."

Vince grimaced and hit his palm against the car door frame. "Damn. I should be there, too. George's been a fixture at our job sites for a long time."

"How about I go as Retro Reproductions' representative?" April said.

Vince smiled. "That'd be nice. Please give my love to his kids, and tell them I'm sorry I can't be there."

Her last stint as Ed's proxy hadn't worked out very well. She had to tell Vince what she hadn't told Ed. "Vince, Mrs. H. kicked Retro Reproductions off the Mirabella job."

He grimaced. "I know. She's left sixteen voice mails on the machine."

April said earnestly, "I'm going to fix it. Tomorrow. She'll change her mind."

He nodded. "Good girl. I've got other jobs

the men can go to tomorrow. But I need them back at the mansion by Monday."

That gave her one day to fix what she'd ruined: the mural and Retro Reproductions' relationship with Mrs. H.

But that was tomorrow. Tonight, she had to find out as much as she could about the short life of Frankie Imperiale.

April ran back to the barn for a quick shower. She chose a pair of black linen pants, hoping that the wrinkles made the statement that she was a free spirit, not a lazy bum. She dug out a lacy black cardigan to tone down the azure blue tank, and slipped on her heavy silver bracelet. Had Ken known the value of the silver and turquoise Navajo cuff, it would be in the same pawnshop as her engagement ring.

In the car, she kept thinking about Yost's bullet fragment. Had Frankie Imperiale been shot? That changed everything. Of course, she knew her father couldn't have killed a man in cold blood like that, but who could?

According to the sign outside the funeral home, the service for George Weber was at eight o'clock in the Willow Pond Room. She opened the main doors and went down the hall indicated by the sign. The quiet surrounded her, and she was grateful that the hall was carpeted so her steps wouldn't disturb the wake. She felt as if she were the only person not in place.

A table halfway up the hall held the Weber funeral cards that they'd stamped last night. She took one. Through the open door, she could see a priest saying prayers over a closed casket. Every chair was full, with people standing in the back of the room. Deana and Mark were side by side under the windows. He leaned in to whisper in her ear. Deana turned to him, hiding an inappropriate grin behind a cupped hand. April felt a stab of jealousy at the intimate exchange. Her friend had a great husband, one she could work and play with. April felt her own failure with Ken.

She didn't see how she could sneak in without causing a disturbance. She stepped away from the door. George's after-wake party would be held downstairs. She turned back and used the wide central marble steps to the reception hall.

On the landing, just before the last three steps that turned into the hall, an easel held a poster board of pictures. Written across the top, arched in rainbow lettering, was "George Weber, 1920–2008."

"Cheers," April heard just before she felt the hearty slap on the back. Clive circled around her, watching her face. He looked as if he expected her to be delighted to see him again. His natural goofiness seemed out of place at a funeral, but he was oblivious.

There wasn't much room on the landing, but she dodged the kiss on the cheek. "Hello, Clive."

"Seen your mother yet?" he asked.

April shook her head. "I only just got here. Isn't she with you?"

"She got away from me. She's probably in the kitchen," he said.

That figured. April felt her face twist, reflecting the anger she felt. She'd wanted to talk to her mother, tell her about Ed, in private. "Figures. She's not happy unless she has a dishrag in her hand."

Clive caught the look. "Look, give her a break. She's shy. Like me."

April reared back, unsure if he was kidding. "Shy?" The rock star was protesting shyness?

He was serious. His eyes narrowed and his pretty mouth pursed. "I am, you know. I've only lived in this town for ten years, and the locals don't take well to outsiders. You wouldn't believe what they say about me sometimes. Call me a bleeding Limey —"

April stopped him. She wasn't worried

267

about his troubles. Her mother was not shy. "What's my mother's excuse? She's lived here her whole life."

He said patiently, "Her reluctance to mingle is of a different sort. She's lived her life under scrutiny."

April felt a twinge of pain. As hard as it had been for her after Ed left, she'd graduated early and escaped to the West Coast. Her mother had remained behind — with the whole town knowing her husband had left her for a man.

Clive took April's arm. He grinned at her. He was used to his winning smile doing all the work for him. "How about it? Shall we rescue her?"

April pushed his hand away. She already had a father. Two, in fact. She didn't need another. "I will help you get my mother out of the kitchen. But only because I want to talk to her. Besides, she's probably getting in the way of Deana's hired help."

"That'll do," Clive said, eyes twinkling.

April felt as though she'd just been conned, seduced into doing something she wasn't sure she wanted to do. Her mother liked being in the kitchen. If she didn't want to come out and be with Clive, that was his business. Not hers.

Clive was leading her down the steps. He

was like the gnats that made it impossible to sit outside on a warm summer night. Small, annoying and resistant to eradication.

She took the rest of the steps and turned into the reception hall. Despite the fact that the Willow Pond Room had looked full, this room was already teeming with people. She looked for a familiar face.

The kitchen was separated from the rest of the room by a wide countertop, nearly the length of the wall. It served as a buffet. A door to the right led into the workspace. She could see her mother moving about, opening the refrigerator and setting out cream next to the enormous coffeepot. Two young people in white chef's coats stood to one side, obviously hired for the occasion but intimidated by Bonnie.

She felt a surge of annoyance as she crossed the room. Her mother was always serving someone. That made it impossible to have a conversation with her. There was always something that needed to be stirred or basted or fried between them.

"Hey, Mom. Come on out."

Clive stayed behind April, hearing in her voice that she didn't need backup.

Bonnie shook her head. "I told Deana I'd keep the bread basket filled."

"Why did she hire those two?" April looked meaningfully at the two servers and back at Bonnie. Bonnie's eyes flashed.

"Mom, please," April pleaded.

Bonnie acquiesced. She took off her apron and came out of the kitchen. April and she stood looking at each other for a moment. April suddenly didn't know what to say.

Bonnie picked up a plate and a napkin wrapped around a plastic fork and knife. She held it over the food and asked April, "Make you a plate?"

The counter was crowded with casseroles of all shapes and sizes. This was a full-on Pennsylvania potluck dinner. April's mouth watered. She knew without looking what the fare was. There'd be hot German potato salad and cold ham and sliced turkey. Cabbage rolls and pickled eggs. Green bean casserole and Jell-O molds with mayonnaise. Not gourmet food, but the very definition of comfort food.

In addition to the counter covered with dishes, two eight-foot tables lined the side wall, filled with enough cookies and pastries to feed a small army. Plastic ziplock bags and paper plates were stacked at the end so that the leftovers could go home with the attendees. Hospitality was important when saying good-bye to the dead.

April shook her head. "No, Mom." Her stomach growled, and her mother smiled knowingly.

Bonnie started dishing up pierogies on her plate. The potato-filled dumplings were a local delicacy, homemade in huge batches by the church women each Friday. Bonnie had put three on her plate before April stopped her.

"Hang on, Mom," she said. "Whoa."

Her mother looked up, startled. "You love pierogies."

April's teeth were clenched. "I'll get my own food, thank you."

Bonnie set the plate on the counter with a jerk. She picked up a clean plate and nodded her head toward Clive. He pointed, and she loaded up the dish. April sighed. Her mother wouldn't stop until everyone had eaten and wouldn't eat until everyone had gone home. Her news would have to wait.

April picked up her plate and went down the line, taking the smallest spoonfuls of the richest foods, a little bit of her favorites and a lot of the green salad she found at the far end. She knew she'd hurt her mother's feelings by not letting her feed her. But she was tired of playing second fiddle to a dishpan.

A wave of people came in from upstairs, at least four dozen people, all talking loudly.

Softer, funeral voices abandoned, the talking grew louder, echoing as the hall filled.

April moved over to a corner of the room, finding an empty spot where she could watch and listen.

She saw a lot of almost familiar people. None she could put a name to, but recognizable just the same. Most people were dressed in black or navy. She smiled thinking about the last funeral she'd gone to in California. It wasn't a funeral at all; it was a Wiccan crossing-over ceremony with everyone dressed in shades of red because that was the dead woman's favorite color.

She heard people talking about Frankie. Despite the police's best efforts to keep the tentative identification a secret, the Aldenville grapevine was thriving. She heard Frankie's name mentioned more than George's. Thankfully, she didn't hear her father's name mentioned. His march into the police station had gone unnoticed.

She dumped her empty plate in a green garbage can. Bonnie and Clive were talking to a group of Bonnie's friends, mostly women from church.

April walked the periphery of the room. She wanted to ask about Frankie. She saw Tammy and Lyle talking to Mike McCarty. She recognized Mary Lou and her daughter, who came in with an older man and younger man. The young man, Kit's husband, steered her to a chair and went to get her some food. Mary Lou smiled at him indulgently, like she was one lucky mother-in-law.

April crossed the room to the dessert table. She didn't see Rocky or Piper. Their lives must not have intersected with George's. He was not country club.

These were the middle-class folks who made up much of Aldenville's population. Who filled the churches and the ball fields, and the town pool in the summertime. Some held jobs in the light-industrial parks nearby or were the hairdressers, truck drivers and grocery-store clerks. Some, like Bonnie, worked at the club. None of the old money she'd seen on the golf course earlier. George was a decidedly solid citizen.

Where was Mitch? She'd thought he would be here. He seemed genuinely upset yesterday morning when he'd heard about George's death.

What did he know about Frankie Imperiale? There had been something in his eyes on the golf course earlier when Suzi told them whom the body belonged to. He'd claimed to be older, and not part of the crowd that partied at the Castle, but she'd seen recognition on his face when Frankie's name came up.

He'd been a college student the summer Rocky graduated. Said he'd still been at school. Most colleges were finished, though, by the end of May. Wouldn't he have been home for his sister's graduation? What was he hiding? Maybe he'd bought the booze for some of the parties. Surely he'd had a fake ID from college. The drinking age was twenty-one, but he was a rich kid with the connections needed. If he had gotten caught providing liquor, he could have gotten into serious legal trouble. Yost had hinted he'd busted someone that night. Maybe it was Mitch.

It was possible Frankie had just died from an overdose, drugs or alcohol. But she'd seen the large dent in his head. He'd been dumped in the fireplace. And maybe shot.

April was greeted by an elderly bald man. He rubbed the top of his head with glee. "Remember me?"

April nodded. "You were at the Castle yesterday. Curly, right?"

Curly's eyes glittered. "I saw Yost take your father in earlier. A tapestry of justice," he sputtered. Saliva gathered in the corner of his mouth, and he wiped it clean with a shaky hand.

"A . . . ?" April started to ask, then realized he meant to say "travesty." He must watch *America's Most Wanted* a lot.

"I live on Main Street," Curly explained. "Across from the police station."

Clive appeared at April's elbow, startling her with his sudden presence. "The police have your father? Does Bonnie know?" he asked, his voice shrill, his eyes big and wide. April couldn't help but remember how on his old TV show, his eyes would bug out whenever there was a new revelation.

April shook her head. She looked up. Her mother was working her way around the room, gathering up dirty paper plates. "Well, I wanted to tell her when I got here, but she was too busy," she said. "Besides, they're just questioning him."

With a scowl, Clive left them. April watched as he drew Bonnie away from the garbage can. Bonnie's eyes flicked to April as Clive told her about Ed, then away as though April couldn't be trusted. April felt very alone. She knew her mother didn't have room in her life for Ed, but she felt as if she was the one being rejected.

April knew there was only one way she could help her father.

She turned to the bald man. "My dad'll be okay, Curly. Did you know the dead man, Frankie?"

"Sure, I watched him grow up. His mother lived on Main Street, too, next to the post office. She was a domestic. Cleaned the bank and some of the offices around town. He was just a kid when he first started working for your dad. Of course, he wasn't very old when he left town, either."

But he hadn't left town. Instead, he'd been killed. "You were at the Castle job back then, right? Did Frankie get along with everyone?"

Curly shrugged. "I don't know." His eyes unfocused. "I'll tell you who didn't like him. George."

That got her attention. "George? Why not?"

She lost his. His gaze grew distant. "Such a shame about George. He'd been so down, so depressed about going into the nursing home. But Tuesday we had lunch, me and Mo and him, like we always did, at the diner. He and Mo'd been over to the Castle site and George was just as happy as could be. Said he had found the answers to all his problems."

April wanted to get the conversation back to Frankie. Hearing about old men's fears of nursing homes wasn't what she was after.

An arm snaked around Curly's shoulders.

Lyle's sharp jaw came into view. "So where are the sidewalk supervisors headed next? Don't tell me. That sewer replacement job in Butler, am I right? I can't compete with the heavy equipment."

Curly smiled sheepishly.

"Nothing like digging up a street to get all the boys out," Lyle told April. "They're convinced they can help things along, if the Ditch Witch gets stuck."

Curly's eyes lit up and his head began to wobble dangerously again. "Have you seen the new one? It goes like a mother —"

"Yeah, Curly, I've seen it," Lyle interrupted. He gave Curly a smile and glanced at April. He was holding a red Solo paper cup. April could smell the liquor in it. She hadn't seen a bar, but there must be one somewhere. She looked for Tammy, expecting her to join her husband, but April didn't see her. April remembered some folks thought she'd been responsible for his death at the nursing home.

"Tammy not here?" she asked Lyle.

He shook his head, saying unconvincingly, "Migraine."

Curly said, "I was just telling Miss Buchert here how happy George was on Tuesday."

"George was?" Lyle said, his smile fading. His eyes searched Curly's.

"Sure, he came back from the job site, just as happy as a kid."

"I think he was excited that he was going to see something blow up. That George liked a big bang as much as anybody," Lyle said with a wink.

Curly laughed lasciviously. "That he did."

April said, "Well, you must know, Lyle. You saw him Tuesday, didn't you? The day before the explosion?"

Lyle shook his head as if searching his memory. "No, I don't think so."

"I thought my dad said you were there, doing something with the dynamite."

Lyle disagreed. "I wasn't there." His eyes got misty. "I didn't see George at all before he died, sadly. The last I saw him was on the Donnybrook job the week before."

"Oh, that was a good one," Curly said. "With the big backhoe." He rubbed his hands together in glee. April looked at Lyle, who shrugged and smiled.

"These old guys got to get their kicks somehow," Lyle said. "The bigger the equipment, the bigger the thrill."

April laughed. Curly enjoyed being teased by Lyle, that much was clear.

And he gave as good as he got. "You get yours blowing stuff up. At this stage, all I can do is watch."

Curly looked off in the distance. The line at the buffet was three deep, and people were sitting in chairs lined up in rows, scarfing down potato salad and Jell-O. The business of burying a friend was an appetite-building one. Several men were passing a flask. In the room, the women and the men were in separate groups, the women arguing over the amount of sugar in the coleslaw and the men disagreeing about how much rain had been forecast.

Lyle leaned into April, keeping his voice low. His features were oversized, like his hands. He said, "By the way, I dropped off some invoices at the barn earlier."

April looked at him in surprise. "You were in the barn?"

"Well, yeah. That's the way your father and I work. He likes stuff put right on his desk. In the special place."

She laughed. That did sound like her dad. She'd have to talk to him. That system had to change now that she was living there. She couldn't have strange men dropping in without notice.

"Okay, I'll make sure he gets them. I'd like to talk to you about the Castle job and what you remember about Frankie Imperiale."

"That's a shame, ain't it? They sure it's him?"

April shrugged. "It's not official."

"There are only a few dentists in Aldenville," Curly said. "They just got lucky that he'd had his dental work done here."

April nodded. That was true. Many people went into Wilkes-Barre for their doctor's appointments. Someone like Frankie, with a hardscrabble upbringing, was lucky to have had any dental work done.

"How well did you know Frankie?" April asked.

"I barely remember working with him," Lyle said. "That would have been way back, at the first Castle job. He was an apprentice."

Yet Ed didn't remember him. April tried to think of something else to ask him.

Lyle looked at the diminishing line at the buffet table. "I'm going to get some food. Do you want something?" he asked her politely.

"Thanks, I already ate."

April tried to spot the other elderly man she'd seen with Curly at the Castle yesterday. "Where's Mo?" she asked.

"Not here." Curly leaned in and whispered. His breath was stale and smelled like old socks. "He couldn't take it. He lives at that damned nursing home. He had a bad afternoon, and they gave him something to sleep. He was agitated."

Tammy wasn't the only one who couldn't face a funeral.

"Can you get me some cookies? I need to rest my dogs a bit." Curly headed to a line of chairs set up under the high windows.

As she approached the dessert table, April heard the Buchert Construction name and slowed near a group of mourners that were gathered around the cookies. They were talking about Frankie. She inched closer, picking up a small paper plate. She put a pizzelle on her plate. She vacillated between cream puffs and snickerdoodles. Did Curly have to worry about trans fat? She decided it was too late for him. He might as well enjoy the turtle brownies. She made her choices slowly so she could listen.

A bosomy woman clucked, "Poor Rita Imperiale. All those years. Never knowing where her son was. Thinking he'd abandoned her."

"He was always trouble," said an elderly woman with a face the color and texture of a well-used paper grocery bag.

The first woman leaned into the group. April strained to hear. "Her only child. She never told anyone who his father was."

281

The group of women resorted to murmurs, and April backed off, now putting cookies randomly on Curly's plate. She'd left home, too, left her mother alone. She'd always been in touch with her parents, though. Still, there had been long stretches of time during college and when she was getting her career off the ground that the phone calls home had been scarce. She looked over at her mom, now walking with Clive, introducing him to the priest, and wondered if she had needed more from April.

April dropped off the plate of cookies with Curly and then searched out Lyle. She found him eating at a banquet table, and sat down in the empty chair next to him.

"Do you think Yost has it in for my dad? Some kind of personal vendetta?"

Lyle looked thoughtful, his mouth moving as he chewed potato salad. "He's always after us to have the proper permits, making sure our tools are locked up every night. I don't think he checks up on every contractor like he does us."

"Did you? Have the right permits for the Castle?"

Lyle's eyes flashed with anger. "You heard me. I talked to the borough yesterday morning. The code enforcement officer said I was cleared."

"Okay, okay," April said. "I'm just trying to figure out what's going on."

Lyle shook his head. "Used to be a man's word was good enough. When George was the code enforcement officer, Yost and George were tight as thieves. There would have been no questions."

All she'd done was make Lyle mad at her. April excused herself.

April mingled, listening to conversations that ranged from the deer population to road construction and back again. Frankie and George, the dead men, seemed to have been forgotten.

Why was Frankie so forgettable? She wanted to know what Frankie Imperiale looked like. The men her father hired back then often came to their house in the mornings for Bonnie's sticky buns and coffee. Maybe she'd remember him if she saw his face. She might remember who his friends were.

According to Curly, he was a local boy. If that was the case, she knew right where to look. She made her way through the crowd and past the kitchen, using the back hall that led to Deana's place.

April turned into Mark's study. Just as she'd remembered, every high school yearbook for the past twenty years was lined up at the bottom of the bookshelves. He had the remainder, dating back to when Mr. Hudock started high school, in storage.

She counted back on her fingers. Rocky's graduation party was held June 13, 1993. Frankie would have been a few years out of school by then, working for her dad. She pulled down the 1990 yearbook and thumbed through. She started in the senior section and scanned the color pictures of boys and girls, with the hairstyles and clothes as anachronistic as if they'd been photographed a hundred years ago.

Nothing in 1990. She pulled down 1991.

Hancock, Huddleston, Imperiale. There was Frankie's name, but next to it was only gray splotch. No photo available. Darn. She tapped her teeth with her fingernail. He had to be somewhere in the yearbook. Maybe he'd been involved in sports. April looked through the team photos with no results. Nothing in clubs. Maybe he'd been voted class clown. Or most likely to end up dead in a Castle ruin. Nothing. Frankie hadn't been the extracurricular type.

She did see a picture of a cheerleading Tammy, smiling, lithe and beautiful, without the worry lines that were now such a prominent feature of her face. Her high, pert ponytail was a bright yellow. It looked so unlike the mousy bob she currently wore. April felt like a voyeur. It was obscene, seeing this pretty girl with such hope and promise, before life dealt her its nasty blows. She wondered what kinds of events had led Tammy to the frown lines and gray hair.

Flipping further through the pages, April saw a familiar face. A group of students were standing around an old car. The teacher was Mo. She read the caption. "The twenty-five-year-old Valiant was completely restored in Automotive Shop by Joe Keener, Barney Zimmerman and Frank Imperiale. The project was underwritten by Weber Insurance."

She pulled the book closer. Frankie's face was tiny, and she couldn't make out his features. According to the caption, he was the one with the grin and the mullet. But the more important thing was that Mo and George had known Frankie. She'd find out more from Mo.

It looked as if a trip to the nursing home was in her future. She swallowed a bit of guilt about using poor George that way, but she needed to get her dad out of Yost's jail.

The door to the study opened. Deana stuck her head in. "Oh, it's you," she said. "I couldn't imagine why the light was on in here. Mark's downstairs with George's family."

April pointed to the pile of yearbooks. "I see you've kept up your father's tradition."

Deana smiled fondly. "Can you believe my dad? He still buys them and has a fit if they're not on display when he comes home from Florida. Mark says this room will belong to my dad until the day he dies."

"Nothing wrong with that," April said. Before she caught herself, she had the thought that it would be nice to have a space in her mother's home that she could call her own.

Deana said, "I'm glad we have a few minutes to catch up. How are you holding up?"

April rubbed a hand across her forehead. "Dads. Can't live with 'em, can't kill 'em. You know my father is being questioned by the police?"

Deana shook her head, her brown eyes troubled. She leaned into her friend. "When did that happen?"

"Late this afternoon," April said, pointing to the high school yearbook picture. "Since Frankie Imperiale worked on the Castle job site, they wanted to talk to Dad."

"That's him?" Deana said, taking the book from her hands and studying the picture.

April wondered if Deana could see the underlying structure of the skull that she'd seen yesterday come tumbling out of the rubble. She shook her head to rid herself of the image of Frankie's head without the flesh and muscle that made the man who he was.

"Is Ed okay?" Deana asked, looking at her friend.

April shrugged her shoulders. Tears popped into her eyes. Her best friend had to be exhausted after a long day of caring for others, but she was serene and sincerely concerned about April. April fought back the tears. "I need to figure out what happened that night at the Castle. Everything seems to track back to that night."

"The night of Rocky's graduation party?"

April nodded. "Exactly. And the night Jesse was born."

Deana was thoughtful. "What does Jesse have to do with it?"

"I'm not sure except that Frankie is his father."

Deana's eyes widened. "Are you sure? That seems like a very unlikely match up. How did they even meet?"

Deana's attention drifted as they heard footsteps outside, and she moved to the door, listening. Someone was heading for this room. April drew her friend back a step, just as the door was flung open.

"There you are," Tammy said, her eyes wide and brimming with tears. April shrank into the room, but Tammy made a beeline to Deana, gripping her upper arms.

"I want you to help me. You can help me. Please," she said, her voice clogged with tears.

Deana gently extricated herself from Tammy's grasp. Deana had plenty of experience with grieving people. April was impressed anew at her quiet strength.

"What can I do for you, Tammy?" Deana's professional voice was soothing.

Tammy drew in a breath. Deana guided her to the couch that they'd sat on last night watching the late news, and squatted on the floor next to her. She put her hands on the woman's knees, as much to ground her as anything else.

"You've got to find out what killed George," Tammy said. "Please, Deana, I know you can find out how he died."

"Tammy, honey," Deana said, "he was an old man. You've got to let him go. He had a full life."

Tammy's shoulders heaved as she let the tears flow. She looked up to the door. April got the hint and closed it. Whatever Tammy wanted to say was private.

"Deana, you saw him. Did he look like he'd been killed? You can't believe what people are saying. I heard someone say he'd been smothered with his pillow or given an overdose of insulin. Can you find out?"

Deana shook her head. "That would be impossible to determine without an autopsy. His family didn't want one. George was very specific in his instructions that his body remain intact. End of story."

Tammy had buried her face in her hands, and her next words were barely audible. "The nursing home is a good place. We do the best we can."

"It's true," Deana said. "I testified to that with the last investigation. Forever Friends takes good care of their clients."

Tammy wailed, "If the nursing home gets a bad rap, it could close and I'll be out of a job. All a place like that has is its reputation. After what happened last winter, we're just starting to fill up again. If people think we're killing our patients . . ."

Deana said softly, "No one thinks you're killing people, Tammy. Slow down."

"That's easy for you to say," Tammy cried.

Why was Tammy so upset? Did she know more about George's death than she was saying?

"Can't you do something?" Tammy said.

"Definitely not," Deana replied. "I have a position of trust in this community. I can't afford the hint of impropriety. I cannot get involved. This is my livelihood you're talking about. Mark's work. My family's business." Deana's eyes were stormy. April hadn't seen Deana's wrath in a long time.

A beeper went off on Deana's watch. "It's time for the family's final moments with George. I've got to go."

Tammy was crying gently now. "Can I stay up here for a moment? I don't want Lyle to see me like this. He's not happy that I'm so upset about George. Says I'm a worrywart."

April said, "I'll stay with her, Deana. Go do what you have to do."

Deana shot April a worried look.

"It'll be fine," April said, her hand on Tammy's shoulder. She kneaded her muscles. Deana left the room.

"This could come back on your dad, you know. George was at the Castle the day before he died, April," Tammy said. "He might have hurt himself over there. Sometimes injuries don't show up until later. They do their damage internally, and then the person dies in his sleep. The Castle is just as much at fault as the nursing home is. More."

290

April wondered about the two deaths since she'd returned to Aldenville. Both were connected to the Castle in some way. Both were connected to her father. What if George's death hadn't been natural?

She didn't want to entertain the possibility. "Yost was investigating that possibility. But he didn't find anything."

"That's only because Frankie's skull distracted him. That Castle was a mess. There were hazards everywhere. Lyle said he twisted his ankle in a hole. An old man like George, he could have easily gotten hurt."

Why *was* George there on Tuesday? The old men liked to watch the work crews, but no one was working that day. Only Lyle, double-checking his dynamite charges. April had a thought. "How did you get here, Tammy?"

"Lyle," she said.

But Lyle'd said she was home with a migraine. April's thought was cut short by Tammy.

"Come to the nursing home tomorrow," Tammy said, clutching her arm. "I'll show you around. You can see for yourself what a reputable place it is. I'm on in the afternoon. Wait until we get through lunches, say, after two."

Mo was at the nursing home. This would be a good opportunity to talk to him.

"I'll come over, Tammy," April said.

"Thanks, April. You'll see," Tammy said, tears leaving red streaks on her splotchy face. April felt a twinge of guilt using Tammy's vulnerability to get into the nursing home. But to keep her father from going to jail she needed to know what George knew about the graduation night party, and Mo was the only one who knew that now.

CHAPTER 14

The next morning, Friday, April woke up later than she'd intended. She felt dry-mouthed and achy, as though she'd spent the night drinking cosmopolitans instead of going to a wake. She was emotionally hung over. The stress of the week had left her feeling wrung out.

She lay in bed trying to figure out what she'd learned last night. She'd seen Frankie's picture but didn't remember him. Tammy was afraid that she was being blamed for killing people at the nursing home. Curly, Mo and George had had one last lunch at the diner before George went back to the home and died. Frankie had not been a nice guy, at least according to Suzi and the other stampers.

In the shower, April remembered with a start that she had to get to Mirabella and meet Rocky before she could do anything else. She'd nearly forgotten. She needed to salvage this job for Retro Reproductions.

Before leaving she listened to a short message from Vince that had come while she was in the shower. He told her that Ed was still being held. He'd spent the night in the holding cell of the jail on Main Street. Vince was going to work. He'd be on the Heights job today if she needed to reach him.

She looked up the number for the local police and called. A secretary answered, informing April that Ed could not receive calls, but he would be able to use the phone later in the day. April left a message with her, telling her dad she loved him and to call her.

April flipped on the radio, ate cereal with one hand and drew with the other. She listened for mention of the Castle story or something about the skull or the bullet, but none came.

She crumpled the napkin she'd doodled on and put her cereal dish in the sink. She'd been drawing dark images. At the stamping party, Piper had created a page about her son going to jail. She understood that impulse now. April found herself drawing bars and gloomy corners. Ed in jail. Whatever she didn't want to think about came through in her sketch pages. She reminded herself he wasn't in jail. He was in the local pokey. There was a huge difference. That was a good thing. But she couldn't get rid of the nagging feeling that Yost wasn't finished with him yet.

The ring of the phone brought her back to reality. It was Rocky. "I just saw Aunt Barbara leave. Ready to go?"

April glanced up. The clock on the microwave read 9:04. "I'm on my way," she said.

Once outside, she slid the big barn door smoothly on the track, locking it with the key Ed had left. But she didn't make it to her car. An unfamiliar blue pickup rattled up the drive, blocking her in. She scowled. She was going to be late. Would Rocky wait for her?

She shielded her eyes and recognized Lyle after he rolled down his window and leaned out. This wasn't the muscle car that he'd been driving when he dropped off Tammy the other night. This was a brand-new four-passenger truck, with fancy wheel covers and shiny tailpipes. The huge tires meant it stood four feet off the ground.

He was holding a folder. "Time cards. It's Friday. Your dad's day to do the payroll."

April's heart sank. "Did you talk to him? This morning?" April asked.

Lyle said, "No. Vince left me a message last night with the crew's work assignments." He looked at her hopefully as if she would enlighten him. "He said we were off the mansion job for now?"

Obviously Vince hadn't thought he needed to know about Mrs. H. kicking them out. "For now," she said, hoping her oblique tone would keep him satisfied. He waited for more, but when she wasn't forthcoming, he tapped the folder.

Lyle said, "I guess he forgot about payroll. Understandable, with everything else going on. But the men have to be paid on time."

She said, "Do you know how to do the payroll?"

Lyle dashed her hopes. "I don't. I stick strictly to the construction side of the business."

April felt her head start to pound. How had she gotten so involved? She'd come back to Pennsylvania to work on one of her dad's jobs. No pressure. No being her own boss. She'd just wanted to be an employee, but here she was the boss of a six-man crew who needed to get paid. She rubbed her temples.

April said, "Leave the time cards with me."

"Want me to put them inside?" Lyle asked.

She shook her head. "That's okay. I just locked up."

He handed the folder to her and started

to put his truck in gear but then stopped. "I already told Vince, but I'll tell you, too. I'll do whatever it takes to keep Retro Reproductions going."

April was touched. "Thanks, we're going to need all the help we can get."

Lyle backed out of the driveway. She tossed the folder on her passenger seat. The payroll would have to wait until she got back. Maybe Ed would be home by then.

The first order of business was getting Retro Reproductions back into Mirabella. If she didn't keep the men working, there would be no more paydays after this one. She jumped into her car and drove to the Tudor.

Rocky was waiting on the back steps. Today she was dressed in a loose sundress, the floral print bringing out her green eyes. She was wearing red huaraches that looked like they came from Mexico. The bracelet she never seemed to be without dangled from her perfect wrist, and an old Schwinn bike with a wicker basket leaned against the porch railing.

April felt her stomach tighten at the thought of what waited for her inside. Vince and her dad were counting on her. "Did you look at the mural?" she asked.

Rocky shook her head. "No, I just got

here, too. Come on."

April hesitated as Rocky stood to go in. She was officially off the job and had no business going into Mrs. H.'s house. If she wasn't breaking any laws, she was at least breaking rules of etiquette. Rocky disappeared and April shook herself. The mural wasn't going to fix itself.

The house was quiet except for the ticking of a clock somewhere and the whirr of the fan of the air conditioner. Drapes were drawn against the heat of a summer day. With no construction workers on site, the house seemed unnaturally still.

"How are you this morning?" Mitch asked. He came from the hall and scrutinized her expression. April saw Rocky stop and look back at the two of them, a bemused expression on her face.

"Fine," she said abruptly, quickly passing him and catching up with Rocky in the dining room. She didn't want Rocky thinking she had any feelings for Mitch. He looked a little confused by her abruptness, but she couldn't worry about him now.

Rocky had installed herself in front of the mural, her eyes narrowed. She picked off a piece of peeling paint and sniffed at it. Squatting, she rubbed her hand over the surface of the wall.

April's throat constricted. She wiped her sweaty palms on her jeans. There was so much riding on Rocky's opinion. But the frown on her face was not a good sign.

Sitting back on her heels, Rocky pursed her lips and brushed the hair from her eyes. April saw a tiny scar that led from the corner of her eyelid up across her forehead. It bisected her frown lines. No wonder she wore her hair the way she did.

She couldn't wait any longer. "What do you think, Rocky?"

"Like I said yesterday, you're screwed. This was painted with oils, so when you used alcohol on it, the paint actually dissolved. There's nothing under there. See?" She rubbed at the spot and showed April her fingertip, covered with gold color. "You're down to blank wall."

April groaned. "So not what I wanted to hear," she said.

Rocky shrugged, her shoulders eloquent. "I don't know what to tell you."

April said hopefully, "Maybe you can convince your aunt Barbara that the mural is too ugly to restore."

"Don't bet on it," Rocky said. "We've grown up hearing how it was a genuine Refregier."

Mrs. H. had said something like that on

Wednesday. "Is that someone well-known?" April asked. Her voice was thick with panic.

Rocky nodded. Mitch looked grim.

"A *famous* muralist painted this?" That was all she needed. She'd destroyed the work of a world-renowned painter. Her heart sunk even lower.

Mitch said, "Supposedly the guy became famous later doing WPA work. You know, like the mural at Coit Tower."

So Mitch had been to San Francisco. Interesting.

April stared at the wall. The picture was so ugly and over the top. The characters were oversized, almost cartoonlike. But the colors did have that 1930s sensibility. Damn.

Mitch's phone rang and he walked away from them to answer it.

Rocky straightened. "I'm sorry, April. I'm fresh out of ideas."

"Well, thanks anyhow."

The mural was hopeless. Her mind shut down, unable to think of alternate solutions. She'd have to let her father know she'd failed. April followed Rocky through the kitchen.

Rocky said conversationally, "I've got to go. I'm meeting Tammy for breakfast."

"Is she okay?" April asked. "She was so

upset last night."

"She's just had a stressful week."

"Yes, with George dying and all. And then Frankie Imperiale, too," April said, watching Rocky's expression. Rocky's face didn't change.

Rocky shook her head, her beautiful hair moving as one sheet. "Why would Frankie's death affect her? She didn't know him. Tammy's only ever had one boyfriend. She's gone out with Lyle since she was sixteen."

Rocky and April were off the porch now. Rocky grabbed her bike and turned it around. She glanced up to see if Mitch was coming and then pitched her voice low, her comments for April's ears only. "Whatever you're trying to do by connecting Tammy with Frankie, you need to stop now. She's an innocent who's being stretched to the max. You have no idea what her life has been like in the last year with the deaths at the nursing home."

"Kind of like the stress of having your father interrogated by the police, I'd imagine," April said sarcastically.

Rocky was fingering the pieces on her bracelet. One piece was made of brass and looked familiar to April. April bent down and touched Rocky's wrist.

"Let me see that," she said.

Rocky pulled away, but April had hold of the piece she wanted to study. She saw the letters "UC" and the front wheels of a truck. "This is part of a Buchert Construction buckle," she said. "Where did you get this?"

Rocky said, "Tammy and I found it in Lyle's dresser a couple of years ago. We were looking for found objects for our bracelets."

April looked at the bracelet more closely. The charms were bits of metal washers, pieces of glass and fiber beads. The eccentric mix was charming.

"Why this?" April asked. "Why the Buchert buckle?"

Rocky looked away as she pulled her wrist from April's grasp. "It's a talisman of sorts. Reminds Tammy and me of graduation night. She has a piece, too."

"That's weird," April said.

"The point is," Rocky called as she rode away on her bike, "Tammy had nothing to do with Frankie. Nothing."

April leaned against her car, heart pounding. What did Rocky have against her? She needed time to think. But the screen door slammed and she jumped as Mitch came out of the house to join her. "Sorry," he said.

She didn't acknowledge him, lost again in thoughts about a long-ago party.

"So now what?" he asked, indicating the mansion behind him. "What are you going to do about the mural?"

She tried to pull her thoughts out of the past and into the here and now, shaking her head as she did so. "I really don't know. I need to get the men back on the job by Monday, or Retro Reproductions will suffer."

Mitch frowned. "Don't forget your dad's part in this. I mean, he's the one who told Aunt Barbara that you could clean the mural."

"True, but I doubt he could have imagined that I'd do enough damage to shut down the whole job."

Mitch's mouth twitched. "You can't lay it all on you. Ed's got to take some responsibility. Your only hope is to get Ed to talk to her and convince her everything'll be all right."

"Kind of tough, from a jail cell." April shrugged. She wasn't successful at keeping her bitter disappointment out of her voice.

She noticed a blue truck in the drive. "What's Lyle doing here?"

Mitch said, "He said something about a shipment of pipe coming here by mistake."

April was annoyed. "Cripes, he was here last night when the pipe was unloaded. I hope he gets up to the Heights job soon. Vince's expecting him."

Seeing Lyle's truck reminded her of the payroll that needed to be done.

"I've got to go, Mitch. I've got paperwork I have to get done."

"Just remember, your father has to bear some responsibility for this."

She headed back to the barn. Mitch's words about her father had her wondering what to tell him. Chances were Vince had already told him about her contretemps with Mrs. H. yesterday. But she'd assured Vince she would fix things. And she hadn't.

She could do the payroll. That would help. She dumped the folder Lyle had given her on her father's desk and flipped through the time cards, trying to place names with the faces of the guys she'd met Wednesday. John Clark, Bernie Dudek, Butch Martin, Carlos Riveria, Mike McCarty.

Retro Reproductions had a total of eight men on their payroll, not including Vince or Ed. Yesterday, there'd been four men on the Mirabella job. Three others were with Lyle on the Heights job. She flipped through the time cards. The workweek ended yesterday, Thursday. The hours had to be allocated to the correct job, and it looked as though Ed used a color-coded system. Lyle's time card was divided between two jobs: the Heights and the Castle. He wasn't involved in the Mirabella job. At least not this week. April noticed his whole day was allotted to the Castle. He said he was getting permits, but he was also out at the job site. He'd said he hadn't seen George and Mo, but Tammy had found out about George's turned ankle from him. She'd have to ask Mo about what happened on Tuesday.

April noticed John Clark was on record as having worked at the Mirabella job yesterday, but she was sure he was the guy who hadn't been there. Lyle, or John, had put the wrong color next to his time.

April wrote a note to Ed, outlining the mistake.

Receipts from the supply house and other vendors were in a neat pile on the metal spike. The ones Lyle dropped off last night. She saw the invoice from the delivery from yesterday on top. Sure enough, the materials had been allotted to the Mirabella job. She made a note to ask Lyle about the pipe he'd moved this morning.

There was an invoice for the dynamite from the Eckley Munitions Company. It was dated a month earlier, so April put it in the folder marked "Mirabella."

April turned on Ed's computer and found

a folder named "Payroll." Inside the folder was a spreadsheet that Ed had designed. April found last week's file. The payroll was complicated; each man had a different rate of pay, as did each job. There were benefits to be figured out, payroll deductions for taxes and union dues. Her heart sank. This would take a while.

She added the hours on Mike McCarty's time card and tentatively plugged in the numbers. The payroll tax was figured automatically, as were the other deductions. Net pay appeared in the final column. As long as she transcribed the number of hours correctly, this payroll should be okay. Then she could write the checks out and have them ready for Ed to sign whenever he got back here tonight. If he got back here.

Her mind wandered back to Frankie Imperiale's time card that she'd seen earlier. In those days, the pay week had run from Friday to Friday. He'd been paid through Friday, June 11. As far as April knew, no one had seen him after that.

The Castle had been boarded up sometime on Monday, June 14. But the Buchert Construction payroll ended the week before. No one was paid past that day. She'd have to ask Ed who had boarded the place up. He couldn't have. He was with her.

She finished writing the payroll just after one and closed the checkbook with a flourish, congratulating herself. It was one less thing her father would have to deal with. That felt good.

She had time to eat before heading to the nursing home. Deana had sent her home with enough leftovers to last her a couple of days. As long as she didn't tire of pierogies, she was set.

Walking toward the kitchen, April spotted her sketchbook on the table. She opened it and looked at the skulls she'd drawn the night before last, one of which had a star-like impression on the side of the head. She opened her camera phone and looked at the real pictures. Her drawings really bore no resemblance to the actual skull of Frankie Imperiale. In her drawings, the star-shaped indentation had been huge, but in reality, it was quite small. Probably not enough to kill anyone.

She looked closer. She couldn't see a bullet hole from this angle. Had she missed one on the other side? Maybe a bullet had penetrated the skull through the crack. She couldn't tell. She didn't have enough information, but she knew where to get some.

April dialed Deana's number without even stopping to think about it. She knew the number by heart. They'd talked to each other every day, several times a day, all through junior high and high school. She had no other friends for whom this was true. She didn't even know what Ken's phone number was. Of course he'd changed numbers so many times to get away from his creditors he probably didn't know what the number was himself.

Deana picked up right away, recognizing her ring. "April? Is your dad okay?"

April said, "Yost's still got him. I'm hoping he'll be home later today. I have a question for you. About the cause of death."

"Anyone in particular?" Deana asked.

"You know I mean Frankie. I saw the skull, Deana, and I saw that it was bashed in. I mean, there was a star-shaped dent in the side of that man's head. Could that be why he died?"

Deana said, "It's very difficult to determine cause of death without the complete body. He could have been knocked on the head without it being fatal, then stabbed through the heart or poisoned. It's not a given, no, that just because he was hit in the head that that's why he died."

Or he could have been shot, April thought. "Yost thinks they might have found a bullet fragment."

"That would change everything," Deana agreed.

"What about George's death, Dee? Is there anything weird about it?"

Deana was quiet for a beat. April was about to check her phone to see if the call had been dropped when Deana said, "People in nursing homes are very vulnerable. Any kind of fall or injury could lead to death."

April knew the end of a topic when she heard one. Deana would say no more.

Her call-waiting tone sounded. She checked the screen. "Deana, it's my dad. I've got to get this." She hung up quickly and picked up the call. "Dad?"

"Hi, honey."

April felt her knees go weak. Her dad sounded okay. "Are you out of trouble?"

Ed's voice was low. "No, not yet. They're still talking to me. Listen, Lyle will be dropping off the time cards."

"He already did. I've got them."

Ed grunted. "The payroll *has* to be done today." His voice got higher. "If the checks aren't in the guys' hands today, their union can fine me. If I get too many fines, I won't get any more carpenters when I need them. And too many fines mean Retro will go busto."

He stopped to draw in a ragged breath, and April interrupted. "Hold up, Dad. You're covered. I figured out the payroll."

"You did? With all the deductions and the different rates for each job? That Heights job is a prevailing wage job, you know."

"I did it. I'm not saying it's perfect, but I think it's okay."

"You're a doll," Ed said, the relief palatable.

"One problem. I can't sign the checks."

Ed's voice deflated. "Only Vince or I can sign checks."

"I'll bring them to you. Yost will have to let you deal with this."

"No, bug. I don't want you here. I'll have Lyle pick them up. He can get Vince to sign and then deliver the checks to the men."

"I'll leave them on the desk. I've got to go out for a while," April said.

"You saved my life today, April."

"I love you, Dad," she said, her heart suddenly swamped by the feelings of love and loss.

"I'll be home soon."

The nursing home was a converted old house that had been added onto more than once. The front door led to a lobby sitting area, which had folks in wheelchairs lined up along one wall. A woman yelled as she passed, calling April a pretty girl. April didn't quite get to the desk before she was waylaid by Tammy.

"April, goody. You're here," Tammy said, greeting her with a hug and a kiss. "Sign in. Everyone has to sign in. For security reasons." She pointed to a clipboard at the unmanned desk.

If this was their security system, it was pretty rudimentary. April could have just walked in.

A woman with her tiny feet encased in bright pink fuzzy socks pushed against the floor. The wheelchair moved forward a few inches before Tammy yanked on the handles and brought her back in line.

"Imogene, honey, just sit now. Pretty soon, it'll be time for Judge Judy."

The woman quieted. April was surprised by Tammy. Away from the stampers, in her work environment, she seemed far more capable. She stood straighter, and although she wore scrubs festooned with cartoon characters, her manner was professional. Her hair was pulled back with two barrettes and her face was made up lightly, highlighted with lipstick. She soothed the woman in the wheelchair, stroking her back and talking softly. April knew she was on *her* turf now.

Tammy said, "I'll take you to Mo and you can ask him about George. You'll tell Deana whatever you find out?"

April didn't see how she had much choice. She wanted to get in to talk to Mo, and this was her way in, so she agreed. George was being buried today, and that would be the end of Deana's connection to this affair, but Tammy obviously thought Deana had some pull.

They found him in a small empty room, lined with shelves holding arts and crafts supplies. Rolls of white paper and jars of paint sat alongside canning jars full of brushes. He was standing at an easel, painting with watercolors, copying a bowl of fruit on the table. He was no artist. His colors were muddy and the shapes were irregular. The oranges looked like pomegranates with distended belly buttons, and the bananas resembled green beans.

Tammy called to him as they entered the room. "Feeling better today? I brought you a visitor. You remember April Buchert?"

He looked up blankly, his eyes watery from staring at his paints. His hand stopped in midstroke, but he smiled wanly when he saw Tammy. He seemed to know she was measuring him and was trying to respond

312

in an upbeat manner.

April said, "We met the other morning at the Castle site. After the dynamite."

"I remember," he said. "You're Ed's kid."

April nodded and approached him. Tammy hung back. "I'm sorry about George. Curly told me you were good friends," April said.

His eyes saddened, and April felt a stab of regret for making him revisit tough times. She steeled herself to ask him more questions he wouldn't want to answer and went on. "You and George were at the Castle the day before the explosion. I heard George took a fall."

Mo shook his head ponderously. "The more I think about it, the more I think we shouldn't have been out there."

This was a different guy than the man she'd met on Wednesday. He'd had too much time to think. When she'd seen him after the blast, he'd been upset with Yost for thinking George had been hurt at the Castle. "Lamebrain" was the word he'd used to describe Yost's theory.

Tammy said, "Mo, do you want to sit? You look a little unsteady."

He shook his head.

He continued, slowly. "We didn't know how overgrown the place had become.

George wanted to check it out. He'd heard about the dynamite permit and wanted to see if it was warranted. He still had connections with the town, even though he hadn't been the code enforcement officer for years."

April didn't want to ask if Mo saw Lyle in front of Tammy. If he was lying, she didn't need to know. Maybe he just didn't want to get involved in case George's family sued Ed.

"And he fell?" April prompted, steering him way from the olden days. For now. As soon as she got rid of Tammy, she'd find out about Frankie Imperiale.

Mo held up a dripping paintbrush and pointed it. "He tripped, but he didn't really fall. I don't think that's what killed him, if that's what you're asking. I mean, he got up, brushed himself off and went on. He didn't even complain of an ache or a pain."

But, April thought, he could have developed one later.

Mo was dabbing his brush on his palette. "I found him in his room later that night, not breathing. He looked awful, like his last moments on earth were hell. His face was twisted in an ugly grimace."

Tammy grunted, making April wonder if the grimace was medically significant.

Mo continued. "I see that expression every time I close my eyes."

Moving to his side, Tammy took the paintbrush from his hand and began rubbing his cheek. She murmured softly. Mo leaned into her. The tableau was so sad, April had to look away. The pain was coming off him like a heat wave.

April could see brightly colored feet coming down the hall. Slowly. Imogene, the woman in the wheelchair, was on the move. Tammy was going to be called out of here any moment. April kept an eye on Imogene's methodical progress. The woman's eyes sparkled with adventure. Mo was saying, "You expect to lose friends at my age, but George was the last one I thought would go."

April racked her brains trying to think of more questions to ask. What would Deana ask?

"How did he behave on the way home from the Castle?" she asked. Imogene was getting closer. Tammy hadn't noticed yet, but her nurse's sense was sure to kick in soon. One of her charges was getting loose.

Mo said, "He was in a great mood. Very upbeat."

With a loud cackle, Imogene broached the doorway. Behind her, a string of wheelchair-confined patients set up a racket, urging her to cross the threshold, like bettors at the racetrack race. Tammy finally saw her and lunged for the handles. She moved swiftly, taking Imogene back down the hall, telling her about keeping in line. The rest of the patients followed.

April took her chance and bent down to Mo. She whispered, "I'm trying to find out anything about Frankie Imperiale. He worked for my dad back when the Castle was being built. You had him in auto shop, remember?"

"Sure, I remember Frankie. I got him into the union . . ." His mind wandered. "George and I spent a lot of time on that job. George was the code enforcement officer, and I was just interested. It was fascinating to watch. I like to watch construction. Still do." His voice caught as if he'd remembered it would just be him and Curly from now on. "I don't know if I will anymore, though."

April needed him to get back on track. "I heard that George didn't really like Frankie."

Mo sighed. "No one liked Frankie much. Your dad couldn't see it, but the kid was a con man. Always playing the angles."

"What kinds of cons?" April remembered her father talking about materials disappearing off the Castle job. "Was he stealing?"

Mo shrugged. "George thought he was. That job was wide open. No one knew what was going on."

"There's always a market for copper pipe and fixtures," April said thoughtfully. She knew rings of stolen goods were always being busted. Maybe that's what Frankie was up to. Mo was right. The Castle was the perfect job to steal from. With Warren Winchester constantly changing his mind, it must have been impossible to keep track of what was going in and out.

She gave Mo a kiss on the cheek and, at his insistence, promised to visit him again.

Tammy was back behind the front desk, her wheelchair wards lined up and quieted. She stopped April.

"What did you find out? Will you ask Deana to investigate?"

April shook her head. "I'm sorry, Tammy. There's nothing suspicious about George's death that I can see." And there wasn't. George was an old man who died in his bed in a nursing home. He was connected to the Castle, and Frankie's death, only in the past. Still, as she left, April felt Tammy's eyes burning holes in her back.

April thought things over as she drove home

from the nursing home. Mo had known Frankie, and it was possible George had suspected him of stealing things. Why hadn't George turned him in? Maybe Frankie had died before George had the evidence he needed. Or maybe they were working together. Would George have killed him?

April wondered if Yost would talk to her about this. Was there a police report about stolen goods back then? Her dad didn't seem to have a clue. He'd been so distracted that summer by his personal issues, the whole job could have been stolen out from under him, and he wouldn't have noticed.

Coming back to the present, April decided she'd stop by the barn and see if Lyle had been by for the checks yet. If he hadn't, she'd bring them to her father. And talk to Yost.

The checks were right where she'd left them, on her father's desk. April scooped them up and headed for the police station.

When she got there she found Officer Yost seated at his desk. The office was small, only big enough for one desk, shared by Yost and the police chief. The phone rang but Yost didn't pick it up.

"Good morning, Miss Buchert," he said, with a sinister curve to his lips. He was enjoying her family's discomfort. April looked down the hall, where the holding cell was. She couldn't hear anyone moving about. Not a cough or a sigh.

"Where's my dad?" she asked.

"Up at the barracks. The state police thought he'd be more comfortable up there. And before you ask, no, you can't see him."

April's cheeks flamed. This guy made her so angry. She wanted to hit him.

She forced herself to sound calm. She didn't want him to get the upper hand. "Did you find any more bones?"

He leaned back in his chair. He must have studied the *Smokey and the Bandit* movies, because he managed to resemble a Southern sheriff by adjusting his body language.

April didn't trust herself to speak. She forced herself to wait. He wanted her to get upset and say something stupid.

Finally he said, "The state police have found more bones."

"With b . . . b . . . bullet holes?" April blurted, all her hard-won coolness leaving her.

He had a satisfied look on his face. "Too early to tell."

April cursed herself for letting him get to her. She tried to regain her equilibrium. Any thought of telling him what she'd found out vanished. There was no way he'd listen to her.

"He's innocent," she said. "You can't hold him forever."

"I can hold him long enough," Yost said, his slick grin returning.

Vince had to get Ed out of jail. Now.

April ran out of the police station, her stomach churning. She had to talk to Vince. And tell him to call their lawyer.

She took the highway up to the Heights, blowing through nearly red lights and risking the ire of truckers by passing them on the right.

At the job site, Vince was on a walk-through with a client inside the stone Federal house. He ignored her attemps to get his attention.

Frustrated, she found Lyle head down in the blueprints spread out on a kitchen island. "What's up? You look upset," he said.

"Yost," she said. Lyle grimaced. "And I need Vince to sign the payroll checks."

"No problem. Leave them with me. I'll make sure he signs them and that the men get paid."

The churning in her stomach lessened. "That would help a lot."

"At your service," Lyle said.

She handed over the checks. As she turned

to go, April said, "So did you get that pipe shipment straightened out?"

Lyle froze, and looked at her queerly. "Pipe?"

"Mitch saw you at Mirabella this morning."

His face relaxed. "Oh that. Yup, all figured out."

"Okay," she said.

When April returned to the barn, Mitch's Jeep was in the driveway. She hadn't realized he knew where the barn was, but of course he'd worked with Ed before. He must have been to Retro Reproductions' offices.

He was sitting on the bench outside the front door. She sensed a little flurry in her belly that felt, oddly enough, like excitement. There was no denying he was a good-looking guy. Even sitting down, leaning on his knees, fingers in his hair, he exuded strength and competence. In her mind she substituted her own hand for the one combing through his hair. And he'd come by to see her. Did he miss her? They hadn't had much time to talk this morning. She tucked her shirt back into her jeans and checked her hair in her rearview.

He stood when she got out of her car. As

she got closer her excitement turned to something else. This was not the laid-back, ready-to-help guy she'd met earlier. His face was shuttered, unreadable.

"Hey," she said hesitantly.

"You need to leave my sister alone," he said without preamble. His mouth was tight, as though he was forcing the words through his lips. "I know she acts tough, but she's not. Stop asking questions about her graduation party. Stop visiting the nursing home. Stop talking to Mo."

April was confused by his angry tone. "Slow down, Mitch. I'm just trying to keep my father out of jail."

How had he known she was at the nursing home? Tammy must have cried to Rocky, and Rocky had complained to her brother. That's the way the small-town telegraph system worked. With cell phones, the word spread even faster.

"I don't know what Tammy told you —"

Mitch was not listening. "My sister was protecting her friend. And she paid a heavy price. Too heavy."

"I don't understand."

"Frankie was a no-good, scum of the earth. He couldn't shine my sister's shoes. After what he did to Tammy, he got what he deserved."

April's heart pounded. What if Frankie had done something to Rocky? Was the whole Winchester clan overprotective? Would Mitch have acted? Could Mitch have killed? She took a step back.

"What did he do?" she asked.

"You don't know?" Mitch searched her face. She shook her head.

Mitch moved his eyes off her and focused on a tall pine tree. April could see a hawk in the very top. Mitch's voice was quiet. "It's not my story to tell."

April's mind was reeling. "I don't understand."

"The only thing that matters is that when Rocky found him, he had a sizable stash of marijuana on him. She can be formidable, my sister, and she threatened him with everything our family name could rain down on him. She told him to leave town or she'd turn his drugs over to Yost."

He was quiet for a few moments. "He left, and she never heard from him again. She thought that was the end of things. Unfortunately, after everyone had gone home, Yost came to the house because of the neighbors' complaints, and Rocky let him in. He found Frankie's marijuana. The quantity was enough to trigger an intent-to-sell charge. Rocky was looking at hard time." He was lost in the past. April's stomach clutched. She'd had no idea what had really gone down at the party that night. But Mitch hadn't even been there.

"I thought you were away at college," she said softly.

He didn't hear her. "It cost my father everything to keep her out of jail. He sent her to France the next day. That's the real reason the Castle never got finished. He went broke making sure she was never prosecuted. Lawyers cost a bundle."

"And my dad went bankrupt," April said bitterly.

"I am sorry about that," Mitch said, coming back to the present. "I've done everything I can to build his reputation back up. I always recommend Retro Reproductions to my clients. I'm your father's personal public relations man."

She shook her head. "My father . . ."

Mitch looked at her, for the first time. "You're not your father, any more than I'm mine. They made mistakes, each of them. But we don't have to let their mistakes define us."

CHAPTER 15

April's mind was spinning as she watched him leave. Rocky hadn't told her the truth about the party. Neither had Piper. Had Tammy? She knew where all of them would be tonight. At the country club, at the all-night stamping party. She'd go and find out. Because someone in the stamping group knew the answer to what happened that night. Everything pointed to them. Many of them had known Frankie. Rocky nearly went to jail over his pot. He was Piper's lover. Everyone else in town seemed to have forgotten him, but not the stamping group.

April gathered her stamping supplies in her old Lancome bag and dressed in ratty sweats and a paint-stained T-shirt. If she was going to stay up all night, she wanted to be comfortable.

Then she remembered her mother was working tonight. It was some kind of casino night at the club. She changed into her good jeans and a button-down blue shirt. Her mother wouldn't need to be ashamed of her daughter for dressing like a bum, pajama party or not.

She got to the club just after nine. Deana had told her the stampers would be in the Hazle Room. She knew where that was, near the kitchen on the opposite side from the bar where she and Mitch had cut through yesterday. The book-lined room was decorated just as she remembered, with nail-headed leather furniture and dark green wallpaper. Several large cherry library tables filled the center of the space. Someone had strung industrial-sized power strips under the table, taping down the cords with duct tape.

Luggage-type rolling carts and plastic bins littered the floor. The stampers were all here and had already started on their projects. Deana greeted April as she entered and dumped her bag at a spot Deana had saved for her. But she wasn't ready to sit just yet; she walked around the room, looking at what everyone was working on.

Mary Lou grabbed her hand. "We're happy you're here."

April was glad someone was glad to see her. She asked, "What are you doing?"

Mary Lou smiled. "I'm making tags. I

hang one on each of the housewarming gifts I send. My clients love the homemade touch." She'd personalized them with items she knew the new owners liked. A dog stamp for a poodle lover, a pig for a collector of all things porcine. A sail for those lucky enough to have a boat.

"Those are lovely," April said sincerely. The tags had nice proportion, and Mary Lou had a great sense of color.

"Check this out," her daughter said. Kit showed her her copy of *What to Expect When You're Expecting.* She'd painted a mustache on the beatific mother on the cover. "I'm altering this to reflect *my* pregnancy." Kit held up the page she was working on. It was a journal entry about swollen feet. A handsome, long-haired man sat on the end of a bed, rubbing the feet of a woman whose face was obscured by her gigantic belly. Kit had stamped words of endearment in a balloon coming out of his mouth.

"Oh, so this is fantasy," April joked.

Kit laughed. "You bet."

Tammy greeted April perfunctorily. No one noticed but April, but she felt the chill. Tammy's hands shook slightly as she showed April the cards she was making. They were straight from the manufacturer's suggestions; Tammy wasn't changing them at all. She was just cutting and pasting. Rocky, sitting close to Tammy, watched April closely.

Piper looked up at Tammy's work. "I thought the idea was to make a card that you *can't* find at a Hallmark store."

Rocky glowered, but Kit was the one who came to Tammy's rescue. "People will love getting your cards," she said. "Just because you made them."

Tammy smiled wanly. "I'm not in a creative mood."

Rocky was working on a new collage. April saw she had already stamped a three-leafed plant and a graduation cap. The Castle was in the center of her piece again. Oddly, there was a picture of a hot dog in a circle with a line through it. April didn't presume to understand what Rocky was thinking.

Piper's table was littered with the papers mothers collect during their kids' school years. Report cards, perfect attendance awards, a program for "Our Town," and even a birth certificate. April saw the birth certificate had been altered. Frankie Imperiale's name had been handwritten in the blank for the father's name in big block letters.

A parent no longer denied. April moved away from Piper without comment. She didn't know what to say.

Suzi was stamping flowers on a silk scarf. She was sitting next to Piper, watching April closely.

Turning away from Suzi's gaze, April saw Mary Lou and Kit laughing as they scrapped together. April felt a pang in her heart that made her look toward the door to the kitchen. She had one thing to do before she could get started. She pushed open the kitchen door.

Bonnie was setting small desserts on a silver three-tiered dish. She looked tired.

"Long day?" April said. It was difficult for her to see how hard her mother worked.

Bonnie looked up, surprised. She used her forearm to brush a hair from her cheek. "I thought you were crafting with your friends," she said.

"Friends? That's a bit of a stretch," April said.

"They're nice people, April."

April heard the warning in her mother's voice. Not to judge so quickly, not to draw conclusions about people because of their social status. But that wasn't the source of April's doubts tonight. Tonight she was worried one of them was a murderer.

"Okay, Mom. I don't want to fight."

"How's your father holding up?" Bonnie asked.

"We don't have to talk about him," April said quickly. "Vince is handling him."

Bonnie wiped down the counter, the pink tile chipped in places. The backsplash was old yellow linoleum attached to the wall with a stainless steel band that was bent and pulling off the wall in spots. The stove was old, with only four burners. Whatever money the club had spent, it hadn't been in the kitchen. This was the last place the members saw. And yet Bonnie sent out wonderful meals each day.

"It's really okay, April." She sighed.

April's scalp tightened. "That's why I came in here, Mom. I wanted to tell you I know you're doing the best you can. I have no idea what it must be like to live in this small town, day after day, with your ex-husband three miles away with his lover. That must be unbearably hard."

Bonnie looked surprised, then snorted. "You should have heard the old biddies at church the first time Vince came to the Sunday social with your dad. Mrs. Gearhart nearly had a coronary." Her face crumpled and her voice filled with tears. "I didn't know what to do."

April put an arm around her mother's

shoulder. "There's not exactly a handbook on how to deal with your husband's homosexuality."

She leaned into her daughter, her voice whispery. "Maybe I need to write it. I'll call it *Meet, Gay, Love.*"

It was a good sign that Bonnie's sense of humor was returning.

"Mom," April said, her laughter quickly turning to tears. She laid her head on her mother's broad shoulder. Bonnie's hand patted her with a familiar heaviness. Her mother's hand fit so neatly between her shoulder blades, it felt like a part of her.

"I don't know what I'd do without you," April said.

"Hush, baby, hush," Bonnie whispered. "It's my fault as much as it is yours. I hardened my heart, God help me, even against my own child. Your father hurt me so much, and I took it out on you."

April protested, "I wasn't very lovable in those days. Before Dad left, I'd been a real creep, just trying anything to get your attention. After he left, all I wanted to do was get out of town."

"I was the adult, April. You were just a kid. A crazy, mixed-up kid. I was supposed to protect you, to love you no matter what, but I couldn't. I was too hurt. I'd thought your father was the love of my life."

She pulled back and smoothed the hair from her daughter's forehead. April could smell the sweet cream-puff dough she'd been baking.

Bonnie said, "For so long, I thought there was something wrong with me. Your father tried to be a good husband. He tried. And he was a good daddy."

He was. That's why April had missed him so. "You did your best, Mom."

Bonnie shook her head. "Maybe. But I can do better now." She brushed the hair out of April's eyes and kissed her eyelids, gently, as if kissing a newborn.

"Go play. I'm making chocolate-covered strawberries. I'll bring them in as soon as they set up."

Her favorite. April kissed her mother. She started to leave but stopped at the door. Her mother had been honest with her. Now it was April's turn to tell her the truth.

"Okay, but first, I've got something to tell you. About my life in San Francisco. About my marriage. About Ken."

April and her mother talked for an hour in the quiet kitchen. She told her mother everything Ken had done to her. She cried and her mother dried her tears. Finally, when April was all talked out, her mother kissed her.

"I'm sorry, Mom. I know you loved Ken."

Bonnie reared back, her eyes wide. "Ken? I don't give two hoots about that little shit. He hurt my little girl, and he should rot in hell."

April burst out laughing. This was so far away from the reaction she'd expected. "What happened to Ken, the darling son you never had?" she asked, gasping for air.

"He's cut out of the will, starting now," Bonnie said. "My millions will have to go all to you."

"Gee, thanks, Mom. I'll try to spend them wisely."

"Let me finish up here," Bonnie said, giving April a shove out the door. She gave April another kiss and smiled. Her face was peaceful, and she didn't look as tired as she had an hour ago. April felt lighter, too.

Back at the stamping room the atmosphere had definitely changed. She heard Officer Yost's name and hesitated in the doorway. Her good mood vanished as she heard angry words. Piper was talking, her hands flying about her face as she stood next to the table. She had a stamp in her hand that she was gesturing with.

She said, "He frickin' grilled me today. It

was ridiculous. Over and over again, asking me the same questions. When was the last time I saw Frankie? What did he say? Where was he going? *Over and over.*"

Rocky and Tammy exchanged a whispered conversation. Mary Lou and Kit were focused on their projects, although April could tell Mary Lou wasn't missing anything.

Piper wasn't finished. "I told Yost the last time I saw Frankie, I was telling him if he knew what was good for him, he'd leave town and never come back."

April looked sharply at Rocky. Seemed she wasn't the only one running Frankie out of town. But he never got the chance to go.

"I bet that shut Yost up," Suzi said, clearly trying to get her friend to stop her diatribe.

Piper said, "My father will so have him fired. The Lewises were here long before he was."

Deana said, "I'm sure he's just trying to establish when the man died. It was so long ago. People's memories fade. I don't remember where I was that night."

April felt she had to step in. She wanted to know what people remembered of that night. "That's because you were home in bed," April said. "If something special had happened to you that night, you'd remember."

"What happened to you?" Piper said snidely. "I mean, I gave birth, and then the father of my child disappeared for good. What did you do?"

April took in a breath. "I outed my father to my mother and caused them to break up."

Silence filled the large space. Every hand hesitated over its project, every eye turned to April.

"April, honey," Deana said. "That's not really true."

"You can ask my mother," April said, pointing to the kitchen door. "I dragged my dad home from the job trailer and told her that their marriage was a sham."

Conversation ceased, even the whispers between Rocky and Tammy. Eyes slid off April's.

Deana grabbed April's shoulder and pulled her aside. She had two deep frown lines between her eyes that April had never noticed before. Deana said, "I'm going out to my car. I've got a big shipment of stuff that Tammy ordered in my trunk. Give me a hand, will you?"

April looked around the room. No one would make eye contact with her. She'd gone too far. Now she would never get anyone to talk to her about Frankie. She felt like crawling in a hole.

"Sure," she said.

The two friends walked outside together. It was getting close to eleven. The night air was soft. April could hear crickets and frogs croaking from the water hazards. She breathed in the summer smells and let the quiet fill her pores. Still, she felt like an idiot.

Deana opened her trunk and pulled out two large bags by their handles. She set them on the ground and faced April, taking April's upper arms and looking at her closely.

"Listen, April, I'm sorry I cut you off, but I feel responsible for this group."

"And my life story is too sordid for them?" April said testily. Deana's sense of propriety was well honed.

Deana tsked. "You know how it is in a small town. We know each other's stories. Intimately. Or at least we think we do. It's better not to flaunt them. We can only get along by pretending not to know that Suzi's Aunt Mary is really her mother."

April swallowed a protest. She was on Deana's turf. This was her scene. The Stamping Sisters was her business.

"I promise to be a good girl."

Deana handed her one of the bags.

"Oof," April said, as the heavy bag threatened to pull her arm out of her socket. "What's in here?"

Deana pulled out a box. "Tammy always orders the complete line every season. All the stamps, papers, inks, matching ribbons and eyelets. It's a huge order."

April was amazed. "That must be expensive," she said.

"Thousands of dollars," Deana said.

"Can she afford that?" April had seen Lyle's paycheck, and nursing homes weren't known for paying their employees well.

Deana shrugged. "She's never bounced a check to me. I know it's excessive, but Tammy gets a little obsessive. Before stamping, she was collecting silver jewelry. It's always something with her."

"Stamping is a disease," April said, hoisting the second bag, leaving Deana free to carry the large box.

"This stuff is as addicting as crack cocaine," Deana said.

"Speaking of crack, did you hear my mom's making chocolate-covered strawberries?"

"Let's go," Deana said, quickening her step.

Bonnie was in the room when they returned, setting out the platter of huge strawberries. The stampers surrounded her, drawn to the chocolate like bees to honey.

April unloaded her burden on a side table near Tammy and gave her mother a wave. "You almost done for the night?" she asked.

Bonnie said, "Nearly. I've just got a little more clean-up."

Tammy jumped up to look at the items Deana and April had brought in. She exclaimed over each one, gently caressing the packages and showing off her finds. She seemed to get happier with each package she opened. Rocky sat next to her, lining up her purchases like a maid of honor at a bridal shower.

April settled in a chair and worked, feeling the stamps in her hand and smelling the inks, relaxing in spite of herself. The repetitive motion soothed her, like rocking in a boat on a gentle sea. She sank into the work, stamping images that were important to her. She'd carved a gently curving ocean wave stamp before leaving California. She combined it with seaweed and an image of the Golden Gate Bridge.

Tammy called to her from across the room. "Your phone's over here, and it's ringing, April."

April looked up. She must have set her phone down near Tammy when she'd carried her purchases in. She listened for the ring. It wasn't a call; it was a text. And only one person texted her. Ken. That was a message she didn't need to get.

"Just leave it," April said. "I'll look at it later."

The phone chirped again. April finished stamping an image of a bird and got up, sighing. She'd have to turn the damn thing off.

Her phone wasn't there. She looked for Tammy to ask her where it was, but she was gone, too. The door to the kitchen was swinging, as though someone had just gone through it.

When April pushed open the kitchen door, she didn't see them at first. The stainless steel prep tables were gleaming. The worn countertop was shiny, and the backsplash shone brightly. A big spaghetti mop lay next to a bucket of water that smelled like ammonia. A noise behind her made her turn.

Tammy was holding Bonnie by the hair. Bonnie looked terrified, her eyes wide. April felt sick to her stomach when she saw the heat gun in Tammy's hands. It was too close to Bonnie's face. April could feel the warmth coming off it.

"What are you doing, Tammy?" April cried.

Tammy shoved Bonnie into the room and dropped the heat gun on the counter. She quickly grabbed a broom that was leaning against the countertop and pushed it through the door handles, barricading them in.

April went to her mother and gathered her in her arms. She felt her mother's heart beating wildly. "Tammy!" she shouted. "What do you think you're doing?"

"Quiet down," Tammy hissed. "What is this?" Tammy held out April's phone. The text-message beep sounded again, but Tammy was pointing to the picture on the phone.

The picture of Frankie's bashed-in skull.

Tammy shoved April away from her mother. April tripped over the mop bucket and fell to the floor, scraping her arm on the way down.

Tammy dropped the phone with a clatter and snatched up the heat gun, holding it again to Bonnie's throat, which was as white as skim milk.

April gasped as Bonnie grunted, "Tammy." The heat gun could produce severe burns.

"Pick it up." Tammy's eyes were like balls

of steel, tiny black rivets. "I want you to listen to me, April. I want all of your attention."

April picked up the phone and stood. She tried to take a strong stance with Tammy. Her elbow smarted and she felt blood dripping. "I can't concentrate with you holding a heat gun to my mother's neck."

Bonnie shook her head slightly. Don't move, she mouthed. April felt her heart harden at the sight of her mother in danger.

"Whatever you want, Tammy, this is not the way to get it," she said through clenched teeth. She opened her jaw to force herself to relax. She could barely breathe in. Her chest felt like it would not expand enough.

"Shut the phone," Tammy said. Then she positioned Bonnie against the barricaded door. There was a small glass window alongside it through which April could see into the room where the stampers were, but none of them had noticed anything amiss.

April wondered where the knives were in this kitchen. Damn her mother's obsession with clean counters. She had to put everything away before she went home. April leaned against a drawer and pulled it open slowly behind her, trying to see what was inside without Tammy noticing.

"You could have saved me that night,"

Tammy said.

"Saved you? From what?" April said.

"From Frankie. You walked right by us. He was raping me," Tammy cried, the pain of that night so present in her voice that April felt it sting on her skin like ice pellets.

"I don't understand," April said. "I never saw you with him."

"I heard you, you and your father. Lyle told me it was you."

April tried to concentrate. She couldn't form a picture of what Tammy was saying. "My father and I were talking inside the job trailer . . ."

Suddenly April remembered the couple she'd seen in the bushes as she biked to the trailer. "Oh my God, I thought . . ."

Tammy's eyes were far away. Someone was pounding on the door now, but she heard nothing. "He dragged me away from the party. He took off his pants and hung them in the tree. While he was . . . on top of me, the pants slipped off the branch and landed right next to me. I grabbed the belt buckle and hit him."

"Tammy, I didn't know you were there, I swear."

Tammy snapped back to the present. "Show me the pictures of Frankie," she demanded.

April opened the phone again, held it where Tammy could see and thumbed through the pictures she'd taken. Tammy jerked with each one. Her eyes were sad. "I knew it. I killed him." She jerked the heat gun near Bonnie's eye.

April flinched and cried out, "Tammy, Frankie was shot. The police found a bullet."

Tammy looked confused and tightened her grip on Bonnie. Bonnie's face was pale, and April wondered when she had last eaten. If she knew Bonnie, it had been hours ago. Bonnie knew how to feed people, but she wasn't good at taking care of herself. April needed her to be strong now.

April saw Rocky's face in the round window. She tried the door, rattling the handles.

"Tammy," Rocky yelled, her voice muffled. Tammy looked that way, then back at April.

"There was nothing on the news about a bullet," Tammy said.

"Of course not," April said. "That's how the police operate. They didn't want the real murderer to know that they were onto him."

Tammy's eyes had widened, and two red spots flamed on her cheeks.

"I hit him that night," Tammy said.

"You didn't kill him. His body wasn't

exposed to the elements." She had to break through to Tammy. "If he had died out there where you hit him, his bones would have been carried off by animals."

That image got to Tammy. She winced, and the heat gun hit Bonnie on the arm. She jerked back in pain.

April bit back a cry of her own and yelled, "Frankie was shot and dumped inside the walls of the Castle."

Tammy looked at Bonnie's arm. The nurse in her took over. Seeing the red welt she'd caused, she dragged Bonnie over to the tap and ran the cold water.

"I didn't kill him," Tammy said. "I didn't kill him?"

"Neither did my father," April said. "But someone did. I need to find out who."

Rocky burst in the door on the other side of the room. April could see the darkened bar beyond. Tammy dropped Bonnie's arm and Rocky ran to her.

Maybe they both killed him. April wondered when Yost had taken Rocky in for the drug possession. Before or after Tammy hit Frankie.

CHAPTER 16

"You okay, Mom?" April grabbed her mother by the hand.

Rocky led Tammy out of the gray metal door. April stared into her mother's eyes. She looked frightened but under control.

Bonnie nodded. "I'm fine, honey. I never believed Tammy would hurt me."

"I did," April said. "She was feeling pretty desperate. She really thought I'd seen her that night and chose not to help her. That's awful."

Bonnie nodded again. She sat suddenly, her face crumpling. April caught her arm and eased her onto a bench under the coat hooks. April grabbed ice from the freezer and wrapped it in a paper towel. She knelt and put the ice on her mother's burn. She brushed a hair away from her mother's face and kissed her cheek. So soft. Just like she remembered as a kid. The softness and the smell of lilies of the valley.

Bonnie took the paper towel away from her. "It's fine. I've done worse to myself cooking."

Clive burst through the door. His boyish good looks were ravaged by worry and sleeplessness. His eyes were puffy, and his complexion paled under the fluorescent lights of the kitchen. He was wearing a pajama shirt tucked into his jeans, with his brown corduroy slippers on his feet.

He took in the tableau in front of him and broke toward Bonnie. "You're an hour and a half late. Are you okay?"

Bonnie was startled to see him. "How did you get here?"

Out of breath, Clive held on to his knees and panted. Mother and daughter exchanged an incredulous look over his bended body.

He answered in short bursts. "I rode. The bike. Garage."

Bonnie turned to April. "Your old one," she said, her eyes flashing at her daughter and mouth twitching in an effort not to laugh out loud. The picture of Clive riding her pink banana-seat bicycle with plastic streamers coming out of the handles was too much.

"You know I can't sleep without you there," Clive said to the floor. Bonnie patted his back and grinned at her daughter and shrugged. She dumped the ice out of the towel.

"Is everything all right?" Clive asked.

"Just fine. Let's go home," Bonnie said.

Bonnie grabbed April and pulled her daughter into her fiercely. She whispered into her neck, "We're okay, you and I."

"Yes, we are," April answered. And they were. She was her mother's daughter, and she would not forget that anytime soon.

"Get your father out of jail," Bonnie said.

April smiled, her mother's priority shift surprising. She grinned. "All right. Come on, I'll take you home." She started back toward the Hazle Room for her keys.

Bonnie said, "Hold on. I've got my car here."

April frowned. Her mother's complexion had not regained its normally ruddy color. "I don't think you should drive. You're still shook up."

"I'll drive," Clive said. He pulled himself up to his full height.

"I thought you didn't have a license," April said.

"Doesn't mean I've forgotten how to operate a bloody car," he said defiantly.

Clive's jaw was set and Bonnie's eyes were twinkling. April admired his tenacity. He was going to do what he could to take care of his girl. She had to let him.

April pulled Clive toward her by his lapels. He was so short, she had to bend to look him in the eye. "Okay, but be careful."

He nodded.

"Watch out for cops," April said. "Officer Yost is out to get our family, remember?"

Bonnie shot April a look. She smiled broadly, her eyes wrinkling in the corners. Her arm shot out and grabbed her daughter. She slung her other arm around Clive's neck. The three of them stood in an awkward hug.

"Our family will be just fine," Bonnie said.

April found Rocky and Tammy in the Hazle Room. They were seated at a table. Rocky was comforting Tammy, who was crying softly. April pulled a chair over. She moved aside Rocky's project.

"Tell me."

"What?" Rocky said, stroking Tammy's hair.

"Everything," April said. "You owe me that. Or I'll call Yost and tell him Tammy kidnapped my mother."

Tammy wailed, and Rocky held her closer. She flashed daggers at April.

"What does your brother have to do with

all of this?"

Rocky's eyes flashed in surprise. That wasn't what she'd been expecting. "Mitch? Nothing."

"But he lied. He was home that summer. He knew what happened that night."

"He didn't lie for himself. He lied for me. He's always trying to protect me."

April knew that Mitch would do that. She thought back to their conversation and realized she'd guessed he'd been hiding something, but it wasn't anything to do with him. It was all about his sister.

"That night changed a lot of lives," April said. She'd thought it had been just hers, but it was far more than that. Rocky had been exiled to France, Tammy frightened into marrying Lyle, Piper a mother without a father for her baby, Frankie dead.

Rocky sighed, and shifted so that Tammy was sitting on her own. Tammy buried her face in her hands. Rocky continued to stroke her, as though she was a nervous cat on its way to the vet. But Rocky remained silent.

Rocky's silence was frustrating. April moved her chair closer, knocking off Rocky's work. She picked up the page. Images of the graduation party were visible. The Castle, the belt buckle. April realized Rocky was collaging images from that night.

The hot dog with the line through it was gone. Instead there were three hot dogs that seemed to be in a progression with the letter following each one.

April remembered Rocky's fondness for rebus. The hot dog was Frankie. It was a picture of Frankie walking away from the party. Rocky was saying Frankie was alive the last time she saw him.

The message was there in the collage. Tammy hit Frankie with the belt buckle, but he walked away. Rocky was reassuring her friend that she hadn't killed him.

April held up the collage. "Why do you have to convince Tammy she didn't kill him? Why does she think she did?"

Rocky turned her head away. "It was my fault. I was so full of hubris back then. I didn't know what it meant to be the child of a rich family. I thought I was so powerful."

She stopped. Tammy breathed slowly, her body rigid with fear. "The party was getting out of control. Kids had left my party at Mirabella, and spilled into the woods, heading for the Castle. Before the roof went on, we'd been partying at the Castle. Climbing in and gathering there. My father had threatened me with boarding school if any more parties were there."

"Frankie had brought a lot of grass to sell. I grabbed his supply and told him to buzz off. Told him the cops were on their way. He wasn't happy, but I threatened him. He backed off, angry, heading for the Castle. He was pissed."

Her eyes filled with tears. "Later, I found out that he caught Tammy on his way home. He attacked her because he was mad at me. I never said a word about it to anyone."

The anguish in Rocky's voice was real. She'd been carrying around the grief of her friend's rape all these years.

April said, "But you took his pot off him, to get him to stop dealing."

"I wish I was that noble," Rocky said. "I was just greedy. I knew I could run him off. My father was powerful enough that Frankie wouldn't mess with me. I just wanted the dope. I would have been a big hit at college with that stash."

April felt the sadness between these two friends who had been locked in this guilt trip for the last fifteen years. Tammy racked with guilt because she hit a man and wondered how badly she injured him. Rocky with her own burden, knowing that she'd sent Frankie out into the woods to victimize Tammy. Neither of them knowing what had become of Frankie.

"But Yost thinks that Frankie was shot," April said.

Rocky turned to Tammy. "I thought I'd seen him walking around later that night," Rocky said. "He was a persistent little shit."

"I believe you now. And I forgive you. You didn't make Frankie do what he did to me."

April left the table. She wondered if it was too late for Tammy to start over and have a complete life.

The question remained. When did Frankie die? Ed said that he'd boarded up the Castle.

Of course, when Ed said "he," he meant Buchert Construction. Not him personally, his men. So who? The answers were back at the barn, in the time cards.

CHAPTER 17

The sun was coming up; the trees were filled with singing birds. The sound was deafening and uplifting at the same time. April raced back to the barn.

Whoever had been at the Castle the morning after Rocky's party had killed Frankie.

April pulled down the box marked "The Castle." She grabbed the payroll file she'd been looking at earlier and then remembered the payroll ended on June 11, two days before the graduation party. Her eyes confirmed it, and her heart sank. She'd been so sure she'd find the answer here. She pounded her fists on her father's desk in frustration.

The job had ended in such chaos after that night, it looked as though no one got paid for boarding up the Castle. As April flipped through the file, an invoice fell to the floor and she bent to pick it up. The invoice was the one from the munitions company. Lyle had ordered the sticks of dynamite a month before the Castle blew up. But according to her father, they didn't have the necessary permits even on that Wednesday morning. Why did Lyle order the explosives so early?

April's blood ran cold. There was only one answer. Because he knew there was a skeleton in the ruins of the building. He couldn't risk the body being found. April's mind raced. Lyle was always around. He'd been her father's faithful employee for nearly twenty years. But why would he kill Frankie?

Maybe George had been wrong. Maybe it wasn't Frankie who was stealing. It had to be Lyle. Maybe Frankie had figured it out and confronted him, and Lyle shot him and dumped his body in the building. Was Lyle still stealing?

She grabbed the file marked "Heights." Mitch had seen Lyle taking the copper pipe off the Mirabella job. Lyle told her he'd moved it to the Heights. There was no invoice for it. And none in the Mirabella job. Lyle had control over the invoices. Unless Ed checked every bill from the supply list, pages and pages, he wouldn't know that the material hadn't gotten to the job it was intended for.

Tammy's purchases from Stamping Sisters, her golf membership — all spoke of someone living beyond her means. Or someone married to a person who was supplementing their income. By stealing. Lyle wouldn't have to pilfer a lot, just enough to allow him to buy a new truck each year. Allow his wife to have all the stamping supplies she could ever want. Allow his wife to work a low-paying job.

April needed coffee. Her brain was fuzzy from being up all night. She went into the kitchen, put water on to boil and spooned coffee into the press, and then stood in the galley kitchen, waiting.

A sickening creak broke the silence. The barn door was being pulled open across its tracks. April turned. Lyle Trocadero was standing in the doorway, legs spread-eagled, one hand in his windbreaker pocket. Her heart leapt to her throat and she swallowed a gasp.

"Lyle! Geez, you scared the life out of me," April said. The barn was out of sight of the main road, out of the sight line of the houses nearby. No one would hear her if she screamed. She decided to treat him as though he belonged in the barn. At five in the morning. On a Saturday.

She tried to sound casual. "I'm just about

to make coffee. Join me?" she said. "I'm surprised to see you here."

Lyle watched her as she poured hot water into the French press. She tried to make sure her body language betrayed no nervousness. She couldn't let on that she knew about him.

"Tammy told me you'd gone home early from the stamping party. I thought maybe you needed help. Is everything okay with your dad?"

April nodded. "As far as I know. I was just tired, that's all."

He wandered over to the office. "Doing paperwork?"

"Not really," she said. "I just knocked over some stuff on my dad's desk."

"Can't mess up the system, can you?" His voice was light, but April saw him react when he saw the invoice for the copper pipe that was lying on top. She froze.

"You're pretty smart, aren't you?" he said.

She knew he knew, and she rushed to reassure him. "It can be our secret, Lyle. I don't need to tell him or Vince. After all, Retro Reproductions is doing okay, right? The company isn't hurt by a little skimming."

Lyle smiled his smarmy smile. "Exactly. It doesn't cost them a cent, really. We just pass it on to the customer."

April knew how close her father's margins were. Lyle's stealing was keeping them close to bankruptcy. And giving Ed countless sleepless nights as he tried to figure out why his estimates always were wrong, why he could never bring a job in with more profit. She wondered about the toll it had taken on him.

"So how do you know what you know, April?"

She decided to flatter him. The barn was a big space, and so far there was lots of room between them. She wanted to keep it that way.

"It was very difficult to figure out. In fact, I wasn't at all sure until you just said that. You hid your tracks very well. Did you pay off one of the salesmen at the supply house? I'm not sure I know exactly how you did it."

April practically felt her eyelashes flutter. Her inner Scarlett O'Hara was closer to the surface than she liked to believe. But Lyle wasn't going to enlighten her. His escapades were less interesting to him than she thought. He sat in Ed's chair, putting his big feet up on the desk. Her blood boiled at this sign of disrespect for her father.

She reached in her purse and took out her

cell. His eyes narrowed. "No service in the barn," she lied. She held the phone up so he could see it. She continued prattling. "God forbid we should ruin our pristine valley with cell towers. The good Methodists decided they didn't want the tower spoiling their roofline."

Lyle leaned back. April heard the chair creek, wondering if it would hold under his weight. "I'm going to leave this burg soon. Florida is sounding better and better."

"That would be best. If you promise to quit Retro Reproductions, I won't tell my dad about your stealing."

"So that's that." Lyle dropped his feet to the floor and stood. He covered the area between the office and the kitchen so quickly, so menacingly, she dropped the phone and it fell apart, battery skittering under the dishwasher.

"Damn," she muttered under her breath.

April didn't want to get caught in the kitchen. She walked toward him, struggling with each step, as though she were mired in quicksand. Her whole body rebelled against walking in his direction. But the door, escape, was behind him.

He stopped at the end of the galley kitchen, arms outstretched, one on each side of the counter. She felt the entrapment deep in her gut, a wrenching so heartfelt, her knees buckled. His smile was feral, his eyes flashing with his powerful position.

She used the stove to prop herself up, still trying to present a strong front.

"Well, Lyle." She tried to infuse her voice with normalcy, but she sounded weak and shaky to her ear. "I should be going to bed. It's been a long night."

"Is that an invitation, April?"

Her name in his mouth made her shudder.

"Look, Lyle, you've covered your tracks. You killed Frankie because he wanted in on your scheme. I bet you killed George for the same reason. It makes sense. George figured out you were stealing. He needed money to pay for the nursing home. You've worked all these years to get where you are. Why should you share?"

Lyle smirked.

April had never felt such hatred before. She fought to keep her rage under control.

The phone rang, shattering their illusion of civility. The answering machine picked up. "April, it's Mitch."

April spoke up loudly, trying to drown out his voice. "He hates me, that guy. And the feeling is mutual. He'd love to put my father in jail for something he didn't do."

Lyle moved in closer, putting his ear close to the machine. He pushed the volume button.

Mitch's voice rang out, clear in the wide open space of the barn, reverberating off the beams and coming right back down. "I heard about what happened at the stamping party. I know you're up. I'll be right over."

Lyle's eyes brightened. He rubbed his hands together. "Oh yeah — a booty call? Man, I was born too late. Girls in my day did not respond to phone calls. I had to get married to get anyone to fuck me in the middle of the night."

"No, no," April said, genuinely laughing off his suggestion. "Mitch just needs something I have of his aunt's. He can't stand me. And besides, I'm married." She pointed to the finger where her wedding ring had resided until last week. The skin under the knuckle was still dented and pale. "I don't know why he thinks I need help."

"I do. Tammy called him for me. Said you'd gone home in a huff and needed some consoling. Nice of him to be so Johnny-on-the-spot, don't you think?"

The pit in her stomach grew icy cold tentacles.

"This way, with Mitch coming, it'll look like a lover's quarrel gone bad."

April's heart stopped. Mitch was going to be the fall guy. The one missing piece of his plan. She was going to be his latest victim, and Mitch would be blamed. She wished she could tell Mitch to stay away.

She scanned the barn quickly. Could she climb over the counter and make a run for it?

He was staring at her breasts now. She felt undressed, vulnerable, naked.

"I've got to make it look good," he said, leaving his post at the end of the kitchen and slowly walking toward her. "Like Mitch had been in your pants."

She shivered. He wanted her to know what he was going to do to her. He wanted to watch her realize and become afraid. Her fear was his power. She let him get a little closer.

He came alongside the refrigerator. April jerked open the freezer door, hoping to hit him with it. He ducked and it fell open harmlessly. She moved away from him, opening the door to the dishwasher and letting it fall in the narrow space between the counters. The dishwasher door hit him across the knees and he fell down hard.

Putting two hands on the edge, she vaulted herself up onto the counter. She reached overhead, pulling the heavy pot rack. The pans rattled as she swung it, just as he was getting up. The rack gained momentum and knocked across his face. He lost his balance and tumbled, his long legs and arms hitting either side of the counters. She heard his grunting exhalations.

When she jumped down from the counter into the great room, Lyle lunged for her. Her stamping supplies were spread out on Mitch's table where she'd left them. She grabbed a pot of embossing powder and threw it at his face. The powder spread into his eyes, and he cried out.

April didn't waste any time. She ran to the ladder leading to the loft and climbed up. As soon as she was in the loft, she pulled up on the ladder. It felt a lot heavier than her father had described. The picture of her father's smiling face describing his latest toy came back to her. He was sitting in jail because of this man. She felt a surge of adrenaline course through her.

She yanked harder, feeling the first two rungs make their way into the loft. She braced herself, pulling so the ends of the ladder were no longer on the barn floor. They were sticking straight out.

Lyle jumped up and grabbed the end of the ladder, ripping it from her hands. She screamed as she felt muscles tear, her fingers burning from the strain. Lyle struggled to pull the ladder down, but his fingers were slippery with exertion and he dropped his end. The ladder sprang back up toward April, bounced and fell to the floor.

April bit back a scream. Now she was trapped in the loft with no way out. And Lyle had a way up. She looked over the edge. The loft was at least sixteen feet off the ground. The floor was hardwood over concrete. If she jumped and broke a leg, she'd be in worse trouble. She needed to be able to run for her life.

Lyle looked up, cackling. He was breathing hard from his trek through the kitchen, but he knew he had her trapped now. His face was dark with embossing powder and white where he'd knuckled his eyes.

She could see him take in a deep breath. He pushed on his side, as though he had a cramp. He was older than her by about twenty years, and his age was showing. He needed to catch his breath.

And he could. The fact was she wasn't going anywhere. She scrambled into the corner of the loft, instinct sending her into the darkness. She had to fight not to throw the covers over her head. She had to keep talking, otherwise she would give up, cocoon herself and wait for her fate.

She wavered but then found her voice and yelled at him, "You could just walk away, Lyle. I don't know anything. Nothing I can prove."

"You know I came to the barn, for one thing," he said. "To plant this so that the cops could find it."

She peeked down. He was pointing a gun. She scrambled to the farthest corner, clutching her sides as she shook.

"Don't worry," Lyle said. "It hasn't been fired in fifteen years. I'm not an idiot, you know. I wouldn't kill you with the same gun I used on Frankie."

April tried to speak, but the gun had scared her speechless. A primal panic had been unleashed. She forced herself to breathe, mouth wide open. She strained to hear him.

She heard Lyle cross the barn, away from the loft. "This is going in the filing cabinet. There's a little hidey hole back here where your father keeps extra cash. I hear the police are getting a search warrant. I'm going to hide the gun, and then you're going to die in a terrible accident."

She heard the metal drawer screech open and felt as though the runners were scraping across her stomach.

"Your white knight will be here any moment. We'll just wait for him, so I can make this look real good. I'm thinking murder-suicide. What do you think?"

She refused to let her brain go where he wanted her to.

"How did you convince Frankie to come back to the Castle the morning after the party?" she asked.

Lyle was breathing heavily; the noises coming out sounded disconcertingly like a lover. April wondered where Mitch was. He should be here by now.

"Your father wanted the Castle sealed. Frankie found me there, working. He knew I'd sold material off the job site, and he wanted in. I didn't want him as a partner, and he took exception to that."

"Did you know he'd raped Tammy?"

She heard him catch his breath. He hadn't known. Damn, she'd made him madder.

Then came the noise she'd been anticipating, fearing. The ladder thwacked against the loft. Her heart nearly leapt out of her chest. She heard him push on the bottom rung several times, testing his weight.

She crawled quietly to the edge of the loft staying low so he wouldn't see her. She positioned her feet on either side of the ladder and braced herself with her hands, knowing he needed to be about midway up the ladder before she could try to push it back and cause use his weight to pull the ladder down.

His face appeared over the edge of the loft. Her body was shaking from not screaming out. She turned her face into her shoulder and pushed with all her might.

The ladder lifted away from the loft two inches and stopped. Lyle's face was creased with surprise, his eyes wide and terrified. He shifted forward, and the ladder changed direction, leaning against the loft again. She kicked again, grunting like a tennis player as the breath expelled from her.

He grabbed her leg, and then she did scream. Loud and piercing, it had the effect she wanted. Lyle let go.

She sat up and tried pushing the ladder with her upper body, twisting away as Lyle reached for her hair. His movement caused the ladder to sway, and April feared the ladder would fall and she would go over with it. She backed away, realizing she didn't have the strength to knock the ladder down with him on it. Still swaying, Lyle leaned forward.

April's breath was coming in short, hard bursts. She felt as if there was no air to breathe. She crawled backward to the other side of the loft, grabbing her pillow as though that would fend him off. Her hand bumped into her sketchbook.

Time slowed as she remembered what she'd been doing the last time she used the sketchbook in the loft: cutting out skulls. Her sharp scissors were here somewhere. She tossed the covers, trying to find them.

Lyle sounded like a train coming, huffing as he rested, getting his wind back. The sound terrorized her.

His hands gripped the edge of the loft. April patted down her bedding.

Just as a leg appeared over the top of the loft, she reached under the bed and felt the cold, smooth edge of a blade. Her hand closed around the scissors.

Lyle pulled himself into the loft and stood, arms reaching for her. Forcing herself to run toward him, she lunged with the scissor blade held out in front of her.

The scissors met his hands and he stumbled back, his foot catching on the end of the ladder. As if in slow motion, Lyle fell backward, over the edge of the loft, landing with a sickening thud.

The ladder crashed down to the floor.

April fell back on the bedding, chest heaving. There was no noise from below. When her heart slowed down until it was just beating rapidly, no longer threatening to come out of her chest, she looked over the side. Lyle was splayed out on the floor, blood under his head.

The barn door creaked open, a sound that wrenched through her. She gasped.

"April?"

Mitch's voice echoed through the barn.

CHAPTER 18

When Ed and Vince stopped by the barn, April was washing her plate. She'd just finished brushing off her sketchbook. She'd gotten crumbs on it drawing while she was eating her toast.

"You two again?" April said. They'd found a pretense to stop at the barn every day for the last week. Just to make sure she was okay. "You could have saved yourselves a trip. I've got five women coming in a few minutes. We're going to stamp."

"We won't stay long," Vince said, restraining Ed, who looked as though he was going to settle in at the table.

"We're off to New York," Vince said. "See some shows, hit the art museum. Just reenergize ourselves."

"You deserve that," April said.

Ed kissed April's cheek. "Monday, we're starting a new job. The old fire station. A couple from Philly bought it and want to turn it into a house."

Vince patted his partner's shoulders. "Simmer down, dude. No shop talk until Monday morning. You promised."

"Don't call me 'dude,' " Ed said with irritation. He took a breath, about to say more, then clamped his mouth shut. He looked from April to Vince. "Okay, you're right. I'm not even going to think about Retro Reproductions until then."

"Clive got us tickets to see the Eagles at Madison Square Garden," Vince said.

"Clive did?" April was amazed. Those tickets had been overpriced and impossible to obtain. "That show'll be awesome."

"Awesome," Vince said, echoing her with a little California Valley Girl in his tone, his eyes dancing. She pulled a face at his gentle mockery.

Ed said, "We just saw Yost at the diner. Lyle has come out of his coma. They're moving him to the nursing home. Under twenty-four-hour guard."

April cringed at the irony. "Poor Tammy." At least she wasn't working there now. Rocky had moved her into her house and was keeping tabs on her.

"I just hope they don't put him in George's old room," Ed said bitterly.

The three of them were silent, thinking

about George, a man with a lot of life behind him, robbed of the years he had coming.

"How are Retro's finances? What did your auditors find?" April asked. Vince and Ed had hired an accountant to come in and see how much Lyle had been skimming over the years.

Vince and Ed exchanged a look. Vince put an arm around him. Ed took in a deep breath and said, "Retro Reproductions will go on. We may not be able to retire as early as we thought we were going to, but we're going to be fine. We've got plenty of time to build the business back up again."

The two men stood, arms around each other's waist. Vince gave Ed a significant look and a nudge. Ed got the message.

"April," Ed said, "we think you're the perfect addition to Retro Reproductions. We'd like you to come work for us. Permanently."

April glanced at the smiling men. She couldn't ask for better bosses. But her first love was stamping, not renovating. "Thanks, but without the Mirabella job, what would I do?" she said.

"Just promise us you'll think about it," Vince said.

Ed held out his free arm for her, and April

stepped in. The three hugged. It felt so good to be a part of their lives.

The hug broke apart, and Ed said, "So? Bright and early Monday morning? You won't be late, right?"

April laughed. Her father could not go out of character for long. "Right. Now go, have a great weekend."

They left, promising to enjoy themselves. April smiled at their backs.

Fifteen minutes later, there was a knock on the kitchen door. Through the eyelet curtain, April's heart did a flip when she saw Mitch's face. She hadn't realized how much she'd missed him in the last week. She'd spent the time mostly at the barn, setting up her own household, making stamps and eating the food that Bonnie made and that Clive bicycled over.

"Having a party?" he asked with a smile, indicating the pile of stamping supplies on the kitchen counter. His face was open and strong, and the way the smile crinkled the corners of his eyes made her weak in the knees. Just a little.

"The Stamping Sisters are on their way over," she said. "My new gig."

Mitch was grinning at her.

"What?" she said.

"My sister's crowd has never had anyone quite like you in their midst."

"What's that supposed to mean?" April's eyes narrowed, and he laughed.

"You're a breath of fresh air," Mitch said. "You didn't give up until you figured out who had killed Frankie Imperiale."

"My dad —" she began.

He held up a hand. "I know, but there was more to it than that. You cared about this guy you'd never met."

April said, "Maybe that was the key. If I'd known him, I might have hated him like everyone else."

Mitch laughed again. His dimple, just one, was deep, matching the cleft in his chin. He smelled like wood chips this morning, and she pictured him, already up early, turning a leg on his lathe or sanding a door. She liked the woodsy smell and breathed in surreptitiously, trying hard to hide her interest in his scent.

He said, "I have a gift for you."

She cocked an eyebrow at him, and he laughed.

"You don't like gifts?" he asked.

"I'm a little suspicious of gift-bearers," she said. She had a feeling her own smile was goofy, too.

"You'll like this one," he said. He pulled a

huge coffee-table book from out of the bag he was carrying. He needed two hands to carry it to the table. She thought about the pictures he'd shared with her earlier. The book opened to a page marked with a yellow sticky note.

"Take a gander," he said proudly. She bent over the page to oblige, conscious that her tank top might reveal too much. She held a hand over her sternum, trying not to think about what she might be showing.

But Mitch wasn't looking at her cleavage. He was pointing to a mural. It looked to her like a WPA type, with thick-bodied men doing menial tasks.

"It's an authentic Refregier. Look right there. See that?"

She looked. "The same guy that painted the mural at Mirabella? So?"

"So, the signature is not the same as this Refregier. Aunt Barbara's is a fake. Probably done after his work became recognizable."

"A fake?" April said.

Mitch crowed, "The mural is worthless. Rocky has a friend who's an art appraiser. She came out and declared it was not part of his body of work."

April felt her mouth open. She was speechless.

Mitch filled her in. "A team of painters is in there right now, stripping the wall and painting over it. And Aunt Barbara has agreed to rehire Retro Reproductions to finish the rest of the renovation."

April caught Mitch by the arm and swung him around. "You're not kidding?"

She pulled him too hard, just as she turned, and he bounced off the table edge and landed in the circle of her arms. She caught him to keep him upright and in doing so, found herself locked in an embrace with Mitch, his sexy eyes inches from her own.

She took in a deep breath, opening her mouth to apologize. She didn't get a chance. Mitch leaned in and kissed her, lingering over her mouth and pressing his body into hers. He shifted so his arms were encircling her, and she felt the strength in his forearms. Visions of what his body was like underneath his khakis flooded her brain, driving out any inhibition.

She kissed him back, fiercely. She felt his surprise, fueling her desire.

Finally, she broke free.

Her voice was raspy with need. "I have a husband, you know," she said.

"I heard it's over," he said, lining her neck with tiny kisses. She felt his eyelashes on her chin. Her knees weakened.

"Technically, I'm a married woman," she insisted. She'd been ignoring Ken, hoping he'd disappear, but it was time to cut him loose. She'd call him later.

"It's okay. I can wait," Mitch said. He stopped kissing her and looked into her eyes. "You're worth waiting for."

His words sunk into her like an insulin shot, giving her body exactly what she'd been looking for: a man who thought she was worth waiting for.

The barn door opened again, and they broke apart sheepishly. By the time the door slid far enough open to let Rocky in, they were on opposite sides of the art book, admiring " '34 Waterfront Strike."

Rocky took in her brother's reddened lips and April's mussed hair, and shot April a knowing glance, but she didn't say anything. She pointed to the book and offered her hand for a high-five. Mitch and April obliged.

"I'll leave you ladies to your fun," Mitch said.

April was amazed at how much she wanted to go with him. She'd been looking forward to stamping with the girls; now, that seemed like a poor substitute. But as he opened the door, Mary Lou and a still-pregnant Kit were there, followed by Suzi and Deana, so April waved good-bye.

Having Mitch for a friend would be okay. A friend, like Rocky. Or Mary Lou. He was someone interesting to talk to. He was wise and steady. He was artistic and creative. The fact that he was good-looking was just an added bonus. She felt Rocky's eyes on her, and she blushed. That was it, no more thoughts of Mitch. No point in fueling Rocky's speculations.

The barn was filling up. The stampers were noisy and congenial, calling to each other and showing off their projects. April felt the empty space replaced with something more.

Bonnie showed up with her seven-layer bean dip and homemade nachos. Clive followed, carrying a box of CDs.

"I thought you might like some music to stamp by," he said.

"I've got music, Clive. But I don't own a Kickapoos album."

Looking through her iPod, he said, "Your music is weird."

"Just because you've never heard of Maroon 5 or Rilo Kiley, don't make fun. You're just an old fart, anyhow. A musical snob. You don't really have too much room to judge. I mean, didn't you write 'Last Bus to

377

Scranton'?"

"I loved that song," Mary Lou put in. Kit rolled her eyes.

"*You* loved that song," Bonnie put in.

"I was ten," April protested.

Clive pouted. "That song has been very good to me. The farm I bought. The Suburban. The last herd of sheep."

April laughed. Clive was irrepressible. She looked to her mother for help, but Bonnie just shrugged. She was very happy that her two favorite people were getting along.

"Don't bother me," Bonnie said gruffly. "I'm going to bake these cheese straws. Leave me out of the musical choices."

Clive found an album he approved of and soon the sounds of the Beatles filled the space. He walked around the room, admiring the stampers' projects.

Mary Lou threw an arm around April's shoulder. "Thanks for having us here." She opened her bag on the table and started taking out papers, scissors and punches.

"How are you?" Deana hugged her and held her close for an extra moment. "Doing okay, really?"

April nodded in her shoulder. "I really am doing okay. Ed's free, the bad guy is in custody. What more do I need?"

"Ken call?" Deana asked.

April shook her head. "Not today. Maybe he's getting the message."

"Which is? You going to stick around Aldenville for a while?" Deana asked gently.

"Dad wants me to work with them. And we're back on the Mirabella job. That will take at least six months," April said.

"And after that?" Deana asked, looking into her friend's eyes.

April smiled. "I'm thinking my parents are of an age where I shouldn't go off and leave them."

Deana looked at her askance. "Your parents are in their fifties, and both have wonderful partners. They need you less than they did fifteen years ago."

"Well, maybe I just want to stick around and see how things turn out. Besides, you need someone to help you with your stamping route, don't you?"

"My stamping *route?*" Deana asked, her eyebrows arched high. Kit started giggling.

April looked around the table. "I figure it's like a paper route, only with franchised paper products."

"You offering to help?"

Her first week back in Aldenville, she'd made more friends than she had the first sixteen years she'd spent here. She liked Rocky and Mary Lou despite, or maybe because of, their wicked tongues. She couldn't wait to see what Kit's babies turned out to be. Piper and Suzi were growing on her. Tammy was a lost soul, for now.

"Maybe," April said.

The stampers went to work. The smell of toasted cheese soon filled the barn. Clive whirled up a batch of margaritas. Her mother smiled at her, and April felt the love across the room.

"Oh, yes, tequila," Mary Lou said over the noise of the blender. "I always work better with a buzz on."

April laid out the project she'd started at the all-nighter, a collage with one of her favorite birds, the cardinal. She'd missed seeing cardinals in California, but she'd been afraid the image might be overdone.

Looking at the page now, she saw her fears were groundless. Even though the image was iconic, her treatment of it was anything but trite. The red bird had only been a jumping-off point. The collage had started with images of California but morphed into images of Pennsylvania. Green rolling hills, pink, full-blooming mountain laurel, white fluffy clouds. The result was a lush panoply.

Her underlying message — one she hadn't even known was in there — came through. She missed home. Nothing more, nothing less. April looked around the table. She had found a deep connection in a place she'd not expected to find one. Home.

She looked out the window. A cardinal came to the bird feeder, his mate as pretty although not as vibrant as he. The juxtaposition of the red feathers against the green pine tree was something she wanted to see again and again.

STAMPING PROJECT

Skull and Scrolls Tag

Supplies
- Black stamp pad
- Skull stamp
- Tag (from office supply store)
- Scroll stamp
- Scratch paper
- Colored pencils (white and gray)

Directions
1. Using a black stamp pad, ink the skull stamp and then press stamp firmly to tag.
2. Use the same black stamp pad to ink the scroll stamp, BUT first stamp it on scratch

paper and then on tag (this will give it a lighter feel).

3. Using a white colored pencil, color in details of skull and scrolls.
4. Go back in with a gray colored pencil and add subtle shadowing.

* Project design courtesy of Holly Mabutas. Visit her website at www.eatcakegraphics .com.

We hope you have enjoyed this Large Print book. Other Thorndike, Wheeler, Kennebec, and Chivers Press Large Print books are available at your library or directly from the publishers.

For information about current and upcoming titles, please call or write, without obligation, to:

Publisher
Thorndike Press
295 Kennedy Memorial Drive
Waterville, ME 04901
Tel. (800) 223-1244

or visit our Web site at:

http://gale.cengage.com/thorndike

OR

Chivers Large Print
published by BBC Audiobooks Ltd
St James House, The Square
Lower Bristol Road
Bath BA2 3SB
England
Tel. +44(0) 800 136919
email: bbcaudiobooks@bbc.co.uk
www.bbcaudiobooks.co.uk

All our Large Print titles are designed for easy reading, and all our books are made to last.